About the Author

Alan Frost is an experienced IT professional being a Fellow of the British Computer Society and a Chartered Engineer. He has spent his life moving technology forwards from punch cards to AI, but always knowing that the key constituent in any system is the liveware, the users.

The Battles of Malvern

Book One in the Merlin Series

Alan Frost

The Battles of Malvern

Book One in the Merlin Series

Olympia Publishers
London

www.olympiapublishers.com
OLYMPIA PAPERBACK EDITION

Copyright © Alan Frost 2023

The right of Alan Frost to be identified as author of
this work has been asserted in accordance with sections 77 and 78 of
the Copyright, Designs and Patents Act 1988.

All Rights Reserved

No reproduction, copy or transmission of this publication
may be made without written permission.
No paragraph of this publication may be reproduced,
copied or transmitted save with the written permission of the publisher,
or in accordance with the provisions
of the Copyright Act 1956 (as amended).

Any person who commits any unauthorised act in relation to
this publication may be liable to criminal
prosecution and civil claims for damage.

A CIP catalogue record for this title is
available from the British Library.

ISBN: 978-1-80074-340-3

This is a work of fiction.
Names, characters, places and incidents originate from the writer's
imagination. Any resemblance to actual persons, living or dead, is
purely coincidental.

First Published in 2023

Olympia Publishers
Tallis House
2 Tallis Street
London
EC4Y 0AB

Printed in Great Britain

Dedication

I dedicate this book to my three nephews: Michael, Adrian and Christopher

Book 1

1

War was Coming

Everyone in the county knew that war was coming to them. Everyone had been expecting it for many years. Everyone knew nothing of importance, but Lord Malander of Malvern knew everything. It was his job to know everything.

But then those that know everything know how little they really know. It had taken Lord Malander a long time to realise how ignorant he was. He was ignorant in the ways of the commoner. He was ignorant in the ways of love and childhood and friendship. But he knew the ways of the Slimenest.

The term 'Slimenest' made him laugh. The ignorant masses had no idea of their correct name. No one knew them as the Sacred Devotees of the Glorious Order of the Apocatastasis. No one could pronounce it or probably understand their philosophy, but to put it simply, they believed that all beings would eventually go to Heaven.

The only prerequisite to entering Heaven was death. Therefore, life was clearly a hindrance and should not be tolerated. Their philosophy only contemplated two options: death or membership of their order. Many would argue that death was the more preferable of the two options.

Lord Malander wondered why the Slimenest had not attacked yet. The Herefordshire forces had been pushed aside, but for some reason, they had stopped. Lord Malander knew that it was the Prophecy that stopped them. A Prophecy that he did not understand but somehow had great significance to the enemy's marauding hordes. He hadn't yet worked out a way of deciphering it, which confirmed that he didn't know everything.

Lord Malander also knew that the Elders had no interest in his theories regarding the Prophecy. In fact, they had threatened him with excommunication, a fate worse than death. The Prophecy was a peculiar phenomenon as it had to be collected. It appeared on walkways and in carvings on trees or even stone. There were many different versions reflecting many different truths, but for the enthusiast, it was possible to collate the varying verses into one coherent but incomplete whole.

It wasn't possible to be absolutely sure about the sequence. It was difficult to decide where new verses should be inserted. There was even a view that verses changed to reflect new realities. Perhaps it was an ever-changing history.

No one knew who the author was or whether it was even of this world, especially as the verses were found all over Grand Britannica.

Lord Malander was also subject to the orders of his Commander: Lord Eleonar. He respected him, but he was very fixed in his ways. The chain of command was everything to him, and there could be no deviance whatsoever even if the local conditions demanded it.

2

The Defence

Lord Eleonar of the High Order's command structure studied the map covering his division. His area of responsibility was Worcestershire. He had commanded a backwater for some time, but as Herefordshire was losing the battle against the Slimenest, it wouldn't be long before his forces would be engaged.
Shropshire was still fighting hard, supported by the forces of the Birmingham conurbation, but anyone with military training could see that they were being worn down. The Slimenest seemed to have unlimited resources and a zealous determination: nothing was going to stop them.

The Home Counties had more or less been devoured. London was surrounded and had requested assistance from the Midlands, but they had their own battles. The Elders had structured their military on county lines with strict instructions not to aid other counties without the High Orders' express permission. But that was another problem that Lord Eleonar had: the Elders had been based in the Malvern Hills for all of eternity. They were not prepared to move. This clearly restricted his options.

His other flanks were protected to some extent by the garrisons of Gloucestershire and Warwickshire. Regardless he had significant forces in Evesham, Pershore, Redditch, Hagley, and Kidderminster, but his two largest armies were in Worcester itself and Great Malvern. The Gloucestershire Division also had substantial resources in Tewkesbury.

The Herefordshire forces were being pushed back towards Bromyard and Ledbury. He also needed to take these somewhat depleted forces into account. He desperately needed an update on their strength and actual location. He commanded a scout to find out.

Lord Eleonar was not convinced that Lord Malander would stand. He would have replaced him years ago, but he was the son of the third Elder. He was ready to move forces from Pershore and Evesham to bolster the Malvern forces, but he was worried about confidence. Time and time again, the enemy had secured victory from the jaws of defeat by just never giving in. Their fervent ruthlessness and ardent faith had been the determining factors. We lacked the belief that we could win: we lacked confidence.

The enemy had defeated vastly superior forces simply by spreading fear. They never took prisoners. They massacred anyone in their way. They enjoyed torturing their foes. The more pain the victim receives, the more exalted the position they will have in Heaven. There were rumours that they even ate their captives.

The more Lord Eleonar thought about it, the more concerned he became about Malander. The Malvern Hills were a natural defensive line running south to north for nearly ten miles. They were a significant natural obstacle that could be easily defended. If Malvern was lost, then Worcestershire was lost, and if Worcestershire was lost, then the Elders may cease to be, and that would be the end.

3

Apocatastasis in Action

It was all about numbers. How many had they saved from damnation? How many had they released from the curse of life? He needed the numbers to justify his existence. He needed them before he could start the evening torture sessions. How he wished it was him and not them.

He could never understand why so many wanted to cling to life. Why cling to an existence riddled with pain, disease, and anguish? Death should be a welcome deliverance. They should be welcomed with open arms and worshipped as the deliverers, but no, there is constant resistance. Resistance that cannot be tolerated.

Anyway, those who didn't die in battle would soon meet their fate. There were about four thousand male prisoners, stripped and chained to racks. It was important that they suffered so that the entrance to Heaven was guaranteed. Each prisoner had their own personal torturer, or as the order preferred, Soul Saviour.

Slimenest Master, 'On my command, start the eternal release program.'

Chief Soul Saviour, 'Soul Saviours, take your position.'

There was an immediate response of, 'Yes, Master,' and the sound of leather boots on wood as they got in position.

Chief Soul Saviour, 'Gouge out the left eyes so that they can see better.'

There was an immediate outbreak of awful screeching and squealing, but the Commander knew that it was for their own good.

Chief Soul Saviour, 'Emasculate them so that all thought of fornication will end.'

Blunt knives were used to tear away at the testicles and penises of every captive. In some ways, it was the worst of all tortures as it removed all hope of survival. They had no future.

The screams were almost unimaginable, but the Commander knew that it was for their own good.

Chief Soul Saviour, 'Remove their right ears so that they can better hear the word of God.'

Ears were removed to the chants of the Saviours. They knew the routine; they had repeated this process many times. They were confident in their knowledge that they were saviours of the many.

The wooden boards were starting to become slippery with the effects of torture. Warm congealing blood and intimate body parts were mixed with the excreta of the tortured souls. Shit and urine flowed as the captive bodies were worn down by intense unnecessary pain. But the Commander knew that it was necessary, and it was for their own good.

Chief Soul Saviour, 'Scalp them.'

Again, blunt knives were used. Some of the captives died from shock. Some died from the loss of blood. They were the lucky ones.

Chief Soul Saviour, 'Use the rectal hot-rods.'

Sharp, barbed iron rods were heated so that they were red hot and then pushed up each victim's rectum. That was beyond being agonisingly painful, but the removal was even worse as the barbs ripped away at the rectal walls. The screams had reached a new peak. A lesser man would have shown some leniency and ordered the death of the captives, but the Commander cared for his new flock. Their continued pain would bring dividends for them in Heaven.

Chief Soul Saviour, 'My Saviours, it is time for the lead.'

The mouths of the surviving captives were forced open with small frames, and a funnel was inserted. Cannisters of molten lead were poured into their mouths. This was the final straw for many as their jaws and windpipes simply disintegrated. Some of the weaker saviours often ended their captives' misery by a quick stab into the heart, knowing that they would suffer the same fate if they were caught.

Slimenest Master, 'How many are resisting?'

Chief Soul Saviour, 'Sixty-two, Master.'

Slimenest Master, 'Boil them alive and feed their bodies to the dogs. Then prepare the remaining bodies for the catapult.'

Chief Soul Saviour, 'Yes, Master. What about the female captives?'

Slimenest Master, 'Are they of breeding age?'

Chief Soul Saviour, 'About half of them are, my Lord.'

Slimenest Master, 'Take the breeders to the slime pit and destroy the rest.'

Chief Soul Saviour, 'Yes, my Lord.' The breeders were stripped and herded off for impregnation in the nearest nesting pit. The remaining women were beheaded and sent to the catapult stations.

The Commander felt that he had done his duty, but what should he do about the Prophecy?

4

The Elders

The Elders never used to meet that often, but it was almost daily now with the current crisis. On their master map of Grand Britannica, it showed that most of the south-east had been lost along with Essex and Suffolk. London was still holding on, but they recognised that it was a lost cause.

Most of Wales had been lost some time ago, and as far as they knew, most of the Welsh population had been decimated, although it was possible that parts of North Wales were still free.

Chief Elder, 'Fellow Elders, these magnificent hills have been our home and refuge for millennia. They are us, and we are them. British Camp has fought off many invaders, both physical and spiritual, but we endure, but the time has come to consider a tactical retreat.'

The very thought of it was anathema to the Elderhood. There were cries of, 'No, not never', and banging on the table.

Chief Elder, 'I understand your reaction. I feel the same. These hills are my hills, but our position is precarious. If we are lost, then perhaps all is lost.'

Elder 3, 'Your position is understood my Lord, but relinquishing these hills is effectively surrendering to the forces of darkness. We must defend them to the very end.'

Chief Elder, 'Will our forces stand?'

Elder 3, 'They will my Lord or the Prophecy is wrong.'

There was an immediate hush in the room as the Prophecy, which didn't exist but was known to all of the Elders, was never mentioned.

Chief Elder, 'You utter what must not be mentioned.'

Elder Three, 'Yes, my Lord. I utter it with intent. That which is never mentioned has relevance. Can I quote the relevant verse, my Lord?'

Chief Elder, 'You may not.'

Elder Three, 'You leave me no choice. The verse must be voiced.

'I quote:

> *The Lords of the Hills must never flee,*
> *Death and destruction, I can guarantee,*
> *For those that ignore their destiny,*
> *Insanity awaits the escapee.*

Chief Elder, 'Enough.'

Elder Three, 'It carries on, stating that the absentee will cause the end of liberty.'

Chief Elder, 'I say enough, that which must not be heard, MUST NOT BE HEARD.'

Elder Three, 'I bow to your wisdom.'

Chief Elder, 'We will vote on our destiny. Those who want to leave, raise your arm.'

Not a single arm was raised.

Chief Elder, 'The Prophecy also says:

> *The devil awaits for the unknown,*
> *Merlin's home on the throne,*
> *Prepare to flee or postpone,*

The coming of your gravestone.

'You know that the Prophecy says everything to everyone. Please read what you will into it.'

5

War was almost here

Lord Malander of Malvern, son of Elder Three, Lord of the Marches and Lord Commander of British Camp, had been busy. Fortifications had been built throughout the hills. The two major passes at The Wyche and Hollybush had been heavily fortified in depth. These were obvious targets. Kill zones had been established at each pass to pour down missiles on the invaders.

Each hill had to be individually protected. From a distance, the Malvern's look like one long continuous hill, but in reality, they are a series of independent hills consisting of the following:

Hill	Elevation (ft)
End Hill	1,079
Table Hill	1,224
North Hill	1,303
Sugarloaf Hill	1,207
Worcestershire Beacon	1,395
Summer Hill	1,253
Perseverance Hill	1,066
Jubilee Hill	1,073
Pinnacle Hill	1,174

Black Hill (north)	1,011
Black Hill (south)	886
Tinkers Hill	700
Herefordshire Beacon	1,109
Millennium Hill	1,073
Broad Down	958
Hangman's Hill	906
Swinyard Hill	889
Midsummer Hill	932
Hollybush Hill	794
Raggedstone Hill (east top)	820
Raggedstone Hill (west top)	833
Chase End Hill	625

Each hill was allocated a 'Hill Master' with instructions to defend their hill to the end. They were assigned a varying number of men at arms and longbow and cross-bow archers depending on the hill's dimensions. They were also allocated manual workers to help construct new defences.

The two beacons contained the majority of the available resources. British Camp had concentric layers of defence and was regarded as the command post.

Lord Malander was the first Briton to use mounted cavalry. He had heard about its use in the very far east in a place called Italiana, but he wasn't sure if he was the first to use mounted bowmen. It formed part of the reserve that could be used to fill gaps in the defence.

The other major innovation that Lord Malander had introduced was training. Every member of his division had been trained as a fighter and then trained in a specific role. They knew what was expected of them. This seems such a simple idea, but it was quite radical, indeed unheard of. Normally individuals with pitchforks just turned up and got killed. Sometimes they got killed before they even reached the battlefield: the battlefield came to them.

The scouts that were sent out found that there were two different scenarios. Fighting was still continuing between the Slimies and the remnants of the Herefordshire forces. In reality, it was more of a mop-up by the enemy. The second scenario was a cessation of warfare. The Slimies were resting: there was no sign of any preparation on their part to attack the hills. This had never been experienced before. Normally they just mercilessly attacked and attacked and attacked.

6

Worcester Worries

Lord Eleonar of the High Order Military Command was wondering what to do. His scout reported back that the Herefordshire forces had either been eliminated or absorbed into the Malvern forces. He also reported that Malander wouldn't accept the forces into his regular regiments without some formal training.

He wasn't sure what was meant by training. Surely it was just a game of numbers. If you had more troops than the enemy, then the chances are that you would win. It wasn't down to the quality of the soldiers but to the quality of leadership. Everyone knew that.

The scout also reported that Malander had soldiers sitting on horses. What madness was that? What was Malander up to? There was no way that he would hold the line. And now he had the added problem that the Elders wouldn't leave the hills. He understood that they had been there for millennia. He understood that their power came from the hills, but this was nonsense. Their safety was paramount.

What was worse was that he had convinced the Chief Elder to leave. To be honest, he didn't take much convincing. For an Elder, he was fairly easy to manipulate. Then Malander's father convinced the conclave that they shouldn't leave. He used the forbidden Prophecy against the Chief Elder. That couldn't have gone down well. The whole Malander family deserved to be killed.

He recalled the part of the Prophecy that worried him: In the lands and hills of Worcestershire, One and all will suffer much hellfire, The death pangs of an honest squire, Cause the armies of man to retire. Was he that honest squire?

If Lord Eleonar had his way, he would draw a line across England to defend the north and as much of the Midlands as possible. He would scrap the county concept and form a national force under a strong leader. Someone like him, but he knew he wasn't that man. It was all just impossible speculation.

7

Lady Malander

Lady Malander had spent her life in Malvern. She knew every crook and cranny on these ancient majestic hills. She loved the undulating peaks and valleys in the springtime when the bluebells were pushing themselves up through the thick foliage to form a shimmering violet mist that wandered with the wind.

She loved the hot summer days when the hard granite hills provided shelter from the sun, and insects abounded busily carrying out their duties. Walks along the bare treeless peaks provided vistas of incomparable beauty that mellowed the anguished spirits.

She loved the reds and golds of summer. She loved seeing the leaves leave their summer home and the wildlife preparing for winter. She even welcomed the wet days of October and November. And as for winter, the beautiful frosted snow-covered hills became magical. And that was what the hills were: magical.

Mankind had loved and cherished the hills for centuries. It had been a place of pilgrimage before recorded history. It had been a place of renewal with magical flowing waters sprouting out in abundance to calm the sick and depressed. It had a soul of its own. A soul that the Elders communed with. Little did they realise that these hills would become the future Camelot.

Lady Malander was casting her spells of protection as she

had done for the last ten days. They were powerful spells, but she had no idea what effect they had on the Slimenest if any. So far, there was no indication that magic affected them, and there were no spells specifically designed to address their particular kind of foulness.

It was still a mystery where the Slimies came from. Lady Malander had used all of her sorcery powers to ascertain their origin. Knowing their home base helps the magician ground their magic, but they didn't seem to be creatures of our Earth.

The few enemy captives turned to slime during interrogation. To be technically correct, it was more like a sludge that could be washed down the sink. All discerning features simply disappeared in a most unearthly like way.

Lady Malander tried to use some of the slime in her evocations, but it was absolutely inert. It lacked any sign of a life-force. She wondered if they were manufactured golems. It was beyond her experience and, indeed, beyond her understanding.

What was even more worrying was that the enemy was using a magic of their own creation. An evil, elemental, magic that stank of pure horror. It was a magic that haunted and confused the mind and turned the brave into cowards and cowards into mindless wrecks. It was older and darker than anything she had ever seen before.

Lady Malander was trying to pin down the smell: yes, magic does have a scent! In this case, it had a sweet putrefying odour at one level and a dreadful, nauseating stench at the other. One whiff was enough to raise the bile. You could almost taste death, decay, and the decomposition of rotting flesh.

The only positive thing that she had discovered so far was that they were seriously allergic to Tanylip. She wasn't sure if it could be weaponised.

8

The Call for the Gathering

Slimenest Master, 'Is the gathering under way?'

Corps Master, 'They come, Master, they come to the sound of the borgonbus.'

Slimenest Master, 'Have the sacrifices been prepared?'

Corps Master, 'Yes, Master, one in twenty of our fighters have been selected.'

Slimenest Master, 'And how is their welcome release being celebrated?'

Corps Master, 'They will be skinned alive and then slowly minced for dinner.'

Slimenest Master, 'It is the will of Slayerdom.'

Corps Master, 'May death be his bride and our salvation.'

Slimenest Master, 'And what are the unlearned doing?'

Corps Master, 'All human forces west of the Hills of Prophecy have been slaughtered and racked.'

Slimenest Master, 'And is the catapult racking ready for immediate use?'

Corps Master, 'Everything will be in place by the end of the Gathering.'

Slimenest Master, 'Excellent.'

Corps Master, 'Master, could I raise a personal point.'

Slimenest Master, 'If it is to do with your welcome release, then the answer is no.'

Corps Master, 'But Master, you promised me the final release when this county was cleansed.'

Slimenest Master, 'I lied. All promises are to be treated as dead starlings, an impossible flight of fantasy.'

Corps Master, 'But I suffer.'

Slimenest Master, 'And by your suffering, you will learn that Slayerdom cares little for your pitiful life and your wanton desires. You haven't earned the welcome release yet.'

Corps Master, 'But what do I have to do, Master?'

Slimenest Master, 'Capture the Hills of Prophecy.'

Corps Master, 'But what about the Prophecy?'

Slimenest Master, 'The Gathering will decide.'

Corps Master, 'But the great book says:

The great horde will advance,
To the Gathering's war dance,
Lead on by the Master's imperious lance,
Absolutely nothing was left to chance.

Slimenest Master, 'I said that the Gathering will decide.'

Corps Master, 'Decide what master?'

Slimenest Master, 'You should read the whole book, not just the bits you like.'

Corps Master, 'Please enlighten me, Master.'

Slimenest Master, 'Just this time:

To capture the Hills of Prophecy,
Will encounter beasts of great monstrosity,
Nothing will prepare you for its progeny,
These killing, fire-breathing monsters of astrology,
Defeat is guaranteed before their ferocity,

Unless you secure the anomaly.

Corps Master, 'But what are these monsters, and what is the anomaly?'

Slimenest Master, 'Now you understand why we need the Gathering.'

9

Change is in the Air

Chief Elder, 'Is it time to let loose the "beasts of great monstrosity"?'

Elder Three, 'Shouldn't that be the decision of our warlord?'

Chief Elder, 'We don't have a warlord?'

Elder Three, 'Exactly.'

Chief Elder, 'The Council of Justinfair decided that warlords were too dangerous. Do you remember what happened after the war against the demon horde?'

Elder Three, 'But that was nearly ten-thousand years ago.'

Chief Elder, 'I still remember it like yesterday?' There were some sly grins in the room as the Chief Elder regularly failed to remember what happened yesterday.

Elder Three, 'But history doesn't always repeat itself.'

Chief Elder, 'Doesn't it? Is there not a cycle of events? The longer you live, the more of the cycle you see. We are at peace; we are attacked. Men die, we win and so on ad infinitum.'

Elder Three, 'The difference here is that there is no guarantee that we will win.'

Elder Six had heard this argument many times, almost ad infinitum. He realised a few decades ago that the Council had ceased to be a decision-making body. It was actually the opposite; it promoted resistance to all change. It suddenly dawned on him that we were going to lose this war if something wasn't done.

He stood up and loudly pronounced, 'It is time for change.'

No one, but no one, shouted in this venerable chamber. No one, but no one, interrupted another Elder. Everyone was shocked. The Elders, the scribes, the men at arms and the Elderguard were all shocked. The statues of previous Elders and the heroes of the Justinium were all shocked.

Chief Elder, 'Order, Order, what do you mean by this outrageous break in protocol?'

Elder Six, 'I've sat here for decades listening to us achieving nothing. Fortunately, nothing has happened for decades, so it wasn't a problem. Now we have a crisis. We have lost at least a third of our territory.

'We are sitting here waiting for the Slimenest to attack. Our people, who depend on us, are being raped, tortured, and murdered in their hundreds of thousands as we speak, and we are leaderless.'

Chief Elder, 'How dare you?'

Elder Six, 'I dare because I care. It is time for dynamic action.'

Chief Elder, 'Master of Arms, take this upstart away.'

Elder Three, 'I stand with Elder Six.'

Chief Elder, 'Master of Arms, Take them both away.'

Elders Eight, Nine, Ten, Eleven and Twelve stood up in defiance of the Chief Elder.

Chief Elder, 'Is this a mutiny?'

Elder Eight, 'We have no desire to replace you, but almost everyone can see that a warlord is required, and required now. We don't have the skills to manage a military campaign.'

Chief Elder, 'If you go ahead with this, I will resign.'

Elder Two, 'In that case, I propose a vote.' Votes were not rapid affairs but long, drawn-out discursive events. The Council agreed to meet in two weeks to finalise the vote.

10

Scouting the Gathering

Lord Malander, 'Any news from our scouts?'

Lieutenant Squire, 'Lord Hogsflesh is currently collating all of the reports.'

Lord Malander, 'Send him to me as soon as he arrives.'

Lieutenant Squire, 'Yes, my Lord.'

Lord Malander had requested additional resources from Lord Eleonar, but there was constant resistance. It just didn't make sense. These hills had to be defended. The Elders had to be defended. While he was considering his response to Lord Eleonar, Lord Hogsflesh was ushered in.

Malander scanned his Head of Scouting. He was an expert in his field and a man who deserved respect which was in direct opposition to his appearance. His name reflected his whole demeanour. He was a large ugly man with outlandishly large ears, a nose that could smell for Britain and eyes that never quite looked at you. Perhaps these were the characteristics of a good spy.

Hogsflesh had a keen intelligence and a wicked sense of humour. He was a natural risk-taker with a genuine liking for danger. Despite his appearance, he was a great favourite with the ladies. That was partly down to his famed love-making skills.

Lord Malander, 'Morning, Victor.'

Lord Hogsflesh, 'Good Morning, my Lord. I have collated

the various reports from our different scouting units. To be honest, it's not looking good.'

Lord Malander, 'Give me the worst.'

Lord Hogsflesh, 'Well, firstly, they have unaccountably ceased all military operations.'

Lord Malander, 'That's not like them, Victor.'

Lord Hogsflesh, 'I agree. Secondly, it looks like they are planning to punish thousands of their troops, or it is some sort of sacrifice.

'But the bad news is that all of their forces from every corner of Wales are congregating near Ledbury.'

Lord Malander, 'How many?'

Lord Hogsflesh, 'It's hard to estimate as there are still a lot of troops on the move, but I would plan for a hundred thousand.'

Lord Malander, 'But that is four or five times what we can muster.'

Lord Hogsflesh, 'And they are all battle-hardened. I know that you have put your men through an extensive training programme, but there is nothing quite like real blood and guts experience.'

Lord Malander, 'I agree, and I'm not getting a lot of support from Lord Eleonar. But I have built some impressive defences.'

Lord Hogsflesh, 'We are going to need them. Somehow, we need to find a way of resisting their kill-frenzy. They don't seem to have any fear of death.'

Lord Malander, 'It's almost as if they welcome it.'

Lord Hogsflesh, 'I've noticed that they always kill their wounded, and they seem to expect and want it.'

Lord Malander, 'Are they positioning their troops in Ledbury to come via British Camp?'

Lord Hogsflesh, 'It's impossible to tell, but it's a good bet.'

Lord Malander, 'I have the classic defender's dilemma. I have the whole range of hills to defend, whereas they can attack at any point they want. I'm hoping that my mobile forces will allow me to react quickly enough, but I need your scouts to keep me informed.'

Lord Hogsflesh, 'You can rely on my men.'

Lord Malander, 'I know, but they are going to be critical to our survival.'

Lord Hogsflesh, 'What plans do you have if the hills are breached?'

Lord Malander, 'None, as far as I'm concerned, this is our last stand.'

Lord Hogsflesh, 'What about the Elders?'

Lord Malander, 'It's rumoured that they have the same view.'

Lord Hogsflesh, 'In that case, Lord Eleonar must reinforce you.'

Lord Malander, 'He won't listen to me.'

Lord Hogsflesh, 'Do you want me to pull a few strings? You know what I mean.' It wasn't common knowledge, but Lord Hogsflesh was sleeping with Lord Eleanor's wife and the wives of many other noblemen.

Lord Malander, 'Yes, please, Victor. But I need real soldiers, not ploughmen.'

Lord Hogsflesh, 'I will see what I can do.'

Lord Malander, 'One last thing this morning, Victor. Did you spot anything unusual?'

Lord Hogsflesh, 'Unusual? Everything has been usual so far.'

Lord Malander, 'I mean not of this world.'

Lord Hogsflesh, 'You mean the hollows?'

Lord Malander, 'Go on.'

Lord Hogsflesh, 'Some of the enemy troops have hollow patches. You can see straight through them. But what is strange is that the hollow moves around their bodies. Sometimes the hollow even replaces their heads.'

Lord Malander, 'Can you explain it.'

Lord Hogsflesh, 'No.'

11

The Reinforcements

Lord Eleonar was under pressure from all sides. Lord Malander had been begging him for reinforcements, and he took much delight in resisting his appeals. Why should he help this arrogant young upstart? He contemplated taking over the defence of the hills himself, but if he failed, then he would get the blame.

And avoiding blame had been the backbone of his military career. He was not a front-line officer. He had received no military training, being originally destined for things spiritual. He didn't even like making decisions or being part of a command structure.

Now that the Elders were talking about staying, his position was becoming untenable. He had to show leadership, support Lord Malander, or stand down and cause considerable family dishonour. Now even his wife was giving him grief. If he didn't know better, he would have suspected that her strings were being pulled. He made a mental note to investigate that later.

Lord Eleonar called for his aide de camp, Captain Mainstay.

Captain Mainstay, 'My Lord, how can I be of service?'

Lord Eleonor, 'Captain, Lord Malander has requested reinforcements on several occasions.'

Captain Mainstay, 'That is correct, my Lord.'

Lord Eleonor, 'What resources can we spare without risking our position?'

Captain Mainstay, 'My Lord, I have had several regiments on standby awaiting your orders. They are ready to march.'

Lord Eleonor, 'What right did you have to do that?'

Captain Mainstay, 'The right of command, my Lord. It is my job to prepare for all contingencies. It was fairly obvious that one of the options would be to reinforce the Malverns. It makes both strategic and tactical sense, and with your permission, I will order the troop movements.'

Lord Eleonor, 'Captain, you have my permission.'

Captain Mainstay, 'Thank you, my Lord.'

Lord Eleonor, 'One last thing, I don't respect Lord Malander. Please let me know if he fails in his duty. I may need you to take over.'

Captain Mainstay, 'Yes, my Lord.'

Lord Eleonar felt even smaller after this encounter. But at least, in the end, he believed that he had made the right decision.

12

The Gathering Continues

The Slimenest Master considered wandering around the campsite and releasing some of his best troops himself. It would be a great honour for them, but he didn't have time to focus on the extreme torture they deserved and wanted. He had to concentrate on the Gathering.

Bands of troops were still arriving from the far-flung regions of Cymru. Practically the whole of Wales had been cleansed. The locals fought well but were disorganised and lacked direction. They lacked determination, but then they were not really experienced in the finer points of warfare. About ten thousand of the locals were recruited into the cause, but they were marked as 'kill-fodder.'

He toured the camp, greeting his subordinate leaders. There was no joy or pleasure in meeting them. That was for the softbellies. But he did feel pride in their joint achievements and satisfaction in how many souls they had saved.

His tour wasn't random. He was looking for some of the other members of the brigade hierarchy. He wasn't sure whether to kill them or to consult with them and then kill them. They probably had similar plans, but then a violent painful death would be most welcome. He could then sit on the right hand of Slayerdom in Heaven.

He went through the Prophecy in his mind again:

The great horde will advance,
To the Gathering's war dance,
Lead on by the Master's imperious lance,
Absolutely nothing was left to chance.

To capture the Hills of Prophecy,
Will encounter beasts of great monstrosity,
Nothing will prepare you for its progeny,
These killing, fire-breathing monsters of astrology,
Defeat is guaranteed before their ferocity,
Unless you secure the anomaly.

Most of it was fairly clear, but they had never used lances and what was astrology? And what was the anomaly? Could that be referring to the strange 'hollow' disease that they had been experiencing? They had no way of investigating it as they had no doctors. Those who became ill were simply killed, but the 'hollowers' still seemed to function perfectly well.

Well, all of this will be discussed later, but he will make the decisions. If it goes well, he might allow himself to go to the nesting pit to spread his seed.

In the meantime, his troops can rest and recuperate before their next exertions: the capture of the hills. He wasn't expecting it to be easy, but he was completely confident that he would prevail. He always prevailed, but a lot of it was down to planning. He checked the catapult teams and made sure that they had enough stock of dead and dying softbellies as ammunition.

He checked the blacksmiths to make sure that their weapons were being sharpened. He checked the courier unit to ensure that they were operational and that the fletchers were building up their stocks of arrows. Those arrows were going to be needed against those 'killing, fire-breathing monsters of astrology'.

He checked the witches, the brewers of foul magic that had served their purposes so well. They didn't belong to the cult of apocatastasis; they just wanted souls.

It was just a waiting game now for all of his brothers and sisters to arrive.

13

The Elder Games

The twelve Elders were appointed to represent the people, but really, they represented the Elders. It was the natural order of things, and the longer it remained the natural order of things, the more permanent it became. In fact, no one could remember a time before this group of Elders. The world had changed, but the Elders hadn't.

It should have been a time for power-broking and alliances. A time for devious shenanigans, deceit, and secret agreements, but none of the Elders had those type of skills. It was a time for hushed meetings in timeless corridors, of bribes in high places and daggers in much lower places, but the Elders lacked the energy to interact.

Among the younger Elders, and they certainly weren't young, they wanted the Chief Elder, or Elderbury as they called him, replaced by Elder Three or Six. But mostly, they just wanted a warlord appointed, but this was anathema to the Chief Elder.

Elders Four and Eleven went to see the Chief Elder in a poor attempt at changing his mind.

Chief Elder, 'I'm completely opposed to the appointment of a Warlord.'

Elder Four, 'But Chief Elder, we are on the precipice of disaster. There is no light at the end of the tunnel.'

Chief Elder, 'What sort of light are you looking for?'

Elder Four, 'At this stage, I'm not even looking for victory. I just want to see a stout defence in the short-term and then someone planning for victory at a later date.'

Chief Elder, 'Isn't that what we have done using the county structure?'

Elder Four, 'No, we have simply appointed grandiose sycophants in well-paid jobs who have no idea how to conduct a military campaign.'

Elder Eleven, 'Look at that prima donna running Worcestershire. What's his name?'

Elder Four, 'Eleonar, he was a failed priest!'

Chief Elder, 'The system has worked so far.'

Elder Four, 'How can you say that. We have lost Sussex, Kent, Berkshire, Hampshire, Dorset, Wiltshire, great chunks of London, most of the eastern counties and all of Wales.'

Elder Eleven, 'No one in their wildest dreams could call that success.'

Chief Elder, 'So are you for or against me?'

Elder Four, 'No one is against you, but we are for a warlord.'

Chief Elder, 'This is all very messy. I just want it to go back to how it used to be.'

Elder Four, 'What if we set-up a sub-committee that managed the war. That would leave you to focus on the more important things.'

Chief Elder, 'Would I still be Chief Elder?'

Elder Four, 'Of course, but you couldn't interfere with anything relating to the war.'

Chief Elder, 'I don't think that is going to work?'

Elder Eleven, 'Why is that?'

Chief Elder, 'Too much change, far too much change. The slippery slope just gets more slippery.'

Elder Four, 'Is there any way we can change your mind?'

Chief Elder, 'No.'

Elder Eleven, 'Perhaps this will?' He stuck a ceremonial knife into the Chief Elder's heart and said, 'I've done this to protect our future.' He then slashed his own throat.

For the first time in living memory, there were two vacancies in the Elderdom.

14

The Magical Conclave

Lady Malander brushed her long black hair. Normally her maid did it, but she was nowhere to be seen. Her hair provided a brilliant framework for her bright blue sparkling eyes, her petite nose, and luscious lips. She wasn't classically beautiful, but she was very attractive.

It was difficult to decide which were her best features. Was it her generous cleavage or her curvaceous arse? Perhaps it was her long, shapely legs or her enticing smile? If you asked Lord Malander, he would mention the unmentionable. Anyway, whatever your view, she was an impressive display of femininity.

But what was really impressive about Lady Malander was her mind. She was quick, very intelligent, and decisive. Once you added her wit, determination and her extraordinary magical skills, you had a very remarkable woman on your hands. What made the package particularly formidable was her sheer, dedicated will power. She was relentless once a goal had been set.

And a goal had been set: help defeat the Slimies. This was a goal set by her husband, the absolute love of her life.

So far, little had been achieved, and it was getting her down. She knew that she was fighting witches. Their scent was in everything they did, but these were not your everyday common witches. They had an otherworldly feel. She realised that they were just hirelings, working for souls. She knew that she could counter them given time, but her magic should have affected the Slimies directly by now.

Her spell of disappearance should have made some of their fighters simply vanish. It had always worked in the past. She now had to decide whether to focus on the enemy or her own side. Should she attack, or should she bolster her own forces? She had several confidence-building spells in her arsenal, or should she be ready to counter whatever the witches did? She decided that she wouldn't want to be a military commander, but that was what she was.

Lady Malander wasn't working on her own. She had gathered together a team of fifty-odd sorcerers and magicians, and there were more on their way. They were extremely pleased to be of assistance. However, the Elders had continued to ignore their offers of help.

Today was going to be the first meeting of the 'Magical Conclave'. She was determined to stamp her leadership on the group despite having considerably more senior necromancers, wizards, and warlocks in attendance. Normally the magical community were not great team-players. There were far too many egos involved.

She deliberately made sure that she was the last to enter the assembly room. Her entrance was trumpeted by her musicians dressed in the Malander coat of arms. She slowly walked to the top of the table and asked everyone to sit down. She remained standing, resting her arms on the back of the chair, and said, 'Fellow members of the occult arts, I've asked you to attend this conclave to help us defend our way of life. Indeed, I'm asking you to help save your own lives. The situation is dire.

'Already we have lost large parts of the country to the

Slimenest hordes and many of our dear colleagues. I can name the following: Deeplove of the Forest of Dean, Merrymore of the Chilterns, Dangleless of Devil's Dyke and Lady Cusspot of Pebbleton. We will never see their like, again. All have been tortured and murdered by the slimy scum in the name of apocatastasis.'

Lorrimore of Lendle, 'What about Gilltav of Goldford and Tallymore of Titfield?'

Lady Malander, 'I'm afraid that they have been lost along with the whole population of Wales. Many of the Druids were ritually sacrificed by drowning in mud. We need to make a stand.'

The Enchantress of Evermore, 'What do we know about these invading scum? We need to understand our enemy.'

Lady Malander, 'Not a lot, but I will list them on the scriber for all to see:

- The Slimenest or Slimies are technically called the Sacred Devotees of the Glorious Order of the Apocatastasis
- They believe that all intelligent life should be extinguished so that they can go to Heaven
- They believe that the more pain that the person receives during the time of dying, the better their position is going to be in Heaven
- They want to die horribly, but they also need to spread their version of salvation
- Torture is a way of life
- We have no idea where they have come from
- As far as I can see, they are not of this world
- There are one hundred thousand plus Slimenest troops on the west side of these hills
- They are using witchcraft

- At this moment in time, they have stopped all military activities.
- Our scouts have reported that there is some sort of Gathering.

I think that is about it.'

Lorrimore of Lendle, 'What about our forces?'

Lady Malander, 'It has been a bit confused due to the death of the Chief Elder.'

Tinton of Taverton, 'What, an Elder has died?'

Lady Malander, 'Yes, it's worse than that. Two Elders have died.'

The Enchantress of Evermore, 'That's unheard of.'

Lady Malander, 'But it was predicted:

>   *There are times to live and times to die,*
>   *The duo came to glorify,*
>   *But now are dead, those poor alumni,*
>   *What reason you will decry,*
>   *There is no value now or need to crucify,*
>   *We need to turn a blind eye,*
>   *And learn to fight and shout our battle cry,*
>   *It's time to enchant and mystify.*

'Note the last line.'

The Enchantress of Evermore, 'This is the Prophecy that can't be mentioned?'

Lady Malander, 'It can be mentioned now after the untimely death of the Chief Elder.'

Lorrimore of Lendle, 'What's going to happen next?'

Lady Malander, 'My father-in-law is taking over as acting

Chief Elder. There are not going to be any elections until this war is over. A national warlord will be appointed in the near future.'

The Enchantress of Evermore, 'And obviously it is going to be your son.'

Lady Malander, 'That has not been decided. The Elders will select the best man or woman for the job.'

The Enchantress of Evermore, 'So it is going to be your son then.'

15

The Regulars

What a difference a day makes. His father was now effectively Chief Elder in everything but name. Captain Mainstay was on his way to the hills with ten thousand regular infantry, despite Lord Eleonar's resistance. Those troops were going to make a huge difference. And his wife was assembling the country's magical resources.

Although he would never admit it, Lord Malander was now starting to feel reasonably confident that they could resist the horde, well, at least their first attack. He still needed more information on the enemy's plans. Lord Hogsflesh now had men stationed throughout the hills with new-fangled telescopnots. These allowed the viewer to see things in the distance. He made a mental note to investigate their use in battle.

He now had the challenge of where to deploy the regular forces that were arriving. A large percentage of mounted force was stationed between Chase End Hill and Tewkesbury. This is where he was probably most vulnerable. There were also significant forces in Tewkesbury, Cheltenham, and Gloucester, but there was this inviting gap. The Slimies could easily attack Chase End Hill and force themselves up the eastern side of the Malverns.

He called for his Head Engineer, who was out supervising their ongoing defensive formations. Every hour spent on this improved their chances of survival.

He also asked Captain Mainstay to see him as soon as he arrived. He then contacted his father to see if Gloucestershire's forces could be repositioned to protect his southern flank. The northern flank was reasonably secure, although Lord Eleonar had lost ten thousand of his finest.

Lindsey Clutterbuck, his Chief Engineer, arrived first, apologising that he had taken so long.

Lord Malander, 'How is it going?'

Lindsey Clutterbuck, 'We are mostly refining our fortifications at the moment.'

Lord Malander, 'That's good because I want you to move all of your resources to Forthampton to build defences there. When the regulars arrive, I will send them to assist. Now here is the challenge. I want you to build defences that are not immediately obvious.'

Lindsey Clutterbuck, 'You are planning a little surprise then?'

Lord Malander, 'Perhaps, but it will be a surprise.' They both laughed.

Lindsey Clutterbuck, 'Do you want me to wait for the regulars?'

Lord Malander, 'No, go now as time is of the essence.'

Lindsey Clutterbuck, 'Certainly my Lord.'

As Clutterbuck was leaving, Mainstay arrived.

Captain Mainstay, 'My Lord Malander, I'm reporting for duty.'

Lord Malander, 'Welcome aboard, Captain, your presence is very welcome, very welcome indeed.'

Captain Mainstay, 'Thank you, Sir. The pleasure is mine. My troops are desperate to have a go at the Slimies.'

Lord Malander, 'I'm very pleased to hear that. Let me take you through our dispositions.' They both walked over to a map on the table.

Lord Malander, 'Firstly, you can see that the Slimenest have gathered at Ledbury or what's left of it. All of their other units that were originally spread along the western side of the Malverns have moved to Ledbury as well. Our Chief Scout, Lord Hogsflesh, has estimated that they have at least a hundred thousand fighters.'

Captain Mainstay, 'How many troops do we have?'

Lord Malander, 'With your reinforcements, we can just about muster forty thousand trained troops. But we have the advantage of good defensive positions and strong forces on our northern and southern flanks. Half of my mounted troops are also based there.'

Captain Mainstay, 'What are they?'

Lord Malander, 'They are foot soldiers who fight on horseback with swords or arrows.'

Captain Mainstay, 'I've never heard of that before, my Lord. Surely horses can't cope with battle conditions?'

Lord Malander, 'It's not my idea. It has been successfully used in several foreign countries. So far, it seems to be working. But we have one desperate weakness.'

Captain Mainstay, 'Forthampton.'

Lord Malander, 'Exactly. I've just sent our engineers there to build defences. I need you and your troops to go there and assist them and then defend to the end. I want you to be well hidden and then to launch a surprise attack against the enemy.'

Captain Mainstay, 'And what are your plans if we are overwhelmed, my Lord?'

Lord Malander, 'My original strategy was to hold the line no matter what, but I've recently been considering building a defensive line behind the River Severn. I've asked my father for additional labour to build defences at Upton.'

Captain Mainstay, 'And your father is?'

Lord Malander, 'The acting Chief Elder.'

Captain Mainstay, 'Wow, some pedigree.'

Lord Malander, 'That may be so, but we need to hold the Malverns no matter what. Can I rely on you to hold the Forthampton gap?'

Captain Mainstay, 'You can, my Lord.'

Lord Malander, 'Excellent, please take up your command.'

Captain Mainstay, 'Yes, my Lord.'

Lord Malander recalled part of the Prophecy:

The gallant captain joined the fray,
Nothing would turn his head away,
From the need to maim and slay,
Our enemies on this, our Lord's day,
Helped by a fighting neigh,
As our foes slipped away.

16

The Gathering

Most of the disparate Slimenest groups had reached the Gathering at Ledbury. It was almost time for the formalities to begin. The torturers were preparing the tools of their trade, and the fires were being stoked.

The Slimenest Master welcomed the other force leaders. The Command structure amongst the Slimenest was fairly fluid. Partly because of natural warfare loss, partly due to challenges from juniors, but it was mostly down to a longing for death. Leaders welcomed death and placed themselves in positions where they were likely to be killed. This made strategic planning really difficult, if not almost impossible, so they had to rely on drug-induced rage.

The Gathering was a vague attempt at imposing some order. It was also a celebration of death and their successes. As it was getting dark, the Slimenest Master went to the main tent in the middle of the temporary village and joined his colleagues at the top table. Several volunteers were tied to posts, covered in oil, and set on fire to create light for the festivities. Their cries and the sizzle of slowly burning flesh helped establish just the right ambience for the event.

There were six leaders sitting around the top table, three short of the required decorum. The Slimenest required a decorum of nine. The Slimenest Master called for three volunteers who would suffer a truly awful death at the end of the Gathering. There were numerous volunteers, and at least sixteen were killed in a rush to sit at the table. One of the volunteers died from blood loss as he sat there.

Eventually, a decorum was formed, and the meeting started. The business was open to all who were in hearing range. Many died trying to get nearer to the action. Some died from the random firing of arrows. Those victims had been blessed.

The Slimenest Master stood up and half expected to be arrowed to death, as it had happened quite a few times before. He prepared to bellow, as bellowing was expected.

Slimenest Master, 'Fellow Slimenest, the time has come to attack the Hills of Prophecy. As you know, we have the Prophecy, but it is hard to interpret its meaning, as you will see.

'I am concerned about the following:

The great horde will advance,
To the Gathering's war dance,
Lead on by the Master's imperious lance,
Absolutely nothing was left to chance.

To capture the Hills of Prophecy,
Will encounter beasts of great monstrosity,
Nothing will prepare you for its progeny,
These killing, fire-breathing monsters of astrology.

Defeat is guaranteed before their ferocity,
Unless you secure the anomaly.
There are times to live and times to die,
The duo came to glorify.

The gallant Captain joined the fray,
Nothing would turn his head away,
From the need to maim and slay,
Our enemies on this, our Lord's day,
Helped by a fighting neigh,
As our foes slipped away.

'What are these beasts of great monstrosity?
  'Who is this gallant Captain?
  'What's a fighting neigh?
  'Where is our lance?'
Slimenest Armourer, 'Fuck the Prophecy. Let's kill the softbellies.'
There was a huge cheer and a rattling of weapons.
Slimenest Master. 'We need to consider the implications of the Prophecy.'
Slimenest Catapultier, 'You no listen, you die.' He threw his dagger straight into the right eye of the Slimenest Master, and he became the new Slimenest Master.
There were more cheers, more rattling of weapons, and more drinking. Anarchy prevailed and the torturers tortured, and most members of the Decorum were eliminated. There was no leadership, no planning, and no strategy, but there was a brawling, bedevilled bunch of bastards, intent on killing. The easiest target was themselves, and in an hour, they had killed a third of their own army. This wasn't the first time that it had happened, but it usually occurred when they were drugged into a killing frenzy.
Tents were burnt. Their entire food and alcohol stocks were consumed. Every living creature in the nesting pit had been pummelled to death. The coven of witches was sexually abused and ripped to pieces. Then the rioters slept. They slept the sleep of a drunken horde.

17

The Alert

Lord Malander heard the sound of horse hoofs. It always woke him up as it normally meant bad news. He recognised the knock on the door as that belonging to Lord Hogsflesh.

Lord Malander quickly got dressed with the aid of his aide and was soon downstairs to meet his friend. Hogsflesh had very dirty boots and smelled of smoke.

Lord Malander, 'How are you, old friend?'

Lord Hogsflesh, 'I have good news, my Lord.'

Lord Malander, 'That makes a welcome change.'

Lord Hogsflesh, 'I'm not exactly sure what is happening, but the Slimies are fighting each other, and their camp is on fire.'

Lord Malander, 'Is it just one of their brawls?'

Lord Hogsflesh, 'I would estimate that about thirty thousand of their warriors have been killed.'

Lord Malander, 'Well, that has evened the numbers somewhat.'

Lord Hogsflesh, 'I agree, but based on previous encounters, they are now likely to attack.'

Lord Malander, 'Will they wait until daylight?'

Lord Hogsflesh, 'Probably due to hangovers.'

Lord Malander called for his aide and told him to find the Firemaster and then send messengers to Lord Eleonar, the Gloucestershire commanders, and the Chief Elder.

The Firemaster arrived in his bedclothes.
Lord Malander, 'Light the bonfires in an hour.'
Firemaster, 'Of course, my Lord.'
Lord Malander, 'Now is our time.'
Lord Hogsflesh, 'It certainly is, my Lord. Let's hope that we are successful.'
Lord Malander, 'If we are, it will be down to preparation.'
Lord Hogsflesh, 'And your leadership, my Lord.'
Lord Malander called for his aides and issued his orders:

- All Hill Masters to prepare to defend their allocated hill
- Captain Mainstay to prepare to defend the Forthampton gap
- Mounted infantry to prepare for battle
- Inform Lady Malander and get her to prepare her magical forces
- Open all munitions stores
- Scouts to take their positions
- Activate field hospitals
- Activate field kitchens
- Activate the signals core.
- Find out from my father if we can use the secret weapon.

A small team scuttled off to fulfil their individual missions.

18

The Battle of British Camp

Lady Malander sent out her maids to wake up the Conclave members. It was time for magic to make a difference. Eight teams of five joined the hillside defences, ready to practice their mystical arts. Ten of the most senior practitioners joined the forces of Captain Mainstay.

Lady Malander stayed with her husband on top of British camp. They had the distinct advantage of seeing the great horde move. It wasn't long before the bodies of their dead comrades were being catapulted through the air. In the past, this was terribly disheartening for the defenders, but now two things were happening.

Firstly, the Enchantress of Evermore had cast a general charm of 'catapultalia' that caused the catapults to be ignored. Secondly, Lionel Wildheart was using his telekinetic skills to throw the bodies backwards in mid-air. However, the sudden change in direction did cause quite a few body parts to fall off.

The Slimenest horde split in two. It was hard to tell if this was a deliberate action or it was just happening by chance. It was hard to know if anyone was organising the horde. It was more like a force of nature or possibly a riot.

Half of the Slimenest army was heading directly for them, straight towards British Camp. The other half, as predicted, was going towards Captain Mainstay's forces. Lord Malander sent a messenger down to warn him, although he probably knew already.

Now was the time to re-structure his forces, and he ordered the following:
- Take 50% of the forces from the following hills: End Hill, Table Hill, North Hill, and Sugarloaf Hill and march them along the western slopes of the hills to attack the enemy from the rear. Do not attack until ordered. Keep out of sight of the enemy.
- Take 50% of the forces from the following hills: Worcestershire Beacon, Summer Hill, Perseverance Hill and Jubilee Hill and march along the summit to Tinkers Hill. Do not attack the enemy until ordered.
- Move all of the mounted troops to the eastern base of the Herefordshire Beacon and await orders
- All mystical forces to move towards areas under attack.

Ideally, Lord Malander would like to utilise the Tewkesbury and Worcestershire forces to envelop the enemy, but that would take far too much organisation and communication to achieve in the short term.

It was quite intimidating watching the horde getting nearer and nearer. Sergeants were issuing stiff drinks to their men, and there were sounds of, 'Stand', and, 'Steady Boys', even though there were several women in the front line. The line was ready for action, although for many, in fact, the majority, it would be their first battle.

The land in front of British Camp had distance markers for the bowmen. British Camp had a series of concentric ditches starting at the bottom of the hill and then a series of layers: about four to seven in total depending on the hillside's actual topography. The exact structure was quite complex as there were three intertwining hills.

Men at arms occupied the bottom level to protect the archers. The next tier contained the longbowmen, with the crossbowmen on the third level. More longbowmen manned the next level, with the other levels containing infantry and the top-level being manned by the command structure and the mystical forces.

As the Slimies got nearer to British Camp, they started to run, but it was tough going as the camber was quite deceiving. The ground was heavy and wet with numerous natural streams. Parts of the land were effectively bog but, nevertheless, they were moving reasonably quickly, but then they were hit by the first avalanche of arrows from the longbowmen and then a second volley.

The slimy mass was an easy target for the bowmen. Regardless, they rallied, but then they were hit by the bolts from the massed cross-bows. Each volley was being choreographed by the Master Archer. It was almost slaughter on an industrial scale. It was too much for the enemy, and they veered away from the arrowhead storm.

The Slimies had their own archers, but for some reason, they were not engaged. Instead, the remains of the horde headed to the Ledbury Road and its cutting through the hills. The pass was heavily fortified by Lord Malander's men with archers on both sides. It wouldn't be a sound military decision for them to do that, but they were buoyed by one success after another. They knew that nothing could stop them.

Lord Malander ordered half of his mounted infantry to head back along the hills and go through the Wyche Cutting and then approach the Slimenest from the rear. Once again, he made it clear that they should not attack until he gave them permission.

He could almost hear them grumbling as he manoeuvred them around, but that was the beauty of his mobile force.

Whilst this was going on, the magicians continued to cast their spells. The key spell was one of misdirection. It encouraged the horde to turn towards the Ledbury Road. It was them that suggested that they should attack the Hollybush Pass. There were no instructions, just subliminal messages, mostly visual. They also reinforced the concept that they could not lose.

As the Slimenest approached the pass in their thousands, the arrows started to rain down on them from three directions, from the hills on each side of the pass and from the barricades in front of them. It was another slaughter with the dead and the dying stopping the movement of the still-living. Despite everything, they continued their journey to the barricades when suddenly hot sticky oil came rolling down the hill.

It became difficult for the marauding Slimies to stand in the slippery, greasy slurry. One would have thought that the Slimies could cope with a slime slick. But it wasn't the case. They came in their thousands and slipped over in their thousands. Then they were shot in their thousands and died in their thousands. What made it worse was that the dead eventually turned to sludge, making the mucky mire much worse.

In the end, the surviving Slimies could not progress and, although alien to their nature, the only option was to fall back and then attack somewhere else. But before they could, the mounted infantry attacked. The Slimies had never seen anything like it. Men on horseback with swords slashed and sliced at will, and, as they retreated, further men on horseback arrived with crossbows.

A once-mighty force of thirty thousand could now be measured in tens. And these were being steadily picked off.

Lord Malander was well pleased with the day's work. It had been a carefully planned joint operation, but what pleased him most was the lack of casualties on his side. Then he wondered how Captain Mainstay was doing.

19

The Battle of the Gap

Captain Mainstay's troops and about eight thousand of Lord Malander's, were either dug in or were using natural features to hide while they waited for the Slimenest onslaught. The captain and most of his aide de camps were located on Chase End Hill and were liaising with the Hill Master. The two Ragged Hill Masters were also discussing the best way that their forces could contribute.

If you took into account the hill forces and the mounted infantry, then the two opposing armies were fairly equal in size. The obvious difference was that the Slimenest was an unruly but very aggressive mob, while their opposition was disciplined and organised. But it was surprising how often sheer brutal power won the day.

Captain Mainstay watched the advancing enemy. It was one long crocodile of evil filth with flags waving and their weapons catching snatches of sunlight. The hill forces carefully monitored their progress as they marched south so that they could turn at the base of Chase End Hill and then march north up the eastern slopes of the Malverns. They planned, if there was such a thing as Slimie planning, to meet their comrades that were going to fight their way over British Camp and then burst through the Hollybush Pass. It was a simple plan, but they would succeed because they never lost.

The Slimenest were making slow progress as the terrain was difficult, with thick woods, deep escarpments and rushing brooks. The landscape's natural features forced the invading army to separate into smaller and smaller groups that suited the defenders. The Slimies would turn a corner and would suddenly be hit by a mixture of arrows and cross-bow quarrels from Malander's troops.

As the Slimenest forces started to retaliate, the defenders would retreat to the next defensive position. Some of the bowmen waited until the Slimies had passed and then attacked them from the rear, causing considerable confusion. This tactic was proving successful, but it wasn't achieving the kill rate that was needed.

Captain Mainstay watched from his vantage point as the Slimenest emerged from woodland into more open pasture. The Slimies had been slowed down, but their dander was up, and they wanted to kill. It was almost an unstoppable force. It wouldn't be long before they would encounter his regular troops. They would show them what for.

The captain decided on some shock tactics and ordered his mounted infantry to attack the Slimenest column from the side with swords. Just over two thousand sword-swirling horsemen attacked. The whole enemy column simply stopped. It was a mixture of shock and sheer amazement. They had never seen a horse before, let alone a mounted swordsman.

Within a few minutes, the cavalry had slain two or three times their own numbers, but they made the remarkably common mistake of lingering far too long, and they were soon overwhelmed by sheer numbers. The officers were shouting at them to disengage, but it was far too late.

Man and beast were being literally torn apart. The screams of the dying men and the neighing bloody horses as they were ripped to pieces were heart-wrenching. It made the hairs on your body stand on end. However, Captain Mainstay now knew that warfare had changed forever.

The captain threw the dice again and ordered the mounted archers to attack. Soon hundreds of bolts were raining down on the Slimies. The firing was synchronised so that half the archers shot their bolts whilst the other half were loading. Whilst this was going on, one of the Slimies jumped onto an unmounted horse and galloped at the bowmen with his spear sticking out in front of him. He was soon shot down, but it took at least four arrows.

This encouraged the other Slimies to charge at the bowmen. You can't reload your bow and ride a horse simultaneously, which made the bowmen very vulnerable. They didn't want to experience what had happened to their sword-wielding brothers and fled.

The Slimenest felt that they had beaten off one attack after another and had now felt confident that they would win. They were effectively in a drug-induced kill frenzy. They were terrifying berserkers who wanted blood.

Captain Mainstay regretted the loss of the mounted troops, but they had done their job in whittling down the Slimenest numbers. The Slimies still had the advantage on the ground, but now they would be facing his pride and joy. His well-protected bowmen unleashed their weapons, but the swarm was too quick, and they were soon overwhelmed.

A trooper shouted that they were all doomed. A second called out that they should flee for their lives, and soon nearly ten thousand men were on the run. They had no defence, and they were quickly smashed by the Slimies. It was a self-inflicted massacre. Tears of shame ran down Captain Mainstay's cheeks. His reputation and military career were in tatters, and worse, he had single-handedly doomed Worcestershire and possibly all of mankind.

But, being a good officer, he ordered the following:
- Send a messenger to Lord Malander immediately
- Move all of the troops from Chase End Hill, Raggedstone Hill, Hollybush Hill and Midsummer Hill north as soon as possible to join the British Camp forces
- Move all the troops on Swinyard Hill, Midsummer Hill, Swinyard Hill, Hangman's Hill and Broad Down off the hills to engage the Slimenest. Archers should remain on the hills if the Slimies are within range
- Round up the remaining horsemen and any of our fighters left behind.

Captain Mainstay turned to the magicians and said, 'Now it's your turn.'

20

Let there be Dragons

The Slimenest had never seen a dragon before. Let alone seven of them. They were massive beasts with huge claws and teeth with wingspans of thirty metres. They were flying straight at the swarm. They could feel the heat of the raging fire emanating from their mouth and the wind caused by the flapping of their wings. They could hear their mind-numbing roar.

It was the most spectacular illusion ever created by magicians in Grand Britannica. The only downside was that it also terrorised the good guys. To be honest, it terrorised some of the magicians as well.

The swarm faltered and then started falling back, but the illusion chased them. And then the multitude realised that death by dragon would be a marvellous way to ascend to Heaven. Many of the Slimenest bent on one knee, ready to martyr themselves, but death didn't come. They reformed and continued their relentless forward march.

The magicians' second attack was to roll imaginary boulders down the hill. Again, the illusion was perfect but mostly ignored. The swarm carried on with giant imaginary boulders crashing through them. The bee attack was more successful as millions of imaginary bees and wasps attacked them. The Slimenest could feel the insects crawling over them. They could even feel their stings. It was interesting to see how a swarm would cope with a swarm. They coped by running and trying to remove insects from their eyes, but again reason prevailed, and one swarm disappeared, and the other carried on.

The magicians had gained valuable time. Enough time to allow Lord Malander to re-position his forces. His crossbowmen formed lines on the lower slopes of British Camp and Millennium Hill. Then there was another innovation which his men had practiced over and over again but never used in anger.

Three rows of men were quickly formed in front of the raging herd. The first row contained the strongest men with long, sharp sticks called pikes which they stuck in the ground with their points facing the enemy. Then there was a line of men at arms to protect the bowmen in the third line. The long thin line had practised moving backwards and forwards as a mass.

The biggest challenge was taking the first impact, but Lord Malander's men were poised and ready. The remainder of his mounted horsemen were protecting his left flank.

Captain Mainstay was doing his bit. His sergeants had rounded up many of his disgraced regulars, and, together with the cavalry survivors, they attacked the rear of the swarm, picking off the stragglers. It was starting to become a war of attrition.

As the Slimenest approached, the crossbowmen poured bolts into them at an alarming rate. The speed was impressive but unsustainable as cross-bows started to malfunction, and the supply of bolts was getting low. Many had to resort to their secondary task of being men at arms. At one time, it looked like the dwindling swarm were going to attack the hills, but the long rows of men in front of them were just too inviting.

The Slimenest threw themselves against the pikes, revelling in their death. The sheer weight of the dead and the dying caused the entire line to retreat a few steps. But the death rush continued, and they were forced to repeat the retreat three or four times.

Lord Malander ordered his mounted swordsmen to attack their right flank. Gradually Captain Mainstay managed to acquire more and more troops, and, having regained their courage, they proved themselves in battle. It was now clear that the Slimenest had lost, but they never gave in, so they had the job of simply slaughtering them. He got his crossbowmen to surround them and pour bolts into the mass. It was a horrible and inhuman task, but it was a necessary one.

21

The Aftermath

As with most wars, the aftermath is often worse than the battle. During the fighting, everything happens so quickly. There is no time to think. It is just instinct, reaction and survival. The more adrenaline in your body, the less conscious thought. Emotions are heightened, and your average man will do things that are far from average.

When fighting your normal foe, it doesn't take long for regret and pity to kick in, but with the Slimenest, it is just them or you, but they are happy to die. But when you see your brother die in battle next to you, it is just another hazy event, but afterwards, it becomes a shocking moment that is repeated over and over again in your mind.

The physically wounded are patched up, but the emotionally scarred are ignored. They have to buck-up and prepare for the next life-or-death encounter. The dead were buried in mass graves, except those whose loved ones cared enough to retrieve their bodies. Used weapons were collected and sharpened for the next gory death ritual. They now had all of the Slimenest weapons available for use and numerous catapults.

The Slimie sludge, which was all that remained of the once fearsome army, made very good fertiliser and was in high demand. Horse meat was also very cheap to buy.

There was a lot of work to repair the damage done to

Ledbury, but it was amazing how resilient mankind was. The Welsh came flocking back to their homeland.

Lord Malander became an instant hero. No one had defeated the Slimenest before. He constantly redirected the praise to his team, the magicians, the bowmen, the mounted infantry, and the locals of Malvern. Despite this modesty, everyone knew that it was his innovations that won the day: the use of mounted infantry, the synchronised firing of arrows, the defensive arrangements, the integrated magical incantations and, above all, planning. It was planning and more planning that won the day along with superbly trained and disciplined troops.

22

Captain Mainstay

The captain was not looking forward to his meeting with Lord Malander. He was ready to hand over his sword. Actually, it was his grandfather's sword, a family heirloom. Now he had covered it in shame. His only defence was that he tried his hardest, but that wasn't good enough.

Lord Malander's aide shuffled him in.

Lord Malander, 'Welcome Captain Mainstay.' The captain was amazed by how well he had been received.

Captain Mainstay, 'My Lord, I'm here to surrender my sword.'

Lord Malander, 'And why would you be doing that?'

Captain Mainstay, 'I failed you, my Lord. I failed to hold the line.'

Lord Malander, 'I accept that there was a failure, but we won.'

Captain Mainstay, 'I may have contributed to the final victory, but it was all down to you and your trained troops.'

Lord Malander, 'Tell me how you failed.'

Captain Mainstay, 'I believe that the planning was acceptable, but the application wasn't. Your troops performed magnificently, although your cavalry — is that the correct term? — failed to retreat quickly enough.'

Lord Malander, 'Was that your fault?'

Captain Mainstay, 'Not directly, but I was in command, and I have to accept responsibility.'

Lord Malander, 'Carry on.'

Captain Mainstay, 'As the Slimenest approached my troops, they turned and fled. That was clearly a failure on my part.'

Lord Malander, 'In what way?'

Captain Mainstay, 'They were my troops. I had total faith in them. My faith and related poor judgement put the entire campaign at risk.'

Lord Malander, 'Had they ever fought the Slimenest before?'

Captain Mainstay, 'No, my Lord.'

Lord Malander, 'Had they ever been in battle before?'

Captain Mainstay, 'No, my Lord.'

Lord Malander, 'I don't see how you can blame yourself.'

Captain Mainstay, 'But I do, my Lord, I cannot shake off the responsibility for it.'

Lord Malander, 'Tell me what happened next.'

Captain Mainstay, 'I ordered the hill troops under my control to join you. I then ordered my aides to collect the disparate forces together and to attack the rear of the Slimenest.'

Lord Malander, 'That was an excellent contribution. Without that, we may have lost the day.'

Captain Mainstay, 'I can't believe that, my Lord.'

Lord Malander, 'Battles can turn on a penny. A battle is normally a series of individual encounters; some are simply two solitary figures in hand-to-hand combat.

'I'm trying to industrialise the process, and I think I've proved the logic of it. Anyway, I'm struggling to see why you want to hand your sword over.'

Captain Mainstay, 'I need some form of penance for my own

sanity.'

Lord Malander, 'In that case, my punishment is that you attend our full set of training courses and that you work with me on a new planning strategy.'

Captain Mainstay, 'Thank you, my Lord.'

23

The Prophetarium

Lord Malander, 'Dear Abbott, it is a pleasure to meet you.'

Abbott Frogmore, 'No, the pleasure is mine. It is not every day you meet a genuine hero.'

Lord Malander, 'My dear Abbott, I was only doing my duty.'

Abbott Frogmore, 'It's a credit to you, but you are far too modest.'

Lord Malander, 'Your kindness is appreciated, and thank you for making the journey to get here.'

Abbott Frogmore, 'Once again, the pleasure is mine. The hills are a natural wonder, and the local water is the best in Grand Britannica. I have asked to have my ashes scattered on those hills.'

Lord Malander, 'Well, the hills are not short of ashes at the moment.'

Abbott Frogmore, 'I guess they are not, blessed be the fallen.'

Lord Malander, 'You are probably wondering why I asked you to come.'

Abbott Frogmore, 'I assumed that it wasn't for spiritual reasons as the Malanders are not known for their piety.'

Lord Malander, 'Absolutely right. I want to offer you a job that may be slightly sacrilegious.'

Abbott Frogmore, 'That is a surprise. Is it just sacrilegious, or is it heretical?'

Lord Malander, 'Some would say that it is sinful, but from my point of view, it is neither. More a case of analytical research and interpretation.'

Abbott Frogmore, 'You are talking about the Prophecy, aren't you?'

Lord Malander, 'They said that you were clever.'

Abbott Frogmore, 'Too clever for my own good, some would say. It has got me into trouble on many occasions. I find it very hard to conform in the face of logic to the contrary.'

Lord Malander, 'Don't you hold the record for being expelled from the most religious institutions?'

Abbott Frogmore, 'To my shame, I do.'

Lord Malander, 'Your qualifications sound perfect for this job. I want you to set-up a team of experts to collect, review and interpret the Prophecy. The operation will be yours to control.'

Abbott Frogmore, 'But don't we have the full Prophecy already?'

Lord Malander, 'So far we have the following verses in the public domain:

> *The Lords of the Hills must never flee,*
> *Death and destruction, I can guarantee,*
> *For those that ignore their destiny,*
> *Insanity awaits the escapee.*
>
> *The devil waits for the unknown,*
> *Merlin's home on the throne,*
> *Prepare to flee or postpone,*
> *The coming of your gravestone.*

In the lands and hills of Worcestershire,
One and all will suffer much hellfire,
The death pangs of an honest squire,
Cause the armies of man to retire.

The great horde will advance,
To the Gathering's war dance,
Lead on by the Master's imperious lance,
Absolutely nothing was left to chance.

To capture the Hills of Prophecy,
Will encounter beasts of great monstrosity,
Nothing will prepare you for its progeny,
These killing, fire-breathing monsters of astrology.

Defeat is guaranteed before their ferocity,
Unless you secure the anomaly.
There are times to live and times to die,
The duo came to glorify.

But now are dead, those poor alumni,
What reason you will decry,
There is no value now or need to crucify,
We need to turn a blind eye,
And learn to fight and shout our battle cry,
It's time to enchant and mystify.

The gallant captain joined the fray,
Nothing would turn his head away,
From the need to maim and slay,
Our enemies on this, our Lord's day,

> *Helped by a fighting neigh,*
> *As our foes slipped away.*

Abbott Frogmore, 'I've never seen so much verse in one place before'.

Lord Malander, 'I'm not sure if it is in the right sequence. I'm led to believe that this is only about 10% of what is out there. I need the rest, and I need it interpreted. Are you interested in the job?'

Abbott Frogmore, 'I am interested, but I would need resources.'

Lord Malander, 'That shouldn't be a problem as the Elders have agreed to finance it.'

Abbott Frogmore, 'I thought that the Elders had banned it.'

Lord Malander, 'Not since my father has taken over.'

Abbott Frogmore, 'Your father?'

Lord Malander, 'He is the acting Chief Elder.'

Abbott Frogmore, 'In that case, you have found your man.'

Lord Malander, 'Excellent, I need a plan on what you need: staffing, property, equipment etc. Please be bold.'

Abbott Frogmore, 'Don't worry, I will.'

Lord Malander, 'Just to get you excited, we recently found these verses:

> *The master of all is for all a master,*
> *With the Abbott onboard as forecaster,*
> *Progress will be much faster,*
> *As strong and clear as alabaster,*
> *That won't help avoid a disaster.*

> *The Man of God was so fat,*

In his cloak and crooked hat,
Don't let him corner you like a rat,
Remember, he hates the regal cat.

Abbott Frogmore, 'I'm that Abbott?'
   Lord Malander, 'And that's your job to interpret.'

24

What say the Elders?

Elder Three, the Duke of Mercia, was looking forward to the next meeting of the Elders. He planned to shake things up, partly because he liked shaking things up, mostly because it was urgently necessary.

For a start, he had issued an agenda. Normally they spent the first few hours trying to agree on what they were going to discuss and then failed to do it because a long lunch got in the way. Of course, the reality was that the previous Chief Elder had his own agenda. One that was never shared.

Previously they had always got together the night before and shared a heavy, rather wet, dinner. Few of them were compos mentis the next day and, in some cases, not even the day after.

The agenda was radical:
1. Agree on the purpose of the Elder Council
2. Allocate roles and responsibilities
3. Establish a budget
4. Establish a civil service
5. Review national Slimenest situation
6. Appoint a national warlord
7. Agree on the appointment of Abbott Frogmore
8. Any other business.

Most of the morning was spent discussing the first four points. In every case, Elder Three got his way. He was the only one with prepared arguments. Eventually, they got onto reviewing the Slimenest situation, and it became apparent that nothing or very little was known. It was embarrassing and frighteningly worrying that so little was known.

Then the Council got onto the key issue of the day: the appointment of a national warlord. Servants circulated some of the finest wine in the duke's cellar.

Elder Three started the discussion by saying, 'Fellow Elders, please take your glass, stand and toast the greatest general in the land and our next warlord: Lord Malander.' It was a done deal.

That night, over dinner, Elder Three told his son about his promotion and congratulated him. The Mercia House was once again on the move.

Lord Malander wasn't sure whether to shout with joy or scream with anguish. He was too young. He was too inexperienced. He wasn't ready for this level of responsibility. But someone had to do it. Who else was there? Who else could do the job better than him?

Lady Malander was thrilled but concerned that he would be away from home a lot of the time. She recognised that the role was critical to the survival of Grand Britannica. She knew that her husband was the right man for the job. She accepted that he was probably the only man who could do the job. She wasn't that happy that their lives were going to change, perhaps forever.

Lord Malander also made it clear that he would need to expand the magical forces, and, as a consequence, his wife would have to establish an Academy of the Mystical Arts.

He went to bed full of ideas. Things were going to change.

25

A Meeting of Minds

Lord Malander woke up energised and ready to implement some new ideas. He was desperate to get things underway. He sent his aides out to collect the key people he wanted for a meeting that afternoon. During the morning, he pondered and developed his ideas. They had no time to waste.

Gradually his guests arrived, and they were led to a large chamber containing a round table and many chairs. At this stage, Camelot was but a dream in the far-flung future!

The guests were as follows:
- Abbott Frogmore
- Annie Dragondale
- Captain Mainstay
- Lady Malander
- Lieutenant Bandolier
- Lindsey Clutterbuck
- Lord Hogsflesh
- Tindell Lambskin
- Faye Mellondrop

Lord Malander, 'Ladies and Gentlemen, fellow victors of our first battle against the Slimenest, your lives are about to change. Firstly, I need to tell you that I have been promoted to the role of National Warlord.'

There was a genuine and heartfelt round of clapping and cheers. No one in the room disputed the fact that he deserved it.

Lord Malander, 'This means that your roles are going to change. As of now, you are all members of the War Council. 'Your positions are as follows:

'Abbott Frogmore, you are now Head of Prophecy Research and Planning. Your role relating to Prophecy research has already been discussed. You will also take on responsibility for strategic planning, which will necessitate your team liaising with all of the other disciplines.

'Are you happy to proceed?'

Abbott Frogmore, 'Delighted, my Lord.'

Lord Malander, 'As discussed previously, I will need your departmental plans and requirements in the very near future.'

Abbott Frogmore, 'I've already started working on them, my Lord.'

Lord Malander, 'Excellent. Annie Dragondale, you are now Major Dragondale. Head of Archery. Are you happy with that?'

Annie Dragondale, 'I'm not sure that I'm ready for that level of responsibility, my Lord.'

Lord Malander, 'We haven't got time for people to get ready. You are the best we have. You will need to set up a School of Archery. Do you accept this role?'

Annie Dragondale, 'Yes, my Lord. I'm pleased that you have confidence in me, a mere woman.'

Lord Malander, 'There are no mere women in my army. You have earned your place. Hold your head up with pride.

'John, you are now Major Mainstay and my Second in Command. Do you accept the role?'

Captain Mainstay, 'Yes, my Lord. I will not let you down for the second time.'

Lord Malander, 'I know that, Major John.' And John grinned one of the largest grins going.

'Lady Jane Malander, you have already accepted the role of Head of Mystical Arts, and you are already planning an Academy.'

Lady Malander, 'Yes, my love. Sorry, Am I allowed to call you love?'

Lord Malander, 'Not really, I will have to punish you later.' Everyone laughed.

Lord Malander, 'Lieutenant Bandolier, you are now Major Bandolier of the Cavalry. You will need to set-up a Cavalry School. Are you happy with that?'

Lieutenant Bandolier, 'I couldn't be happier, my Lordship.'

Lord Malander, 'That's what I like to hear. Lindsey, my dear friend, do I have a list of jobs for you?'

Lindsey Clutterbuck, 'That's just what I was worried about.'

Lord Malander, 'Do you want the list now, Major Clutterbuck?'

Lindsey Clutterbuck, 'You honour me, Sir. Fire away.'

Lord Malander, 'Here is the list:
- Great Malvern will be our HQ and Centre of Operations. This is partly because the Elders are based here and that it is a great defensive position
- We need buildings for the Academy of Mystical Arts, the Cavalry School, the Archery School, the Prophecy Research Centre, Command Centre, the Infantry School, the Scouting School, an Armoury and stores complex, stables, barracks and probably lots more
- We need castles at each end of the Malvern Hills
- We need a castle at Upton upon Severn
- We will probably need castles in Worcester, Gloucester,

Ledbury, and Tewkesbury. I need your guidance on that
- We need a good pathway along the eastern side of the hills
- We need to retake Wales. I've no idea what needs to be done
- Ledbury needs a lot of construction work.'

Lindsey Clutterbuck, 'I think that is enough, my Lord, for now.'

Lord Malander, 'Fair enough. You are going to need a lot more resources.'

Lindsey Clutterbuck, 'I will probably need a new building.' Everyone laughed again, but there was truth in what he said.

Lord Malander, 'Dear Victor, you are now Major Hogsflesh, and you are charged with building a Scouting School.'

Lord Hogsflesh, 'I'm honoured, my Lord.'

Lord Malander, 'Tindell, you are now Major Lambskin of the Infantry.'

Tindell Lambskin, stuttering, 'I'm a simple ploughman and not worthy of the role.'

Lord Malander, 'I accept that you are a bit simple, but there is no one braver or more deserving of the role. You have no choice.'

Tindell Lambskin, still stuttering, 'Yes, Sir.'

Lord Hogsflesh, 'Don't let him bully you.'

Tindell Lambskin, stuttering even more, 'I won't, Sir.'

Lord Malander, 'I will bully you if I want to.'

Tindell Lambskin, still stuttering, 'Yes, Sir.' On the field, there was no chance of bullying him. He was totally loved by his troops. He was one of them: hard-working, committed, down-to-earth. A real hero!

Lord Malander, 'I'm glad to hear that you are onboard. Faye Mellondrop, I want you to be head of everything else: supply, transport, medical, administration, accounts, canteen, uniforms etc. Are you happy with that?'

Faye Mellondrop, 'As happy as a Slimie in the shit.' She never minced her words, but she was just an amazing no-nonsense administrator. As they say, an army marches on its stomach.

Lord Malander, 'You will be Quartermaster-General.'

26

It's not all quiet on the Slimenest Front

It wasn't long before the Slimies heard about the defeat. It was an affront to their cause. It was an affront against God. It was totally unacceptable. Part of the Slimie mystique was their infallibility, their invincibility, and their determination never to give in.

The effect on humans was already noticeable. They now knew that the Slimenest could be defeated. They now had a hero. The humans fought harder and for longer. And the humans now wanted revenge. Resistance was growing throughout Grand Britannica.

In terms of Malvern, thousands of volunteers were flocking to the cause. Untrained ploughmen, blacksmiths, housewives, schoolboys, and even members of the priesthood were dropping the tools of their trade and signing up as soldiers. Every place in the Academy of Mystical Arts was taken. There was a buzz. A buzz of excitement. A buzz associated with winning.

Lord Malander's name was now a byword for hope. He was conscious that the euphoria would soon end. The first failure would burst the bubble, but for now, it was worth ten regiments of soldiers. Well, perhaps five!

Lord Malander realised that the Slimenest would not tolerate this. He would be a target. They would come in their thousands, perhaps hundreds of thousands, determined to wipe his name from the annals of history. He needed to prepare for this.

The Slimenest leaders in the south of England secretly met at Horsell Common, near Woking, where H.G. Wells' aliens would land in years to come. Normally they would call a Gathering to make decisions, but this was too important, too urgent. And also, a Gathering usually cost them between ten and fifteen per cent of their fighters.

The current extent of the Slimenest 'empire' included all of the home counties but not London, Essex, Herefordshire, Hampshire, Wiltshire, Norfolk, Suffolk, and Dorset. The Isle of Wight was still free. Oxfordshire and Gloucestershire were under attack but still resisting strongly. The only human victory was the freeing of Wales, but the good news was that Wales had many resources invaluable to the cause.

However, the Slimenest were suffering the classic problem encountered by all invaders. How do you defend what you have and still continue the invasion? They had an obvious advantage over other invaders: they wanted to kill the entire populace of the conquered areas, but it took resources. What should they focus on?

In reality, Lord Malander had the same problem. Do you build up the defences of your base, or do you assist Gloucestershire and Oxfordshire? And what should he do with the Northern forces? After some deliberations, he decided that once Malvern was secure, he would use the Cotswold edge as his next defensive position.

It would have suited him better if the escarpment was facing the other way, so he didn't have slopes behind him, but you have to work with what you have got. Gradually he would push forward to utilise the hills of Oxfordshire.

27

Where are they?

Lord Malander called for Major Hogsflesh. He always enjoyed the company of this great bon vivant.

Lord Malander, 'Morning, Major, or do you still prefer Lord?'

Major Hogsflesh, 'The ladies seem to prefer Lord, but when you are a Hogsflesh, you get used to being called lots of names. I've often thought of changing it, but that name has shaped me.'

Lord Malander, 'I agree. I can't imagine you as anything but a Hogsflesh.'

Major Hogsflesh, 'How can I help you?'

Lord Malander, 'I need intelligence.'

Major Hogsflesh, 'I've been saying that for a long time, but not everybody can have my gifts.'

Lord Malander, 'Very droll. There is a lot that I need to know.'

Major Hogsflesh, 'Tell me what you want, and I will get it.'

Lord Malander, 'This is my list.' He handed over a scroll with the following on it:
1. I need to know the exact position of the Slimenest incursions
2. I need that to be constantly monitored
3. I need to know what's happening in London
4. I need to know how Gloucestershire and Oxfordshire

are doing
5. I need to know what resources we have in each free county in Grand Britannica
6. I need to know who is in charge of each county
7. I need couriers to go out and inform the above that I'm the new national Warlord.

Major Hogsflesh, 'That's quite a list.'
Lord Malander, 'And I need the information now.'
Major Hogsflesh, 'Of course you do. What is your priority?'
Lord Malander, 'One, two and four, but I can't spare you.'
Major Hogsflesh, 'I understand. I picked up a lot of good men who know the territory well. I will send the scouts out now. I will create a team to address the other points.'
Lord Malander, 'What do you think of Lord Eleonar?'
Major Hogsflesh, 'As a man or as a soldier?'
Lord Malander, 'Both.'
Major Hogsflesh, 'As a soldier, he is a total waste of time although he is a good administrator and knows the basics.'
Lord Malander, 'And as a man?'
Major Hogsflesh, 'Honest, straight as they come, hard-working. His heart is in the right place. He wants to serve and make a difference. In many ways, he is a natural diplomat.'
Lord Malander, 'Would he fit into your team?'
Major Hogsflesh, 'I could definitely use a man of that calibre.'
Lord Malander, 'Go and see him and sign him up.'
Major Hogsflesh, 'Yes, Sir. Before I go, I wondered if there is any way we could use magic to help with the scouting?'
Lord Malander, 'I will ask my Lady.'
Major Hogsflesh, 'Thank you, Sir.'

Lord Malander had noticed that since the victory, he was shown a lot more respect, but then the proof was always in the pudding. He wondered what that really meant.

28

Decisions were made

The Slimenest were not used to making decisions. When you are hoping to die and achieve everlasting happiness, decisions become rather boring and tedious. And when you have to think about other things, you are not focusing on releasing souls. They were not there to conquer land. What use was it to them? Their reward was in Heaven.

But sometimes, to maximise the kill-rate, you have to plan. And if planning is too much, then you have to make a decision. And if that is too much, you have to assess the situation and come to a resolution, and if there is a verdict, act on it. And if that is too much, just fight.

When a decision had been made, it was not always shared because the chain of command was vague, but somehow things got done. There was, in fact, an outcome of the meeting. One key resolution was made and pronounced: Fifty per cent of the forces on this grotty, smelly island would be used to attack Malvern and raze it to the ground.

Retribution would be total. No living soul would survive. Perhaps even the hills would be flattened.

To celebrate the outcome, a Killfest was organised. About two thousand 'human volunteers' were rounded up and tied to posts in the camp. The ever-popular festival events were enacted:
- Eye gouging

- Disembowelling
- Impalement
- Breast ripping
- Bone crushing
- Genital mutilation
- Boiling alive
- Drowning
- Flagellation
- Force-feeding
- Scalping
- Stoning
- Tooth extraction

One of the most popular events was to bet on who could do the most damage to a victim but still keep it alive. Normally there were twelve less than enthusiastic volunteers. The torture had to follow a prescribed process which started with multiple rapes. Then all of the fingernails and toenails were slowly ripped out. This was followed by the extraction of teeth one by one and then the slicing of the tongue. Salt was then rubbed in to cause further agony.

The genitals were then roasted and ripped off. This was then followed by the systematic stabbing, scraping, and burning of arms and legs before they were sawn off. The wounds were then braised to stop bleeding.

The victim was then skinned and scalped. The ears and nose were then sliced off and pushed into the mouth along with some sulphuric acid. The poor victim still had the pleasure of seeing everything, but that wasn't the end. His belly was slashed open to release his guts. Then his eyes were gouged out.

If the victim was still alive, he was honoured by being fed to the hogs, although sometimes drowning was an option because the hogs had been too well fed. The winning torturer was then tortured to death, as was his or her want. They did have the dubious pleasure of choosing their own end.

Once the festivities were over, the march to Malvern was on, but not before another verse was found:

> *For our enemies, we will torture and kill,*
> *For our friend's death will be our goodwill,*
> *We do it for love as they have free will,*
> *It's not because we are mentally ill,*
> *That we destroy all on Malvern Hill.*

29

Bad News on the Horizon

Major Hogsflesh never really liked being the bearer of bad news, but that was frequently his job. And this was bad news. He ran down to Lord Malander's Command Centre. It was a glorious name for a converted barn. And running wasn't that easy when you had an extended belly to support. He didn't see himself as fat, but he accepted portly.

Lord Malander was pleased to see his old friend but not so pleased when he heard the news.

Major Hogsflesh, 'My Lord, Groups of the slimy turds have been congregating at Swindon. So far, we have estimated about two hundred and fifty thousand of them, probably half of the whole Slimenest population in the country. That includes all of them who were attacking Oxfordshire and Gloucestershire.'

Lord Malander, 'That wasn't the start to the day that I wanted. Obviously, we need to track them, but I guess that they are coming this way?'

Major Hogsflesh, 'I fear so, my lord.'

Lord Malander, 'Can you organise meetings with the Lieutenant-Generals of the Gloucestershire and Oxfordshire forces.'

Major Hogsflesh, 'Of course, my Lord. They are both good men that you will find to be invaluable assets.'

Lord Malander, 'Another question. If they marched

normally, how long would it take for them to get to Malvern?'

Major Hogsflesh, 'There are some "'ifs and buts". Firstly, will they march as one column or many? A decent army would probably march by division. It would make sense to have at least five columns, but I suspect that it will be one big procession as they are not a professional army. But that will slow them down considerably.'

Lord Malander, 'I agree with you, but they might send an advance force against us.'

Major Hogsflesh, 'That's possible, but you have a reputation now. I believe that they will not attack us until all of their forces are in position.'

Major Hogsflesh, 'Secondly they will have to stop regularly for rations. That will be a challenge as they normally feed off the land. An army that size will have to forage far and wide. Then, there are the catapults, great big clumsy things.'

Lord Malander, 'Do they need them? They weren't particularly effective against us.'

Major Hogsflesh, 'The answer is yes. They are creatures of habit. Their organisational structure and their complete outlook, doesn't encourage or even allow innovation. They will do what they always do.'

Lord Malander, 'But last time they only used catapults to fling corpses.'

Major Hogsflesh, 'They rely on terror to intimidate the opposition. Catapulting dead friends and neighbours at you is a key part of their terror campaign. So, like most marches, the column will be restricted to the speed of its slowest component: the catapults.'

Lord Malander, 'And the road from Swindon to Gloucester is not the easiest, especially for very large loads.'

Major Hogsflesh, 'And getting down Birdlip Hill will not be easy if you let them get that far.'

Lord Malander, 'That needs to be assessed. So what's the answer?'

Major Hogsflesh, 'I would say eight to ten days. But the more I think about it, I would say that it's going to be at least ten days.'

Lord Malander, 'If I have my way, it's going to be a lot longer. Can you also invite the Lieutenant-General of Worcestershire to our meeting?'

Major Hogsflesh, 'Of course, my Lord.'

30

More of Frogmore

Lord Malander, 'My dear Abbott, how are things going?'

Abbott Frogmore, 'On what front?'

Lord Malander, 'On all fronts?'

Abbott Frogmore, 'Well, the Prophecy team are still settling down. Those academic types don't move that quickly. On the planning front, I've thrashed out a few ideas for you to review.'

Lord Malander, 'Go on.'

Abbott Frogmore, 'Look at the map on the wall. The black area is what we believe to be the extent of the Slimenest incursion. It looks like their forces in the eastern counties are meagre, and we could easily recapture them.'

Lord Malander, 'By my reckoning the Slimies have conquered Dorset, West and East Sussex, Kent, Essex, Suffolk, Hertfordshire and most of Southern Norfolk.'

Abbot Frogmore, 'They have also captured most of Wiltshire and Hampshire.'

Lord Malander, 'You are right. I can see it now.'

Abbot Frogmore, 'At least London is still resisting the incursion, my lord.'

Lord Malander, 'I see that you have two black lines on the map.'

Abbot Frogmore, 'That's correct. The northern line goes from the Severn Estuary to the southern part of the Wash and the western lines dissects Somerset in half.'

Lord Malander, 'And what is the purpose of these lines?'

Abbott Frogmore, 'I'm proposing that all of the Northern and Midland forces form a defence behind the top line, and the South-Western forces do the same behind that line.'

Lord Malander, 'Are you proposing that we surrender Oxfordshire, Cambridgeshire, Northamptonshire, Berkshire, Hertfordshire and Buckinghamshire?'

Abbott Frogmore, 'Of course not. The area between the lines is our field of engagement. There is no point in having forces in Cheshire and Yorkshire. If we continue with that structure, we are lost.'

Lord Malander, 'I agree we need to concentrate our forces as soon as possible.'

Abbott Frogmore, 'Then we need well-organised armies designed for attack. I'm still thinking about it, but I'm considering the following:

- Recapturing Norfolk and Suffolk, then we could move our defensive line further south
- Reinforcing London, from there, we could strike out in many different directions and even divide their forces in half
- Invade from the Isle of Wight.'

Lord Malander, 'That's excellent work. I'm impressed.'

Abbott Frogmore, 'Thank you, my Lord.'

Lord Malander, 'Start the planning process for the lines of defence, but we have a bigger challenge on our hands.'

Abbott Frogmore, 'What's that, my Lord?'

Lord Malander, 'The Slimenest will shortly be on the move.'

Abbott Frogmore, 'So you were right. How many are

coming here?'

Lord Malander, 'Two hundred and fifty thousand.'

Abbott Frogmore, 'Bugger, sorry, my Lord.'

Lord Malander, 'Bugger is too mild.'

Abbott Frogmore, 'Fucking Hell.'

Lord Malander, 'That's more like it.'

Abbott Frogmore, 'So we have ten days then.'

Lord Malander, 'How did you know that?'

Abbott Frogmore, 'They will travel at the speed of the lowest possible denominator: the catapult.'

Lord Malander, 'So I need you…'

Abbott Frogmore, 'To consider ways of slowing them down whilst you build your defences.'

Lord Malander, 'Exactly.'

Abbott Frogmore, 'Well, the obvious comes to mind.'

Lord Malander, 'Go on.'

Abbott Frogmore, 'From the top of my head, I would suggest the following:

1. Burnt Earth Strategy
2. Slow down the catapults
3. Hit and run raids
4. Roadblocks
5. Fires
6. Flooding
7. An attack on the rear of the column
8. Traps.'

Lord Malander, 'Please start the planning process as soon as possible.'

Abbott Frogmore, 'Certainly my Lord.'

31

Lady Malander has her Way

Lady Malander hadn't seen her husband for a few days. She understood that his time was precious, filled with meetings, planning, reviews etc., and she was just another cog in his busy schedule, but she was a young woman who had needs. Well, not so young, but she still had needs. Consequently, she planned a romantic evening, but really, she was going to fuck his brains out.

One of the side effects of magic was that it made you randy. She had been on the edge of an orgasm for some time. She needed her husband to help push her over the edge. And it was getting urgent. It had started to affect her work.

Lord Malander knew something was wrong as soon as he opened the front door. A man can often sense when things are not quite right, but there were no servants for a start, and there were fewer candles than normal. And there was a very sweet scent in the air. He prepared for danger, but he hadn't fully realised how precarious his position was.

Lady Malander walked into the room in a flowing, almost transparent, nightdress, one he hadn't seen before. Not that there was much to see as it hardly covered her hips or ample breasts. In the candlelight, she looked stunning. He could see the dark triangle of her minge, and his manhood responded accordingly. He couldn't remember the last time that he had a good fuck.

Lady Malander, 'Good Evening, handsome.'

Lord Malander, 'Hello, my darling wife. You seem to be in a rather romantic mood?'

Lady Malander, 'I plan to give you the best fuck of your life.'

Lord Malander, 'Do you now, but I've got lots of work to do?'

Lady Malander, 'That might be the case, but you have got a job to do at home.' She took her nightdress off and stood in front of him, stark naked.

She was a very attractive woman, not beautiful in the classic sense, but very fuckable. His member was now fully rigid. She came over and removed his right boot.

Lord Malander, 'I really can't spare the time.' She took off his left boot.

Lady Malander, 'I understand.' And she took off his jerkin.

Lord Malander, 'I've got a really important meeting to get ready for.' She pulled his tights down to expose a cock on guard duty.

Lady Malander, 'It must be terrible for you.' She kneeled down and placed his very stiff cock in her mouth and gently licked away. At the same time, she stroked his hairy balls as she knew that he liked that. She also knew her husband's body well, and she could tell that he wasn't far from coming, and that wasn't what she wanted.

It reminded her of the long hot summers when they first got married. When Lord Malander, a shy youngster, had no idea what to do, but then they spent long nights together investigating each other's bodies. The investigations had gone well but had not borne fruit, and six years later, she was still childless. There was talk about her being barren.

Lady Malander grabbed her husband's arm and dragged him to the nearest bed. She laid on her back and opened her legs, exposing her cunt to him. He bent down and licked her labia as he knew that she liked that. He also knew his wife's body well and could tell that she wasn't far from coming.

His cock was now aching with desire. It urgently wanted satisfaction, and he plunged his stiff prick deep into her womanhood. He was shocked by her reaction. She had the monster of all orgasms. She experienced a series of cataclysmic climaxes. Her body literally shook with pleasure as she suffered one peak after another. She was on the crest of an erotic wave.

Lord Malander couldn't hold back any longer, and his cock exploded. Prodigious amounts of seed were pumped into her. She felt that it was probably the best fuck of her life, and if that didn't generate a baby, then nothing would.

They cuddled and cuddled some more, and then they both slipped into a deep sleep that only lovers could achieve. They both woke a few hours later, still in the most intimate of positions. They made love again, but this time it was a safe, soft married type of lovemaking, which was nice.

Then it happened. Lady Malander was turned into a hog, warts, and all.

Lord Malander shouted for help, but there were no servants as the lady of the house had sent them away because of her romantic inclinations. He quickly pushed his pig of a wife into the bedroom and locked her in for safety. His aides were soon there, and he told them to get magic assistance as soon as possible.

32

Hogs Everywhere

Lady Malander wasn't the only person who had been hogified. Captain Mainstay, Abbott Frogmore and Major Hogsflesh were also victims. Lord Malander couldn't help laughing to himself as Major Hogsflesh was now genuinely hog's flesh. What a twist of fate.

Lorrimore of Lendle, Tinton of Taverton, Lionel Wildheart, and the Enchantress of Evermore were with Lord Malander discussing the situation.

Lord Malander, 'What has happened?'

The Enchantress of Evermore, 'This is clearly the work of a very powerful magician.'

Lorrimore of Lendle, 'I would say so. It would have to be a very skilled practitioner of the mystical arts to turn one person into a hog, let alone four.'

Lionel Wildheart, 'I have to agree. It's beyond anything we could do.'

Lord Malander, 'So what are you going to do about it?'

Tinton of Taverton, 'What do you want us to do?'

Lord Malander, 'Turn them back to their normal selves.' He sometimes wondered if magicians lived in the real world. He had always admired his wife for being down to earth at one level and quite magical at another.

The Enchantress of Evermore, 'Our studies suggest that

involuntary therianthropy is often permanent.'

Lord Malander, 'Therianthropy?'

The Enchantress of Evermore, 'It's the ability of a human to change into an animal. Werewolves are probably the best example of this. Here it has been forced on them by an external agency.'

Lord Malander, 'So is there no hope. We need these people back, or we are all doomed.'

Lorrimore Lendle, 'There is always hope. Firstly we need to identify the person who cast the spell and then identify the spell itself. When we have that, we can try and develop some counter-measures.'

Lord Malander, 'How can you identify the magician involved?'

Lionel Wildheart, 'Every spell contains the traits of the person that cast it: a bit like a personal signature.'

Lord Malander, 'So how long will this take, and don't mention string.'

Lionel Wildheart, 'Less than a month.'

Lord Malander, 'Come on, we need this whole thing rectified in hours, a day or two at the most.'

Tinton of Taverton, 'It will take as long as it takes.'

Lord Malander, 'Fuck you. That is my wife and friends we are talking about. I need results, and I need them now.'

The Enchantress of Evermore, 'Please calm down, my dear Lord. I can understand your position, but we are dealing with the unknown here.'

Lord Malander, 'Please start work on this immediately and keep me regularly informed.'

Lord Malander didn't know that there was a verse covering this:

Some prefer a pig to a hog,
Others would rather play leapfrog.
But who, but who is the demagogue?
Is the barren womb the epilogue?
If this tale ends in no dialogue.

33

On the March

The Slimies were on the march. Their sense of direction was appalling: they marched in the wrong direction for the first ten miles in one long column as Major Hogsflesh predicted. By the time one of the senior Slimies realised the error of their ways, the catapults had sunk into the mud.

They managed to turn the front of the column, but they weren't sure what to do with the rest of it. In the end, they decided to let it continue. So, by the end of the day, they arrived at where they started. In human terms, that couldn't be regarded as successful, but the Slimies were quite pleased with their endeavours.

Foragers were sent out to collect food, but this was never successful as the foragers generally consumed what they found and then they went to sleep. As a consequence, the whole army tended to forage. That was militarily acceptable when you had a few hundred or even a few thousand troops but not when you had a quarter of a million. At best, the roads were mud tracks, and now they were being churned up, making it almost impossible for the catapults to be moved.

Slimies could eat almost any fauna or flora, although they much preferred fauna. Any living thing was simply ripped to pieces and consumed, and that included humans, especially humans. When food got really difficult to find, they were quite happy to resort to cannibalism. Some even started eating their own bodies.

Anyway, the countryside had been stripped in all directions, including the next ten miles, which meant that food was going to be in short supply in the days to come.

34

Delaying Tactics

It wasn't long before Lord Malander learnt that the Slimies were on the move. He went from relief back to despair, when he got confused accounts of the direction they were going in.

He called for a meeting of what was left of his War Council, which included:
- Major Dragondale, Head of Archery
- Major Bandolier of the Cavalry
- Major Clutterbuck, Engineering
- Major Lambskin of the Infantry
- Quartermaster General Mellondrop.

Lord Malander, 'Welcome to this somewhat depleted War Council. Our magical friends are still trying to return our colleagues to their normal selves, but progress is very slow. In the meantime, the war continues, and the Slimies are on the move.

'We are steadily building up our resources, but we now have to do whatever we can to slow down their progress.

'Abbott Frogmore was working on a plan before he was transmogrified into a hog. The key points of his plan were as follows:
1. Burnt Earth Strategy
2. Slow down the catapults

3. Hit and run raids
4. Roadblocks
5. Fires
6. Flooding
7. An attack on the rear of the column
8. Traps.

'Does this make sense?'

There was a general nodding of heads.

Lord Malander, 'These are my orders for Major Clutterbuck:
- Build roadblocks
- Set traps
- Identify if there are any flooding opportunities
- Identify any other ways of delaying them. I know from experience how inventive you can be.'

Major Clutterbuck, 'Yes, Sir.'

Lord Malander, 'These are my orders for Major Lambskin:
- Explain to the local population what is happening and take them to safety
- Bring livestock with you
- Destroy all arable crops
- Destroy all other sources of Slimenest food
- Delay the enemy where you can, but do not engage them
- Work with Major Bandolier to damage or destroy the catapults.'

Major Lambskin, 'Yes, Sir.'

Lord Malander, 'These are my orders for Major Bandolier:
- Carry out a series of hit and run raids
- Do not engage the enemy in a serious battle

- Cause fires at night
- Work with Major Lambskin regarding the destruction of the catapults.'

Major Bandolier, 'Yes, Sir.'

Lord Malander, 'These are my orders for Major Dragondale:
- Assist the others as required.'

Major Dragondale, 'Yes, Sir.'

Lord Malander, 'These are my orders for Quartermaster General Mellondrop:
- Support the other services
- Create a new department to develop new types of weapons. I have quite a few ideas in mind. You will need carpenters and ironworkers.'

Quartermaster General Mellondrop, 'Yes, Sir.'

Lord Malander, 'You are dismissed.'

35

The Pig Farm

Lord Malander was looking forward to a good night's sleep. He struggled to get three or four hours in one go before getting interrupted. He also found it strange sleeping without his wife by his side, and, although he loved his wife, he didn't want a pig in his bed. Its toiletry and table manners had a lot to be desired.

Nevertheless, he made a habit of saying goodnight to her. None of the magicians could tell him whether it was just a pig or a hog with a living, thinking human consciousness. If it was the latter, he was going to be in serious trouble as he hadn't shown a lot of affection to the animal.

Anyway, he trotted down to say good night to her, and she was gone. He immediately called the head maid to ask where she was. Apparently, all four of the pigs had been rounded up, and taken to the nearest sty.

Lord Malander, 'Are you telling me that you have put Lady Malander in a pigsty?'

Head Maid, 'Yes, my Lord.'

Lord Malander, 'How could you?'

Head Maid, 'I'm sorry, my Lord, but she was making a terrible racket. It got so bad that I consulted your herdsman. He said that she needed to root around with the company of other pigs. It was an important part of being a pig. It turned out that the others were in a similar state. So we rounded them all up and put them in the sty. I'm really sorry if I did wrong.'

Lord Malander, 'No, that's fine, off you go.' He wandered down to the pigsty, tracked down his herdsman, and said, 'Where is my wife?'

Herdsman. 'With all the other pigs, my Lord. That's just how they like it.'

Lord Malander, 'Show me.'

Herdsman, 'She's over there with the big porky on her back.'

Lord Malander, 'What's he doing?'

Herdsman, 'He's giving her one. It's his way of showing her who the boss is. Since she arrived, she has been very popular with the male pigs. That is at least the fifth time she has had sex this morning.'

Lord Malander, 'That's got to stop.'

Herdsman, 'Your Major Hogsflesh wouldn't leave her alone.'

Lord Malander, 'I want Lady Malander to have her own pen, and the other three can share a pen.'

Herdsman, 'I will do whatever you tell me to do, but she won't be happy. Don't blame me if she pines and dies.'

Lord Malander, 'Are you being serious?'

Herdsman, 'I certainly am.'

Lord Malander, 'In that case, leave her be.' He decided to chase the magicians again.

36

The Lieutenant-Generals Dance

Lord Malander met with the Lieutenant-Generals of Gloucestershire, Oxfordshire, and Worcestershire in a barn in Tewkesbury. He had met a couple of them before, but he didn't really know them. It was difficult explaining that the Head of Scouting had been transformed into a pig. He was also conscious that he had to stamp his authority over them. To be honest, that wasn't going to be that difficult as he was a recognised hero.

Lord Malander, 'Gentlemen, as you know, I have been appointed as the National War Lord, and I have setup a War Council consisting of the following:
- Abbott Frogmore, Head of Prophecy Research and Planning
- Major Dragondale, Head of Archery
- Major Mainstay, Second in Command
- Lady Malander, Head of Mystical Arts
- Major Bandolier of the Cavalry
- Major Clutterbuck, Head of Engineering
- Major Hogsflesh, Head of Scouting
- Major Lambskin of the Infantry
- Major Mellondrop, Quartermaster General.'

Lieutenant-General Oxfordshire, 'So we have a new dance-leader?'

Lord Malander, 'That is right, and you better dance properly to my tune, or you are out.'

Lieutenant-General Oxfordshire, 'OK, but what is Prophecy Research?'

Lord Malander, 'It was a banned subject, but the ban has been revoked. It would appear that a lot of verses in the Prophecy of the Hills seem to reflect reality. Consequently, we are carrying out research into it.

'For example, these verses seem to describe parts of our recent battle in detail:

> *In the lands and hills of Worcestershire,*
> *One and all will suffer much hellfire,*
> *The death pangs of an honest squire,*
> *Cause the armies of man to retire.*
>
> *The great horde will advance,*
> *To the Gathering's war dance,*
> *Lead on by the Master's imperious lance,*
> *Absolutely nothing was left to chance.*
>
> *To capture the Hills of Prophecy,*
> *Will encounter beasts of great monstrosity,*
> *Nothing will prepare you for its progeny,*
> *These killing, fire-breathing monsters of astrology.*
>
> *Defeat is guaranteed before their ferocity,*
> *Unless you secure the anomaly.*
> *There are times to live and times to die,*
> *The duo came to glorify.*

'There may be clues in the poem that will help us get out of this mess.'

Lieutenant-General Worcestershire, 'Do we need a Head of Mystical Arts. It's hardly of military interest?'

Lord Malander, 'I wish that was the case, but we have certainly been under magical attack from the Slimenest. They have been using human witches.'

Lieutenant-General Worcestershire, 'Witches will work for anyone who has a piece of silver.'

Lord Malander, 'True. We have also been successfully using magic against them. It mustn't be underestimated.

'The next thing I want to share with you is our grand strategy.'

Lieutenant-General Oxfordshire, 'It's about time that someone had one. This county-based approach is doomed to failure. It was just jobs for the boys and girls.'

Lord Malander, 'What we are proposing will upset some of you but wait until I finish.

'We plan to isolate the South and the South-East by building defensive lines from the Severn Estuary to The Wash and from North Devon to Weston-Super-Mare.'

Lieutenant-General Gloucestershire, 'That was close, I've got a nice little retreat on Knightstone Island in Weston.'

Lord Malander, 'I will take that into account. We will then move all of our national forces to defend those lines. Let me show you on the map. As you can see we are moving all of our forces behind the two defensive lines.'

Lieutenant-General Oxfordshire, 'But you are sacrificing my county.'

Lieutenant-General Gloucestershire, 'And mine.'

Lord Malander, 'No, you are mistaken. This is the plan:

1. We create the two defensive lines
2. We move all of the troops from the free counties to man them.
3. We then create effective armies to recover all the territories inside the lines. Initially, our battles will be in Gloucestershire and Oxfordshire.'

Lieutenant-General Oxfordshire, 'I accept that it is a good start, but where are you going to get those armies from?'

Lord Malander, 'We are going to create them. Your forces are going to be the nucleus of our first army. I have extensive training facilities at Malvern, which will continue to be our HQ.'

Lieutenant-General Gloucestershire, 'My men are trained.'

Lord Malander, 'Can they fire arrows whilst on horse-back? Can they form a phalanx? Can they build strong defensive position? Can they march at double-time? Can they read maps?'

Lieutenant-General Gloucestershire, 'Of course not, they are only casual soldiers.'

Lord Malander, 'There are only professional soldiers in my army.'

'So do you want to know why you are here today?' They all nodded.

Lord Malander, 'There is a Slimenest army on its way here. Currently, it is near Swindon, but it plans to attack and destroy Malvern. It will go straight through your counties.'

Lieutenant-General Gloucestershire, 'It has been rather strange recently. We were in a bitter fight with them, and frankly, we were starting to lose ground. They just kept going, no matter what, and then they suddenly disappeared.'

Lieutenant-General Oxfordshire, 'Same here.'

Lord Malander, 'That's because they were all summoned to Swindon.'

Lieutenant-General Oxfordshire, 'So you are saying that

they were all recalled to Swindon to form an army to come back here.'

Lord Malander, 'Correct, but we know that their sense of geography and direction is very poor.

'Currently, we are carrying out a campaign to slow down their progress which includes the following:
1. Burnt Earth Strategy
2. Slow down the catapults
3. Hit and run raids
4. Roadblocks
5. Fires
6. Flooding
7. An attack on the rear of the column
8. Traps

'I think that sums it up. These are my orders for Gloucestershire and Oxfordshire:
- Explain to the local population what is happening and take them to safety
- Bring livestock with you
- Destroy all arable crops
- Destroy all other sources of Slimenest food
- Delay the enemy where you can, but do not engage them
- Move all of your troops to Malvern
- Your best troops should be utilised to delay the enemy.

Please provide recommendations.'

Both Lieutenant-Generals responded positively.

These are my orders for Worcestershire:
- Move all troops to Malvern for training.

'Gentlemen, these are going to be the days of your lives. Please carry out your duties with urgency.'

They all said, 'Yes, Sir.'

37

Magical Failures

It was important not to give up hope, but as time went by, he had lost the little faith he had in his magical team. Regardless he decided to go and get an update.

Lord Malander, 'Thanks for seeing me. Has there been any progress?'

The Enchantress of Evermore, 'There has been some progress, but it has been of little value. We have identified a signature, but sadly we can't recognise it. We are beginning to wonder if it is of this world.'

Lorrimore of Lendle, 'I would go further and say that it is definitely a type of magic that has never previously existed on this planet.'

Lord Malander, 'So are you saying that this magic comes from another planet?'

Lionel Wildheart, 'Or possibly another dimension.'

Lord Malander, 'You don't know?'

Lionel Wildheart, 'How can we know?'

Tinton of Taverton, 'We have been wondering why you weren't targeted.'

Lord Malander, 'That thought had crossed my mind several times. I even tried to identify any distinguishing factors, but none are obvious. And what's to stop them doing it again?'

The Enchantress of Evermore, 'We have a team of magicians

maintaining a spell of protection. It doesn't entirely stop an attack, but it does weaken it, and it also warns us.'

Lord Malander, 'Why didn't we do this before?'

The Enchantress of Evermore, 'It takes a lot of resource to maintain it twenty-four hours per day. At the time of the incident, we didn't have the resources, and to be fair, the danger wasn't apparent.'

Lord Malander, 'Have we reached the point where there is nothing you can do?'

Lionel Wildheart, 'Do you want the truth?'

Lord Malander, 'Of course.'

Lionel Wildheart, 'We are completely out of our depth. It's a bit like a domino player against a chess master. Their magician is in a different league to us.'

Lord Malander, 'Can't you give me any hope?'

Tinton of Taverton, 'Someone said that there was always hope, but in this case, I can't see any.'

Lord Malander, 'So I might as well eat my wife for breakfast?'

Lord Malander had missed yet another verse:

Magical failures lead to gloom,
Around the corner, you meet your doom,
But hope lies in a new butcher's broom,
And a well-loved family heirloom.

38

On the Road Again

On the road again to Oxfordshire,
Sheer hard work one had to admire,
The obstacles were getting quite dire,
But nothing worse than sinking mire,
Gave us victory to aspire.

The column started its advance in the pouring rain. It wasn't the all-pervasive misty rain or the rather annoying drizzle or the intermittent downpours. It was the sort named after animals: cats and dogs. It was a continuous sheet of never-ending precipitation that drenched you to the bone.

It was the sort of rain that turned sideways and attacked your eyes. Torrents of water were converting the muddy passageways into veritable quagmires. It was becoming difficult to even stand in the deluge, and you simply couldn't see where you were going. Into this water-drenched environment came over two thousand mounted archers who attacked the front of the column. In a five-minute period, over ten thousand arrows hit the nearly blinded leaders of the drenched procession. That alone caused quite a few deaths, but what raised the death toll dramatically was the crushing.

The column just rolled on. The dead and the dying were crushed as those behind just trampled over them. Many fell, and they, in turn, were crushed by the following troops, who then carried on with the gruesome debacle. No one knew how to stop the convoy, and the death toll simply grew and grew.

The archers continued with their attack, hidden by the atrocious weather conditions. They continued until their stock of arrows was depleted. Then the column hit a series of deep water-filled trenches. The front of the marching army tried to stop, but they were just pushed into the stake-infested pits. Again, crushing was the cause of most deaths. Eventually, there were enough crushed bodies in the pits to make it crossable.

The rain started to calm down, which meant that they could see that the road ahead was blocked by fallen trees, well, almost a forest of trees. As they cleared the trees, further trees came rolling down the hills on each side. They all had to be removed so that the catapults could pass. There were few deaths, but there were long delays which was the purpose of the exercise.

It was time to make camp, but they had only travelled five miles. The foragers could find little to eat. The fields had been burnt, the wells had been poisoned, and the farm stock had been removed. They ended up eating their dead comrades. Then the mounted archers attacked the camp with burning arrows. The few tents that existed caught fire along with some of the catapults. This attack wasn't that successful because everything was too wet. But burning arrows still killed Slimies, and it stopped them resting.

Major Lambskin then led twenty groups of men to attack the catapults. They weren't sure what the best approach would be, so they decided to cut the ropes and remove as many catapult wheels as possible. It was a relatively easy action as there were no sentries, and most of the Slimies were fast asleep after their cannibalistic orgy.

When the Slimies woke up and found wheelless catapults, they decided that the best solution was to pull them along as they were, which definitely slowed the column down even further. So far, the delaying tactics had worked well.

39

The Butcher

His aide de camp informed him that a young tradesman wanted to see him, but Lord Malander was genuinely too busy. He told his aide to send him away. But the tradesman waited and waited.

Lord Malander continued to meet and greet, to carry on running meetings, to raise and sign orders, to plan and inspect, and occasionally he managed to grab some time to eat a chicken leg and sip a glass of red wine. Then he spotted the tradesman sitting outside his door. He told his aide that he could see him now.

The tradesman stood in front of the Lord with his cap held in his shaking hands. Lord Malander could see that he was very nervous and quite anxious.

Lord Malander asked his aide to get the man a seat.

Lord Malander, 'Please sit down.' The tradesman or rather tradesboy, as he was very young, sat down on the very edge of the seat as if he might be asked to go at any moment.

Lord Malander, 'Would you like a glass of wine?'

Thomas, 'Yes, please, my Lordship.' The aide took a glass over to him. It was probably the most expensive thing he had ever held, and the wine was not really to his taste. He was more of a mead man, but he felt very honoured.

Lord Malander, 'And what is your name?'

Thomas, 'Thomas, my Lordship.'

Lord Malander, 'Just Thomas?'

Thomas, 'Yes, just Thomas.'

Lord Malander, 'And what do you do, just Thomas?'

Thomas, 'I'm a butcher's boy, my Lordship.'

Lord Malander, 'And how can I help you?'

Thomas, 'I'm here to help you, my Lordship.'

Lord Malander, 'That makes a very pleasant change. And how do you intend to do that?'

Thomas, 'Well, I was near the pigsty intending to buy a few porkers for the chop when I spotted your wife and three other men. She grabbed my attention because she was trying to fight off the attentions of a rather fat pig.'

Lord Malander, 'You saw my wife?'

Thomas, 'Yes.'

Lord Malander, 'Where?'

Thomas, 'Inside the body of a pig, of course.'

Lord Malander, 'You sound as if it is quite common.'

Thomas, 'Not common, but I have seen it before. It's one of the tricks played by Decour de Charlene.'

Lord Malander, 'Decour de Charlene?'

Thomas, 'She is quite a famous witch in these parts.'

Lord Malander, 'Really.'

Thomas, 'Yes, absolutely. She must be at least three hundred years old. What she doesn't know could be written on a playing card.

'So did you want your wife back?'

Lord Malander, 'Of course.'

Thomas, 'Oh, that's not always the case. Many men have got rid of their wives by transforming them into animals and selling them.'

Lord Malander, 'That's shocking.'

Thomas, 'That may be the case, but it happens. Do you want the other three released as well?'

Lord Malander, 'Of course.'

Thomas, 'OK, I will need something precious from each of them.'

Lord Malander, 'Jewellery?'

Thomas, 'It could be, but ideally, I need something that is emotionally precious. Something more much valuable than money.'

Lord Malander, 'A family heirloom.'

Thomas, 'That would be perfect if they love it.' Lord Malander rushed off to get his Mother-in-Law's sewing set. It was valueless, but it was used every day by Lady Malander. Strangely it was what got her into magic, although he could never see the connection.

Thomas took the sewing set into the pigsty, made several incantations, and then attempted to smash the set with his butcher's broom. There was no flash or even a sonic boom; the pig just gradually changed into a naked woman trying to defend her sewing kit.

Lord Malander rushed to hug her. She grabbed his jerkin to protect her modesty.

Lord Malander, 'How are you?'

Lady Malander, 'I had the strangest dream that I was a pig.'

Lord Malander, 'That's really weird.'

Lady Malander, 'What's even stranger is that my fanny is really sore.'

Thomas eventually restored the other three, and he got himself a much better job.

40

Back on the Road

The Slimenest were not early risers. There was no hurry to save souls, and most of the army had no idea what they were doing. But once they had breakfasted on their dead colleagues, they were ready to go.

At that moment, the mounted archers attacked again, causing disarray among the Slimenest. This time it wasn't raining, so the Slimie archers could return 'fire', but they weren't organised enough, and their response was sporadic. The mounted archers retreated and decided to go for a series of hit and run raids whenever they weren't expecting it. To some extent, the element of surprise was lost.

The lack of wheels on the catapults was really slowing things down. The supervisors, or at least those who took some control, were finding it harder to get volunteers to pull. Those who refused were executed, which led to an outbreak of volunteer martyrs. In the end, the column stopped because psychologically, they needed their catapults. It was one of their crutches.

Then the mounted riders decided to use their secret weapon. They had arrows that contained flimsy packets of Tanylip. None of the archers had any confidence in it, but they had been ordered by Major Dragondale to give it a go. Over two thousand arrows with their little packets shot through the air. Then the Slimenest went wild. The whole convoy turned into one big mass of animalistic scratching.

Slimies were rubbing up against trees, boulders, each other, and the catapults. In their maddening fury, they effectively destroyed more than half of their catapults. Then the mounted riders launched thousands of normal deadly arrows into the mix. There were now three categories of Slimie: the dead, the dying, and the itching.

Major Lambskin, a sheep in wolf's clothing if there ever was one, had two companies working. One company had the job of killing any scouts, and there were a few. They also killed any foragers who strayed too far. The other company picked off any stragglers. They were always one step ahead and one step behind.

Wherever there were hills, there were trees and boulders that could be dropped onto the enemy. The Slimies were expecting it now. Their nervousness slowed them down. It also meant that the humans had to wait for them to turn up, but the Slimie progress was getting slower and slower.

Whilst this was going on, the three shire forces were marched into Malvern. When they arrived, they were amazed to see such an impressive military base. They were shocked to see such a hive of activity and so much organisation.

The arriving troops were fed and watered and then measured up for uniforms, a totally new innovation. They even got new boots. They were less enthused when the training started. It was hard, gruelling work. Both officers and men trained together, and then they were divided into their specialist functions for further classroom or on-the-job training. This was not their normal way of doing things, but even the most conservative of officers saw the long-term benefits.

The verses were coming thick and fast:

Soldiers come from where they dwell,
To fill the chambers of the citadel,
Malvern's butcher boy could quell,
The evil witches diabolical spell.

Our catapults destroyed by the ditch,
Burning arrows make us itch,
More than ever, we need our witch,
To destroy the revengeful bitch.

41

Human Again

Now that four members of the team were back from the bestial experience, he decided to call a meeting of the War Council. And talking about bestial experiences, he had taken full advantage of his wife last night, although he kept getting images of Hogsflesh fucking the pig version of his wife. Rather than make him jealous, it made him feel randy.

Three new members joined the meeting:
- Earl Winterdom, Lieutenant-General Worcestershire
- Count Mannering, Lieutenant-General Oxfordshire
- Lord Birdlip, Lieutenant-General Gloucestershire.

Lord Malander, 'Firstly, I would like to welcome back my colleagues who have been through a rather porky experience. And a very special welcome back to my wife.

'Secondly, I would like to welcome the three new members of the War Council.

'So, let's get down to business. The first item on the agenda is planning. Abbott Frogmore, can you update us, please.'

Abbott Frogmore, 'I believe that the overall plan for the two defensive lines has been accepted, and as we speak, regiments are marching south from all of the northern and midland counties. There is a lot of work to do building fortifications and defensive entrenchments, but we will soon have the labour.

'We still need to convince the counties of Cornwall and Devon that the plan will work. So far, they have shown no signs of cooperation.

'I believe that we need to visit them and bang a few heads together.

'The delaying tactics referring to the Slimenest army that's on its way here appear to be working, but I will let the others update you.

'From a planning point of view, the next tasks are more tactical. How do we re-take the south? I'm still working on that.'

Lord Malander, 'Any questions?'

Major Bandolier, 'What did you have for breakfast? Bacon and eggs perhaps.'

Abbott Frogmore, 'Very funny, how would you like a hoof up your nose?'

Lord Malander, 'What progress has been made regarding the Prophecy?'

Abbott Frogmore, 'Not a lot, my Lord, although we have managed to collect some additional verses.'

Lord Malander, 'I'm looking for some progress in that area in the very near future.'

Abbott Frogmore, 'Yes, my Lord.'

Lord Malander, 'Major Dragondale, your update, please.'

Major Dragondale, 'Our archers have been assisting Major Lambskin, and of course, our mounted archers are now part of the cavalry. The Tanylip arrows have been a huge success. Fay's team are busily producing more stock.'

Lord Malander, 'Thank you. Major Mainstay, your report, please.'

Major Mainstay, 'Nothing to report. I've mostly been making a pig of myself.'

Lord Malander, 'Can we get all of the pig-related jokes out of the way, please.'

Major Hogsflesh, 'It looks like you have saved our bacon.'

Fay Mellondrop, 'This little pig went to market.'

Lord Malander, 'I don't want to be a boar, but please stop.'

Major Mainstay, 'Very good, boar!' They all laughed, and it was important to keep the spirits up.

Lord Malander, 'Lady Malander, your report, please.'

Lady Malander, 'Am I allowed to mention pigs?'

Lord Malander, 'No, please carry on.'

Lady Malander, 'Yes, boss. I do have a few things to report:
- We have cast a protective field over Malvern, which appears to be working
- The recruitment of Thomas the Butcher as a magician has been a godsend. He is a magical superstar and a good butcher. Expect to be impressed
- We are working on a stronger version of Tanylip. The Slimies are seriously allergic to it
- During the Battle of Malvern, there were several reports of Slimies with hollow patches. Our magic caused that.
- We are working on perfecting it.'

Count Mannering, Lieutenant-General Oxfordshire, 'I hear that you can create illusions of dragons.'

Lady Malander, 'That's correct.'

Count Mannering, 'Can you create a real dragon?'

Lady Malander, 'If you asked me before Thomas arrived, I would say no, but it may be possible now.'

Lord Malander, 'Thank you. Major Bandolier, your report, please. And no pig jokes.'

Major Bandolier, 'I wouldn't stoop that low, my Lord. I have

a few things to report:
- The mounted archery attacks on the Slimenest column have been very successful. If we take our combined endeavours, it looks like we have reduced their forces by a fifth.'

Lord Malander, 'But that is fifty thousand Slimies.'
Major Bandolier, 'Yes, my Lord. I will continue:
- The Tanylip arrows have been a huge success. We need more.
- In five days, the Slimenest column has only travelled ten miles and is now stationary.'

Lord Malander, 'Congratulations to everyone who has been part of the delaying team. That's excellent news. We need to brainstorm later how we can intensify our attack on the column.
'Major Clutterbuck, your report, please.'
Major Clutterbuck, 'I can't claim my credit, but whilst I've been on holiday, my team have created many traps and challenges for the Slimenest column. They need to be congratulated.'
Major Bandolier, 'Hear, hear.' And there was a clap of hands as engineers rarely get the praise they deserve.
Lord Malander, 'Excellent work. Major Hogsflesh, your report, please.'
Major Hogsflesh, 'I think most things have been said, but this is our latest status position:
- I can confirm that the column is stationary. We believe that they are waiting for replacement catapults
- Our burnt earth strategy has been a great success. They have been forced to eat their dead
- We mustn't forget the Slimies that are not in the column.

They were all withdrawn back to Swindon. They must have plans to re-engage
- We believe that we know the whereabouts of Decour de Charlene. We are considering the best way of capturing her
- There is a possibility that the Slimenest know about the northern troop movements.'

Lord Malander, 'Any questions?'

Lady Malander, 'Do you need our assistance regarding Decour de Charlene.'

Major Hogsflesh, 'Yes, please.'

Lord Malander, 'Major Lambskin, your report, please.'

Major Lambskin, 'I would like to thank both the engineers and the archers. It has been a great combined effort. I have a few things to report:
- We managed to damage or destroy most of the catapults
- We have killed off thousands of stragglers and most of their scouts
- The training programme is working to its full extent
- New uniforms are being issued.'

Lord Malander, 'Once again, well done to you all. The Quartermaster General's report, please.'

Quartermaster General, 'Everything is fine.'

When Fay said that things were fine, they were fine.

Lord Malander, 'What about the Tanylip arrows.'

Quartermaster General, 'The quantity that was ordered is awaiting collection.'

Major Dragondale, 'That can't be true. I only ordered them yesterday.'

Quartermaster General, 'My girls worked all night. There is a war on, you know.'

Major Dragondale, 'Thank you, Fay.'

Lord Malander, 'Yes, thank you very much. Let's stop for lunch and then brainstorm our plans this afternoon. I believe that we have roast pork for lunch.'

42

Tactics

Lord Malander, 'I hope you enjoyed lunch. Now it's time to review and consider our tactics over the next few weeks. Our first task is the Slimie column. I guess that we just carry on with our current tactics?'

Major Clutterbuck, 'The road ahead for the Slimenest is pretty well planned out already. We have a range of different pits. We have blockaded a river and plan a minor flood and further tree and boulder obstacles. We are also preparing to set a forest on fire.'

Lord Malander, 'So more of what we are already doing.'

Major Clutterbuck, 'That's true, but they will have to cross the Severn, and as per your instructions, we are building significant fortifications there. Your men will have to defend the river bank.'

Lieutenant Bandolier, 'I'm planning significantly larger mounted archery attacks. So far, we have used a force of about two thousand. After the training has been completed, we should be able to utilise six thousand mounted archers. We are also looking at taking more of our static bowmen and teaching them to ride a horse.'

Major Mainstay, 'I had a dream last night that we had a force in Swindon that threatened the Slimie rear. After thinking about it, we could create a dummy army.'

Lord Malander, 'How would you do that?'

Major Mainstay, 'At night it would be campfires and tents. During the day, it would be noise. The sound of men and horses with some feigned attacks. It would need some planning.'

Abbott Frogmore, 'That is genius, my boy. We could stop them in their tracks and reverse their column. Let's get started on the planning.'

Lord Malander, 'That does sound like a good idea, but let's finish our discussion first.'

Lady Malander, 'On the same theme, we could help create the illusion of an army. It would be a dummy show of strength.'

Lieutenant Bandolier, 'When they turn, which will be a complex manoeuvre for them, let's attack them with a small army.'

Lord Malander, 'Please get together and produce a detailed plan for my approval. Let's carry on with the brain-storming.'

Earl Winterdom, 'How do you plan to use us?'

Lord Malander, 'How is the training going?'

Earl Winterdom, 'Well, as you probably know, I was totally opposed to it at first, but I have to be honest, I have really enjoyed it. I didn't know how much I didn't know. Mind you, I do have a few aches and pains.'

Lord Birdlip, 'You can say that again.'

Earl Winterdom, 'I do have a few aches and pains.' Everyone laughed although it was an old joke.

Count Mannering, 'I do agree with the Earl. The training has been excellent.'

Lord Malander, 'My plan is that once the training has been completed, which will include some genuine forays, you will be reformed as the Gloucestershire Regiment. The same with the others.

'Each county will have its own regiment, but there is no guarantee that they will fight in the county of origin. For example, the Worcestershire Regiment might defend Norfolk. The regiment will be utilised as a part of a larger battle plan and as the command structure demands. Each regiment will have a Lieutenant-General. Three regiments will form a division under a full General.'

Count Mannering, 'That makes a lot of sense. I'm happy with it.' The other two nodded in agreement.

Abbott Frogmore, 'At a later date, I would like to discuss the following:
- The defence of the Severn
- What do we do if the Severn is breached?
- Training of the northern forces
- Defensive strategy for the line.'

Lord Malander, 'I think we have some agenda items for the next meeting.'

Lady Malander, 'Can you add magical services to that list? I want suggestions on how we can assist the other disciplines.'

Lord Malander, 'That's been a good meeting. Let's get back to our posts.'

43

Which Witch Hunt?

Lady Malander, Major Hogsflesh and Thomas were outside a small, somewhat derelict cottage in a disused close in Evesham called Charlie's Yard. They had about twenty armed troops supporting them. They were pretty sure that it was the right place as there were magical wards protecting it.

They had been observing the property for about an hour. There were no signs of any magical or mystical activities. It didn't even look lived in. The crumbling walls were covered in ivy, and the roof was holed in a couple of places. The garden was completely overrun to the point that gaining access to the front door would be difficult.

They wondered what to do next when Thomas suddenly levitated the three of them upwards and then transported them through the wall of the house into an upstairs bedroom. Lying on the bed was a very old woman, the one the locals called an old crone. She was breathing heavily through cracked, parched lips. There were a few remaining grey hairs on her head, and one of her eyes had a strange milky appearance. She was the epitome of feebleness.

Lady Malander shouted, 'Thomas, get us out of here now.' They were instantly transported to their previous hiding point. It was just in time as a giant pig came flying through the air and smashed the cottage to pieces. There were pork chops and ham joints everywhere mixed with a vast quantity of sickly, sticky blood and what seemed like endless snakes made from guts. The smell was putrid. It didn't smell like a fresh pig, but the meat looked edible.

Major Hogsflesh, 'How did you know?'

Lady Malander, 'I can't explain it. I just knew.'

Thomas, 'I didn't sense it.'

Lady Malander, 'You will pick it up as you experience more dangerous situations.'

Major Hogsflesh, 'Who was the old lady?'

Thomas, 'That was Decour de Charlene.'

Major Hogsflesh, 'It's just dawned on me that her name more or less means Charlie's yard in French. But why a giant pig?'

Lady Malander, 'It was partly her sense of humour based on what she did to us earlier and a warning. And possibly it was in recognition of your name.'

Thomas, 'I guess that it is slightly humorous.'

Major Hogsflesh, 'Careful boy, it's a very honourable name.'

Thomas, 'Sorry I didn't mean your name. I meant the whole pig thing.'

Major Hogsflesh, 'Careful, you are digging a bigger trough for yourself. Anyway, what do we do now?'

Lady Malander, 'Go home, have some tea and consider our options.'

The Prophecy is drawn to magic:

> *The derelict house with its yard;*
> *Suffered a giant beastly bombard,*
> *From hell came more than lard,*
> *Now ripped apart and charred,*
> *Beware if you don't want to die-hard,*
> *Prepare to use your trump card.*

44

A Poetic Moment

Abbott Frogmore, 'Sorry to disturb you at this early time, but we have found two more verses.'

Lord Malander, 'Let me see them.'

Abbott Frogmore, 'Here they are:

> *Rivers rise, and rivers fall,*
> *The scum are up against the wall,*
> *It's time to make them crawl,*
> *Before the deadly killing fireball.*

> *Their journey was most pitiful,*
> *Less a column, more a sprawl,*
> *Less of a fight, more a maul,*
> *What's the point of it overall?*

Lord Malander, 'That all looks rather encouraging regarding our campaign against the Slimie column.'

Abbott Frogmore, 'It's made me start thinking about our next endeavour, so I started reviewing the prophecy for clues, and there are quite a few unanswered questions.'

Lord Malander, 'Such as?'

Abbott Frogmore, 'The following for a start:

"Merlin's home on the throne,
The devil waits for the unknown,
Unless you secure the anomaly,
Nothing will prepare you for its progeny,
But who, but who is the demagogue?
Is the barren womb the epilogue?"

Lord Malander, 'I think the last line refers to my wife and her childless state.'
Abbott Frogmore, 'But she is pregnant.'
Lord Malander, 'You are joking.'
Abbott Frogmore, 'No, its common knowledge.'
Lord Malander, 'You are joking.' It looked like his wife had some questions to answer.
Abbott Frogmore, 'And who is Merlin? I can't find any mention of someone or thing called Merlin.'
Lord Malander, 'And what is the devil waiting for?'
Abbott Frogmore, 'Some of the lines only become clear over a period of time.'
Lord Malander, 'Which is generally too late to help us.'
Abbott Frogmore, 'Exactly, but the line I'm particularly interested in is:
"Unless you secure the anomaly."
'I think this relates to the origin of the Slimenest. We need to find out where they come from. And who gave them that name.'
Lord Malander, 'When we try and investigate them, they turn to a slime and then mud.'
Abbott Frogmore, 'Does that mean that someone or something is making them from mud?'
Lord Malander, 'You are making good points. I was always

told to know your enemy.'

Abbott Frogmore, 'And what gave them this drive to kill to save our souls?'

Lord Malander, 'It must be bred into them.'

Abbott Frogmore, 'Are they born or are they made. Do they have souls?'

Lord Malander, 'And what are we having for breakfast?'

Abbott Frogmore, 'That sounds like a good idea.'

Lord Malander, 'Will you join me?'

Abbott Frogmore, 'Not if it includes any pork-based products.'

45

The Right Road

The weather was getting better, and the Slimenest were on the road again after waiting for new catapults to arrive. But, so far, progress had been pitiful and very expensive in terms of men and equipment.

The level of wariness in the Slimenest camp was palpable. They weren't frightened of death, they welcomed it, but they wanted to make progress. They knew that the enemy was waiting for them. They were always waiting.

By their very nature, the humans wanted to try something different, but the old tactics were still working, so why try anything new? So, as soon as the Slimenest moved, about two thousand mounted archers attacked. The same thing happened as before. The dead at the front caused a pile-up, and the arrows kept coming.

What was different was that another two thousand mounted archers attacked the rear of the column, causing them to push forward, crushing their colleagues. It was like a domino effect all through the procession. Then to make it worse, groups of archers with Tanylip fired into different parts of the Slimenest army, causing itching chaos.

The archers were getting a bit too confident. They thought they could ride around at will unmolested and strike whenever it suited them, but the Slimies had learnt. They deliberately established groups away from the main column that immediately rushed in and caught the archers unawares. It was a slaughter. Highly trained archers were simply ripped apart and, in some cases, consumed for breakfast.

Almost every group of archers was trapped to some extent. Then Major Bandelier appeared with about fifty men behind the enemy forces. What was strange was that rather than bows, they had firesticks. And these noisy devices killed hundreds of Slimies and put them on the run.

Out of nearly five thousand archers, less than two thousand escaped. And without Major Bandolier's opportune arrival, the casualties would have been far greater. It was a lesson that needed to be learnt. The Slimies were dangerous. They may be stupid, but they were still a formidable force.

This tragedy put a damper on the rest of the day. But this was a war for survival, and losses had to be expected, but it still hurt. It hurt really badly.

The engineers, however, had tried something new. They took the main Swindon to Gloucester Road and added two additional parallel roads about a mile long with dead ends. One ended in a cliff and the other in a marsh. They had done such a good job that the two new roads looked much more realistic than the original route. So realistic that humans couldn't decide which road to use themselves.

When the Slimenest hit the junction, it was total confusion. The ones at the front had little time to decide because of the pressure from behind. In the end, the pressure won, and the column split into two. Sadly for them, they had made two incorrect choices. The engineers who were watching from a distance were ecstatic.

The engineers watched as one of the columns trampled down

an increasingly narrow lane and then cheered as the leaders were pushed over the cliff face. It was hard to stop the Slimenest on the move, and many achieved their goal and met their maker.

There were also cheers along the other road as the column marched steadily into a swamp. It was another Slimenest disaster, but they discovered something interesting: the Slimies could breathe underwater. No one knew that, and it would be a consideration regarding the defence of the River Severn.

Both columns tried to reverse, but the confusion was comical. No one was managing the situation. It became even more confusing when burning trees were rolled down the hill with gallons of tar tied to the trunks. No one knew that Slimies exploded when they caught fire, but then no one had ever seen a Slimie on fire before.

A fresh group of archers poured arrows into the mix. For the first time ever, the Slimies were on the run. They fled, leaving their precious catapults behind, but everyone knew that they would reform and continue. Most of their clumsily built fighting machines were destroyed, but some were hitched onto horses and taken to Malvern.

Despite the early losses, it had been a good day for humanity. Early estimates suggested that over a hundred thousand Slimies had been killed since they started their journey. At that rate of attrition, they would be a spent force by the time they reached Malvern.

One of the archers picked up a note which said:

> *The field was empty except for a tent,*
> *And devil's brew for those who relent,*
> *It's a long way down, a deep descent,*
> *A never-ending twisting road of torment.*

The victims gave no formal consent,
Or evenly unwillingly agreed to the event,
Some need to seek apologetic consent,
Or will eternally burn while they lament.

46

The Wrong Road

As soon as Lady Malander walked in, she noticed the cold atmosphere in the room. It wasn't due to a lack of heating. It emanated from one man: her husband.

Lady Malander, 'So you know?'

Lord Malander, 'I do, but it looks like I was the last to find out.'

Lady Malander, 'That's not entirely true. Thomas told me in front of at least thirty people, and the news spread like wildfire. And to make it worse, I can't tell if I'm pregnant or not.'

Lord Malander, 'That changes things.'

Lady Malander, 'I have another concern. When I was a pig, I was fucked many times. There is not much you can do to stop it.'

Lord Malander, 'I know I watched you rutting away quite a few times.'

Lady Malander, 'And you didn't stop it? You didn't try to protect my honour?'

Lord Malander, 'By the time I tracked you down, your honour had well and truly gone. You were some sort of pig siren. You couldn't get enough.'

Lady Malander, 'That's not true.'

Lord Malander, 'It certainly was, ask the herdsman. Apparently, sows are like that when they want to get pregnant, although technically you were a gilt as you hadn't given birth.'

Lady Malander, 'You should have protected me.'

Lord Malander, 'I had arranged for you to be put into a sty on your own, but the herdsman said that you would wither and die, and I wasn't having that.'

Lady Malander, 'So the problem is, I don't know who the father is.'

Lord Malander, 'It must be me as I gave you a good seeing to on the day you decided to become a pig.'

Lady Malander, 'But what about the pigs. I may have gone down the wrong road?'

Lord Malander, 'Fuck the pigs, the boy is mine!'

Lady Malander, 'Or a girl?'

Lord Malander, 'It's a boy. It's mine and let's not talk about it again.'

Lady Malander, 'Or it could be a brood of seven or eight.'

Lord Malander, 'A complete family in one go. That wouldn't be a bad idea.'

Lady Malander, 'Yes, my love.'

Lord Malander, 'Now I plan to give you a good fucking before you get too pregnant.'

Lady Malander, 'Don't you dare think that pregnancy is going to stop you doing your duty.'

Lord Malander, 'Yes, my love.'

47

Magical Meetings

Lady Malander called for a meeting of her top magicians, which included:
- Lorrimore of Lendle
- The Enchantress of Evermore
- Tinton of Taverton
- Lionel Wildheart
- Thomas the Butcher.

Lady Malander, 'I think we need to assess the current situation and plan for the future.

'Although the military forces have been quite successful, we have failed miserably. I'm talking about the pig incident and the old crone in Evesham. Both incidents made us look foolish.

'Any comments?'

The Enchantress of Evermore, 'They all seem rather pig-related.'

Tinton of Taverton, 'I think I need to apologise on behalf of your magical team for failing to revert you.'

Lady Malander, 'Thank you, but I'm in debt to Thomas. It's disappointing that an untrained youth has got more magical power than the rest of us put together. And I'm including myself in that.'

Lionel Wildheart, 'We can only work with what we have got.

Thomas is a natural wonder, and we bow to him.'

Thomas, 'Please don't bow to me. I'm just a common butcher.'

Lady Malander, 'I don't want it to go to your head, but you are anything but common. We need your skills, but you are going to need some formal training. You might find it rather simplistic, but you will find it of great benefit in the long run.'

Thomas, 'Frankly, I'm looking forward to it.'

Lady Malander, 'It's going to be hard work as we will also need your contribution as part of our ongoing projects.'

Thomas, 'I'm used to hard work. It's quite tough being a butcher.'

Lady Malander, 'I appreciate that, but magic strains the body, the mind and the soul.'

Thomas, 'I'm sure that is the case, but I've found that it makes me feel randy. Is that just me?'

The Enchantress of Evermore, 'After a prolonged bout of magic, I feel like I could fuck a regiment of soldiers.'

Thomas blushed because he had never heard a lady swear before. He also thought that if the regiment were not available, he would be. He quite fancied the enchantress. There was something enchanting about her, even though she must be twice his age. It wasn't easy being a virgin in a room of hardened professionals.

The Enchantress of Evermore, 'You are a virgin, aren't you?'

Thomas just blushed again.

The Enchantress of Evermore, 'Well, come around tonight, and we will cure you of that.'

Lady Malander, 'Betty, leave the boy alone.'

The Enchantress of Evermore, 'Yes Mistress.' And she winked at the boy.

Lady Malander, 'These are our current projects:
1. Protect Malvern from magical attacks
2. Create an illusion of a military camp at night
3. Capture Decour de Charlene
4. Find out where the Slimenest come from
5. Build up our skills for the final encounter
6. Any Other Business.'

Thomas was thinking about sex with the Enchantress. He thought about sex a lot, but he couldn't believe that her name was Betty. He was worried whether he would get an erection if he went to her house. Would she laugh at his spots and the three boils on his back? And he noticed that his breath often smelled. And he didn't have any clean underwear.

Lady Malander, 'Thomas, are you with us?'

Thomas, 'Sorry, my Lady, I was just thinking that I could cast a protective spell that would last for a year without renewal. I could do the illusion, but I don't know what a military camp looks like. I know where Decour de Charlene is. I don't have the words to describe where the Slimenest come from. Was there anything else?'

Lady Malander, 'Thank you, Thomas. Can you show us the protective spell?'

Thomas, 'Shall I do it now?'

Lady Malander, 'Why not? Do you need your Book of Spells?'

Thomas, 'What's that?'

Lady Malander, 'It's where you keep the details on your spells, incantations, herb mixtures etc.'

Thomas, 'I don't do that. It's all in my head.'

Lady Malander, 'It's not a bad idea to record them.'

Thomas, 'That might be the case, but I can't read or write.'

He blushed again and felt embarrassed. Betty, his new love, would think that he was an idiot.

He cast the spell, which was at least ten times stronger than the current one. The others looked at him spellbound. The good news was that it freed the regular magicians from a never-ending, tedious task.

Lady Malander, 'A military camp at night would contain thousands of tents, camp-fires, munitions and stores. There would be singing, shouting, horse noises and the sound of blacksmiths.'

Thomas, 'Would it look like this?' And he displayed on the table a mini-version.

Lady Malander, 'Probably more tents and more noise.'

Thomas did his magic, and there it was. Lady Malander sent one of her aides to get her husband. He reluctantly came along and was astounded. He sent for his senior team, and they were astounded. Soon everyone in the camp was astounded. The only person who wasn't astounded was Thomas, although he didn't know that he could do these things.

Lord Malander, 'You have done well lad, very well.' The Lord asked one of his aides to dress Thomas properly. He arranged for two complete sets of new clothes.

Major Hogsflesh, 'So where is Decour de Charlene.'

Thomas, 'She and her coven are meeting near the old bridge in Pershore as we speak.'

Major Hogsflesh, 'Why didn't you tell us before?'

Thomas, 'Firstly, no one asked me. Secondly, whenever I search for her, she knows. At this moment, she is preparing a concealment spell.'

Major Hogsflesh, 'Can you kill her from here?'

Thomas, 'I'm not sure if I can, and I'm not sure if I want to. I've never killed anyone.'

Major Hogsflesh, 'We are at war, son. No one likes killing, but it is them or us.'

Thomas, 'Things are more complicated than that. Nothing is black or white any more.'

Major Hogsflesh, 'Don't give me that shades of grey crap.'

Thomas, 'It's more rainbow-coloured with dashes of black and white. I have known Decour de Charlene all my life, yet I never knew her. I see both the good and the bad in her. She does have an evil streak, but to some extent, humankind and especially men, have made her that way. I will not kill her, but I will tell you where she is, and she is planning another attack, soon, very soon.'

Lady Malander could see that Thomas was stressed and decided to call the end of the meeting.

48

The Dummies Win

Lord Malander met with Majors Hogsflesh and Lambskin to discuss the planned decoy camps. Both Lady Malander and Thomas were also in attendance.

Lord Malander, 'Let's imagine that the Slimenest column is at rest. Where would be the best place to set up the illusion of a Human dummy camp, also at rest? Obviously, the options are in front of them, behind them or both.'

Major Hogsflesh, 'What is our objective?'

Lord Malander, 'To delay their advance for as long as possible.'

Major Hogsflesh, 'Then the only option is behind. We don't want them rushing forwards.'

Lord Malander, 'So, Thomas, are you confident that you can do this?'

Thomas, 'Yes, my Lord.'

Lord Malander, 'Majors Hogsflesh and Lambskin will escort you with a squadron of troopers. Lady Malander will also go with you to assist. Do not do anything to put yourself at risk. Do you understand?'

Thomas, 'Yes, my Lord.'

Major Hogsflesh, 'He will be safe with us.'

Lord Malander, 'I hope so.' He then waved them off. He was worried about putting his pregnant wife in danger, but she was a tough old boot. Almost certainly tougher than him. His father, the Chief Elder, was even tougher. He made a mental note to go and see him. He was also concerned about Thomas. The loss of him now would be catastrophic.

The small cavalcade travelled through the wilds of Oxfordshire. It looked glorious with the sun starting to set and shining its final shafts of amber light through the early autumn trees. Thomas had never travelled this far before. It made him feel quite manly, almost manly enough to visit Betty.

He was excited about the journey and the job he had been allocated. He was, at last, making a serious contribution to the war effort. Lady Malander was good company, but Major Hogsflesh made him nervous. He was the epitome of manhood. His conquests were legendary, as was his temper. Thomas was concerned that he had slighted him, but nothing had been said.

At one stage, they had to lay low to avoid a Slimie foraging party numbering nearly a thousand. It was the first time Thomas had seen one, and it was quite a shock.

They remained hidden and undiscovered, and when it was clear, they continued their journey. About an hour later, they found their target area, and Thomas started work. His illusion was time-phased, beginning with an army's noise arriving with all the sounds of command and the chatter from the troops. Horses neighed, fires were lit, tents were erected, stores were set up, there was banging and whistling and singing. But it was all one big illusion of sight and sound.

Would the Slimenest take the bait? There was no way that they could miss the commotion, and they didn't. Slimies didn't like getting wet, and they didn't like fighting at night as their eyesight wasn't that good. Nevertheless, they were woken up, lined up and ordered to charge. And charge they did. And some of them kept charging. Their small brains found it difficult to comprehend the illusion, so the easiest thing to do was to charge.

When one hundred and fifty thousand Slimies charge at night in uncertain territory with poor eyesight, you will expect a few accidents, and there were many. One of the challenges was identifying a friend from a foe in the dark. Friendly fire became very unfriendly. Natural obstacles were also remarkably unfriendly. And some Slimies were lost, never to be seen again.

Chaos ruled. Trying to get the Slimies to reform after the scattering was a monumental task.

At this stage, Major Lambskin wished that he had significant forces with him. It would have been another massacre, but his job was to keep the youngster safe.

Back home, things were far from safe.

49

Witches at War

Thomas had established a very effective protective spell that would stop the majority of magical attacks, but it wouldn't stop a physical invasion by witches. Thirty experienced members of the Pershore coven, all hardened practitioners of the dark arts, just walked into Upton-Upon-Severn and started killing anyone they came across.

The new fortifications that were being built at Upton were simply blasted apart. The new Gloucestershire Regiment that was on guard duty, were mown down like a scythe cutting corn. Lord Birdlip died where he stood. The defender's arrows simply bounced off the witches, and Upton was left a burning wreck.

The witches flew along the Hanley Castle Road and then turned left towards the Malvern Hills. The fires at Upton were spotted, and the alarm was raised in Great Malvern. The planned defensive positions were soon occupied.

Bugles rang, ordering both the Worcestershire and Oxfordshire regiments to present themselves. Annie Dragondale's archers also took their preplanned positions. The munitions storeroom was opened to issue stocks of arrows and weapons to anyone that could walk. Lord Malander calmly walked around directing activities as he saw fit.

Scouts started searching both Little Malvern and Malvern Wells, trying to identify the threat, but nothing was apparent. The

Hill forces were alerted, and fires were lit on the hills to let the locals know that a threat was imminent. This was also a signal for the civil militia to present themselves.

Before the scouts could reach Upton, the witches attacked the troops in Malvern Wells, who were marching along the Worcester Road. Some of the soldiers simply dropped dead; others stabbed themselves. Others exploded into blood-splattering pools of bone, flesh, and guts. What was worse was that the witches were almost invisible, flying through the dusky skies.

The cries of the dying could be heard in Great Malvern. Those in the new but incomplete citadel could hear the noise of war. They felt safe as the citadel had been built into the hills, giving it a brilliant view over the Severn plain. But still the enemy had not been identified.

Then they appeared, the black murderers of four or five hundred fine troops. The actual figure was much higher than that. They started picking off anyone they saw. Then the citadel's magical team came out to challenge them. This was going to be a classic confrontation between magic and witchcraft.

Spells and incantations were thrown back and forwards. The witches were probably the most experienced and were certainly less worried about collateral damage. It was a classic contest between the 'nice' and the 'naughty'. One side had rules, the other didn't. In terms of actual numbers, they were fairly evenly matched.

The Enchantress of Evermore hit the witches with an extinction enchantment. The witches shook it off and countered with a beheading bewitchment. This, in turn, was countered. Lorrimore of Lendle returned fire with a slaughter hex which didn't work.

At the same time, arrows were being shot at the witches at a terrific rate which distracted them as some of their power had to be directed towards physical defence. One of the witches died when an arrow got through her defences. Magic was a limited resource, and the witches were getting through their supply at an alarming rate.

The magicians sensed that they were starting to win when Lorrimore of Lendle was killed by an evil eye explosion. This hit them hard, but they carried on. The various smells of magic were now in the air making the laymen feel quite giddy. Two more witches dropped dead with arrows in them.

The Enchantress of Evermore then told her team to all focus on one witch at a time. This proved quite successful, with one of the witches simply disappearing, while another was converted into primordial slime. And the arrows kept coming.

One of the mounted riders lassoed the nearest witch and started swinging her around, crashing her into two other witches. All three of them had no choice but to let their defences down, and in the confusion, they were arrowed to death. And the arrows kept coming.

The Enchantress's tactic was working, but in revenge, the witches caused her head to expand until it cracked apart, and her brains dropped out all over the place. Thomas was not going to get his wicked way with her, after all. And the arrows kept coming.

Further mounted riders tried the lasso trick, but it was a dangerous manoeuvre with all the arrows flying about, but it certainly distracted the witches. It distracted them so much that they didn't spot the hundred-odd spears that were thrown at them from the top of the citadel. This took out four witches and injured two others. The remaining witches got their revenge by making the spear throwers throw themselves off the battlements. More brave men and women died doing their duty.

Lionel Wildheart used the Enchantress's extinction enhancement for a second time. However, this time, he deliberately put all of his remaining magic into the spell. It worked as every witch dropped dead, but so did he. He had made the ultimate sacrifice.

Lord Malander walked around the site trying to build-up morale and give solace to those that had lost dear ones. He was amazed by how much death and destruction could be caused by thirty old crones. He wasn't sure how his wife was going to take this.

And on the citadel wall was pinned a note:

While Merlin is away, there is a hitch,
What's in witches' time but a stitch,
Death of heroes on the pitch,
Was this the end, or just a glitch?

50

The Dummies Returned

The illusion's success was short-lived when they saw the carnage in Upton and then the devastation in Malvern. Lady Malander was in tears. She felt guilt, pride, and relief. Guilt in that it should have been her and not poor Betty that died. Pride in the way her team fought and sacrificed themselves for the common cause. Relief that her unborn son still lived.

Lady Malander ran to her husband, and they embraced. She held her husband close to her. He could feel the tears run down her cheeks and then the sobs as her chest heaved.

Lord Malander, 'I will have revenge. Too many good men and women have died.'

Lady Malander, 'Of course, my Love.'

Lord Malander, 'Pershore will suffer.'

Lady Malander, 'We can't punish a whole town because of one coven.'

Lord Malander, 'It's not about punishing a town, but clearly it is a place of great evil. The town has supported at least thirty witches. They will have families and friends who must be in league with them.'

Lady Malander, 'That's true. I can see where you are coming from.'

Lord Malander, 'These witches are supporting evil. The Slimenest kill everyone; they eat our children. They represent the end of the world. My son cannot enter a world with this sort of filth in abundance.'

Lady Malander understood now. It wasn't just revenge, it was the first pangs of fatherhood, and she felt pride, although she knew that she would have to soften his views.

Lady Malander, 'Yes, my love.'

Lord Malander, 'And we have to show strength. Our men and women will demand action.'

Lady Malander, 'I can see that, but we also need a ceremony to mark this loss, and somehow I need to find magical replacements.'

Thomas was devastated that Betty had been killed. He had had wet dreams about her every night. Now the love of his life was dead. He hated war. What was the point of it? But now that he had seen the Slimies, he couldn't think of an alternative.

He couldn't decide who he hated the most, the Slimies or the witches. Then he decided that it was the witches as they had a choice. They decided to help the enemy. They killed fellow humans for greed and their own evil beliefs.

The job of restoring Malvern began fairly quickly. It gave them something to think about, and it was needed to ward off any further attacks. The fortifications at Upton were restarted as the damage was more superficial than it looked. Bodies were buried. A replacement was needed for Lord Birdlip.

It wasn't long before Malvern was back on its feet, but there would be consequences.

51

The Elder Ways

Lord Malander fixed an appointment to see his father. He loved him and admired him immensely, but, like a lot of the aristocracy, they never had a close relationship. In fact, over the last couple of years, they had got closer. They even laughed about the way the world was.

The acting Chief Elder, Duke of Mercia, was looking forward to meeting his son. In many ways, his son was seen as the national leader rather than him, but he was happy with that. He preferred to be the power behind the throne, not that there was a crown. Perhaps that was the role that his son should aim for?

Lord Malander opened his father's front door and walked in to see his father sitting by an open fire sipping a glass of brandy. He had already poured one out for his son. They both appreciated the sickly sweetness of the well-matured brandy. It wasn't the best as the best was almost impossible to get hold of.

Lord Malander, 'So how is life as Chief Elder?'

Chief Elder, 'Acting, my son.'

Lord Malander, 'In name only. You have always been the Chief.'

Chief Elder, 'Very true, but I only want the best for mankind.'

Lord Malander, 'Don't you mean our family?'

Chief Elder, 'I've always seen them as the same. What's

good for our family is good for the rest.'

Lord Malander, 'Anyway, I thought that I better update you.'

Chief Elder, 'There's not much that I don't already know: Thomas, the witch attack, the delaying tactics, the pig incident. It's all in here.' As he pointed to his head.

Lord Malander, 'So you know that you are going to be a grandfather?'

Chief Elder, 'Let's drink to my grandson.'

Lord Malander, 'I certainly will.'

Chief Elder, 'I hear that there might be a question mark regarding your fatherhood? It must have been galling seeing your wife being rogered in public.'

Lord Malander, 'She was in the form of a pig at the time.'

Chief Elder, 'Even so, it might cause issues when you become king.'

Lord Malander, 'What do you mean?'

Chief Elder, 'That is your destiny, my son.'

Lord Malander, 'What will be, will be.'

Chief Elder, 'That is where you are totally wrong. The man with a plan knows where he is going. Anyway, I wanted to say how proud I am of you.'

Lord Malander, 'That's the first time ever that you have praised me.'

Chief Elder, 'It's true that I don't give praise lightly.'

Lord Malander, 'Thirty-six years.'

Chief Elder, 'That is a long time, but then the praise is more appreciated when it does come. Anyway, we Malanders don't need praise. We are men of action. We know when we have done well.'

Lord Malander, 'Did you want an update?'

Chief Elder, 'Not really, but I would like to know what you

are planning to do in the next few months.'

Lord Malander, 'These are my plans:
- Continue building up the Malvern defences
- Stop the Slimenest column coming our way
- Work on the two defensive lines
- Create an army structured on county regimental lines
- Build up the magical force
- Recapture our lost lands and eliminate the Slimenest
- Punish Pershore for the witch attack.'

Chief Elder, 'That's enough to go on. But let me give you some advice, don't be too harsh on Pershore. Make sure that the punishment fits the crime. Be careful.'

They parted with Lord Malander feeling quite loved. As he walked out, he found this on the door:

Elderly father met the dashing son,
Grandiose news, but is it his grandson?
Is it someone else's or homespun?
The sun and the moon belong to someone.

The troops march in one by one,
Is Pershore doomed by the son?
Will it thrive, or will the plums be overdone?
Has it just begun, or will it be overrun?

52

Pershore Suffers

He had been warned many times. The harsh leader comes to regret harsh actions. He knew that he should treat the locals with respect and dignity, but they had spawned a nest of vipers. There was no way that they could have lived amongst the locals undiscovered.

Someone was feeding them. Someone was selling them cloth for their death-cult outfits. Someone was giving them lodgings. Someone was married to them. They had children. Thirty witches meant thirty homes. Thirty witches meant thirty filthy infestations.

On the road from Malvern to Pershore, his anger grew. He passed the grave of Lord Birdlip in Upton. He passed the wrecked fortifications that men had toiled over for weeks. He remembered Lorrimore of Lendle, Lionel Wildheart and especially the Enchantress of Evermore. He remembered his men, who had fought so hard against the Slimenest.

As his anger built, his respect declined. As he almost cried for revenge, his sense of fair play deserted him. When he reached the outskirts of Pershore, he shouted, 'Let's teach them a lesson.'

Four hundred mounted bowman shot four hundred burning arrows into the town. They continued their volleys until almost every wooden house was on fire. Then the mounted soldiers attacked with blades, eager to prove themselves.

They proved themselves by stabbing the butcher, the grocer, and the blacksmith. They proved themselves by decapitating men and women, the young and the old. They proved themselves by stabbing babies and flinging them into the flames. They proved themselves by raping young girls and slashing their throats. There was a lot of proof that night.

Lord Malander arrived and tried to stop the onslaught that he had unleashed, but the orgy of destruction just continued. There was hardly a property left standing or a person left alive. Even the cats and dogs had been murdered, but there was a sense that revenge had been satisfied.

But not in Lord Malander's mind. What had he done? This would always be his lowest point. His feelings of guilt were worsened by the sheer delight on the faces of his troops. They had answered their master's call with cruel and efficient intent. The blame was his.

His guilt became considerably worse as his troops tracked down the homes of each witch. Not one of them lived in Pershore. What had he done?

Every witch lived on or around Bredon Hill. The epicentre seemed to be Elmley Castle, and more specifically, the wooden castle.

The victorious army returned to Malvern, jubilant in their victory. Most of the men were relieved that they hadn't been eradicated by demonic spells or transfigured into frogs. Lord Malander just felt shame. He wasn't sure how he was going to get over it. He wasn't sure how he could face his wife or his father.

Stuck on a fence, the note said:

*Poor, poor, Pershore,
Did they hear the roar of war?
Did they feel the hammer of Thor?
Was it their crime or the devil's whore?*

53

The Slimies Recover

A new leader appeared. Was he, she, or it one of the horde? Did leadership ability just manifest itself? No one knew, but the fact was that the Slimies had a new leader. One with intelligence and some military expertise, and organisational aptitude.

The column was restructured into three separate columns with vanguards and rear guards. There were outriders and sentry systems. Formal foraging parties were established, and a request was sent back to the South-East Commander for additional resources. The catapults were just left behind as they had no real martial value.

Of course, this was all unknown to the human forces. They continued as normal. The archers arrived as normal, but they were confused by the new columnar structure. Regardless, they attacked as normal, but once again, they were surprised by Slimenest tactics. The Slimies returned fire from two or three different directions, and then a large force attacked them head-on. For the second time, the bowmen were ripped to pieces. This loss of archers was becoming untenable.

The engineers waited as normal for their Slimenest friends to arrive, but they arrived behind them. The Slimies had never tasted engineers before. Generally, they were a bit meatier. The traps failed because the Slimies weren't following the expected route and also because they had scouts operating well ahead of the columns.

Again, it was hard to explain, but the leader's increased ability seemed to improve the overall performance of the Slimie troops. Was there some sort of telepathic connection?

Under the new leader, they had made more progress in a day than they had made in two weeks. And for the first time since the trek started, the humans had lost more troops than the Slimies. For humanity, it was a very worrying and inexplicable trend.

The Slimenest were approaching Cirencester, which had been stripped of anything of value to them. The local population had moved out sometime earlier. Their new leader decided to make camp there whilst his foraging teams were sent out to find some sustenance. That was now getting critical.

He sent scouting teams out to check the route ahead. The Slimenest leader had no maps. He relied on sketchy information obtained from the witches, and they were hardly famous for their orientation skills. He knew that once he got to Gloucester, he had to turn north, but then what?

54

Shame

Lord Malander rested his head against his wife's breasts and cried. And then he cried some more. She rubbed his head, pushing her fingers through his thick dark hair. She simply said, 'I forgive you.' And he started sobbing again.

Lord Malander, 'The problem is that I can't forgive myself.'

Lady Malander, 'I was going to say that there is nothing to forgive, but I would be wrong. What you and the soldiers did was shocking and unforgivable, except that wasn't your intent. Or was it?'

Lord Malander, 'That's a very good question. Like the rest, I wanted revenge.'

Lady Malander, 'But you didn't get it. Instead, you murdered innocent men, women and children.'

Lord Malander, 'Please don't go on. I know that.'

Lady Malander, 'Well, what do you want me to say?'

Lord Malander, 'You could say that I'm not responsible for the actions of my men.'

Lady Malander, 'You always told me that the leader is always responsible.'

Lord Malander, 'I can't argue with that. In that case, I need to fall upon my sword.'

Lady Malander, 'Don't be stupid. Resignation will not be of any value unless there is someone better to take your place, and you know that is not the case.

'And if there were, it would be crazy to change leaders halfway through a war.'

Lord Malander, 'So you are saying just carry on.'

Lady Malander, 'You might as well. No one is criticising you. In fact, most people in Malvern think that you took strong, decisive action against a town that had been infested. You are even more of a hero than you were before.'

Lord Malander, 'So you are suggesting that I add deception to my list of crimes.'

Lady Malander, 'I'm not suggesting that, but I'm saying just go with the flow. It's not easy being a leader. Mistakes will be made. Sometimes mistakes lead to horrible consequences, but they are still mistakes. You didn't go to Pershore with evil intent.

'Now buck-up and resume your duties. We have a war to fight.'

Lord Malander, 'I love you.' And then their love was consummated again.

55

Another Council of War

An urgent meeting of the War Council was called. The following attended:
- Lord Malander, Commander-in-Chief
- Abbott Frogmore, Head of Prophecy Research and Planning
- Major Dragondale, Commander Archery
- Major Mainstay, Deputy Commander
- Lady Malander, Commander Mystical Arts
- Major Bandolier, Commander Cavalry
- Major Clutterbuck, Commander Engineering
- Major Hogsflesh, Commander Intelligence
- Major Lambskin, Commander Infantry
- Fay Mellondrop, Quartermaster General
- Earl Winterdom, Lieutenant-General Worcestershire
- Count Mannering, Lieutenant-General Oxfordshire

Lord Malander, 'Colleagues before we start, I would like a minute's silence for the following:
- Our troops who defended Upton-Upon-Severn
- Our Troops who defended Malvern
- Our bowmen who fought valiantly against the Slimenest
- Our lost engineers
- Lord Birdlip

- Lorrimore of Lendle
- The Enchantress of Evermore
- Lionel Wildheart
- The civilians of Upton, Malvern and Pershore who died pointlessly.'

There was a very poignant period of silence.

Lord Malander, 'We urgently need to review the current position which is as follows:
- The northern and midland forces are now in position on the planned defensive line. They need training
- The south-western forces are almost in position. I'm grateful to Major Hogsflesh for gaining their support
- The Slimenest column divided into three and is now under far better leadership than before
- They are currently resting in Cirencester. We think that they are short of food
- We have experienced an unacceptable loss of mounted bowmen
- Our defences in Malvern were wide open to a witch attack
- Our magical forces are now very limited
- The reprisal against Pershore was pointless.

'So that is where we are,
    'The key discussion points are:
    1.   The Slimenest Column
    2.   Training of the defensive lines.

'The rest can wait.
    'How do we stop the column?'

Major Hogsflesh, 'Our burnt earth strategy seems to be working. Their lack of sustenance is definitely slowing them down.'

Lord Malander, 'I agree that it has worked brilliantly, but it's also causing us problems. We have a lot of mouths to feed. There are a lot of refugees and a huge army.'

Fay Mellondrop, 'I will take on the feeding challenge.'

Lord Malander, 'Thank you, Fay.' As far as Lord Malander was concerned, if Fay took the problem on, then it was solved.'

Major Hogsflesh, 'The burnt earth strategy extends to Gloucester, then we are not really sure what route they will take.'

Lord Malander, 'You will have to monitor the situation and then move quickly.'

Major Hogsflesh, 'Yes, my Lord.'

Major Dragondale, 'I could carry on if I had more bowmen.'

Lord Malander, 'I guess that we need to review our tactics. They seem to be waiting for us now.'

Major Hogsflesh, 'It took them some time to learn.'

Major Dragondale, 'Regardless of the casualty rate, it is slowing them down.'

Lord Malander, 'Any suggestions?'

Abbott Frogmore, 'What about another illusion but this time we back it up with arrow and steel?'

Major Dragondale, 'That's a good idea.'

Lord Malander, 'Go ahead then. Any other ideas?'

Major Hogsflesh, 'There must be something we can do with Birdlip?'

Major Lambskin, 'Why don't we attack them in force whilst they are descending?'

Lord Malander, 'Any objections?'

There were none.

Lord Malander, 'Go ahead then. Any other ideas?'

Abbott Frogmore, 'Where are they going to cross the Severn? Is it definitely, Upton?'

Lord Malander, 'They could cross at Gloucester.'

Abbott Frogmore, 'Where do we want them to cross?'

Lord Malander, 'Upton.'

Abbott Frogmore, 'Then we need to destroy all of the other bridges.'

Major Hogsflesh, 'I'm on the case.'

Lord Malander, 'Excellent. Any other ideas?'

Abbott Frogmore, 'What about ships on the river defending it?'

Major Hogsflesh, 'I'm on the case, again.'

Lord Malander, 'Well done, Abbott, you are on fire. That's all been very useful.

'Now I want your two new regiments to train the defensive lines. Let me know what additional assistance you need.'

Both lieutenant-Generals said, 'Yes, Sir.' Then everyone was dismissed.

56

Is it an Illusion?

The first illusion caused confusion. Would a second illusion work? If it worked again, then they planned to take full advantage of it. The following mounted regiments rolled out:
- First Gloucestershire
- Second Gloucestershire
- First Malvern
- Second Malvern
- First Ledbury
- First Welland
- First Upton
- First Castlemorten
- Second Colwall
- First Mathon.

They were accompanied by Lord and Lady Malander, Thomas, Major Hogsflesh and Major Lambskin (Commanding).

The distances involved were getting less as the Slimenest were getting nearer. There were also more Slimie outriders and sentries than before. Generally, the earlier, easier, victories were a thing of the past. Nevertheless, the defence had to continue, and the scouts had handpicked an area for a trap between Edgeworth and Miserden. This was hilly Cotswold countryside at its best.

The plan was to have two camps halfway up a hill directly

in front of the approaching Slimenest. It was timed to coincide with the Slimies normal retirement time. It was assumed that they would see the encampments in front of them and charge. Effectively they would have to charge uphill, which would slow them down, especially when a volley of arrows hit them.

The bowmen would then retreat, and, as the Slimies followed, they would be hit by another volley of arrows, and this would continue until it wasn't practical. The regiments of mounted infantry would attack at the appropriate moment or not at all if it was too dangerous.

Major Lambskin had given his captain a fair degree of autonomy as it would be dark and the terrain would be difficult to navigate. At least human night-sight was better than that of the Slimenest.

The engineers had completed their work on the hill, digging trenches, covered pits, and erecting stakes. It wouldn't be the sort of thing you would want to charge into.

Thomas did his magic: two ridiculously realistic camps were formed. The Slimenest arrived at just the right time and were preparing to charge when a whistle blew. The Slimenest divided into three, with one group charging right and the other left. The middle started steadily climbing the hill looking for any traps as they went. As far as the humans were concerned, this wasn't normal Slimie behaviour.

The captain of the bowmen was in a quandary. Should he stay and fight or retreat? As the order of the day was to avoid slaughter, he decided to withdraw. It was the logical thing to do, but as they rushed down the hill, they were annihilated by the arrows of their own men on the opposite hill. Those men had been confused by the sounds of the Slimies attacking at the base on the wrong side. Anyway, war was confusion.

The First Welland regiment joined the fray but found Slimies to the right of them, Slimies to the left of them and Slimies to the front of them. They attempted to fight, but theirs was not to reason why but to do and die. A few escaped, but most fell.

Meanwhile, the Slimemaster had ordered a considerable part of his army to quickstep towards Miserden. This was two or three times faster than their normal speed. It wasn't long before the human force had been cut-off. Majors Hogsflesh and Lambskin discussed the situation with Lord Malander. There was every chance that they were encircled or in the process of being surrounded.

They had to break out now before it was too late. They decided to divide into three separate groups, but they would all flee south-west as best they could and head towards Bisley and Stroud. The more direct route to Painswick was particularly difficult ground, especially for horses.

It was decided not to meet up as it was a long route back to Malvern, and there was no way of knowing the fate of the other groups. This had not been a successful venture.

Then Thomas piped up and said, 'What are you trying to achieve?'

Lord Malander, 'It's quite simple, our attempt to entrap the Slimies has backfired, and they are attempting to trap us. Now we need to escape before they destroy us.'

Thomas, 'What would you like me to do?'

Lord Malander, 'Could you kill the attacking Slimenest?'

Thomas, 'I'm not allowed to do that.'

Lord Malander, 'Why not?'

Thomas, 'I honestly don't know. It just seems to be one of the rules.'

Lord Malander, 'What could you do to them?'

Thomas, 'I could change their colour, or shrink them, or make them forget or put them to sleep.'

Lord Malander, 'You could make them go to sleep.'

Thomas, 'I could try, but there are a lot of them.'

Lord Malander, 'Go for it.'

Lady Malander, 'Alan, that is a lot of magic for a youngster.'

Lord Malander, 'What choice do we have? The alternative could be his and our lives.

'Thomas, please go ahead.'

Thomas, 'Yes, my lord.'

The magic was magicked, and the Slimies slept, and so did Thomas. He just collapsed into a catatonic stupor. Lady Malander rushed to him and held him against her chest.'

Lady Malander, 'This is serious. I've only ever seen this once before, and it took the magician six months to recover.'

Lord Malander, 'Things are really not going our way. Let's get him home. Before then, we better make sure that his magic has worked.'

It wasn't long before they came across piles of sleeping Slimies. Some of the men jumped down to kill them, but Lady Malander said that it would not be in the spirit of the magic used. Lord Malander said that we haven't got time to slaughter Slimies. We had to get home.

And home they went.

There is always a verse somewhere:

> *Give us today our daily bread,*
> *That won't help the dying or the dead,*
> *Crushing blows are cherry red,*
> *As we rush to our homestead.*

There are many troubles ahead,
Fighting the scum that are inbred,
Never a child and always unwed,
Clinging to their beloved godhead.

57

Malvern Magic

The weather had always been very changeable on the Malvern Hills. The locals will tell you that sometimes you can experience three or four different weather conditions in one day. But they had never experienced anything like this.

It started with snow, serious quantities of the white fluffy stuff. In a couple of hours, it was two foot thick. No one in the county of Worcestershire had ever experienced anything like this winter wonderland. All attempts at transport and construction were pointless. Then there was another shock: avalanches. Great Malvern was covered at one stage by a series of them.

As the local population began to cope with the unseasonal frozen temperatures and icy conditions, it started to rain. This wasn't your normal drizzle or even a downpour; it was the hot torrential type. And hot meant hot. It was boiling hot. You couldn't walk in it without being scolded.

The resultant floods caused the banks of the River Severn to burst. Upton-Upon-Severn became an island community. Worcester itself was one large lake. The river had disappeared in the Lakeland scenery.

Then the lightning came. Not your everyday type that lights up the sky but horizontal bolts that followed the ground and then destroyed buildings and people. It was the sort of lightning that could turn corners and go up and down stairs. It was the sort of lighting that could hunt down burnable stocks and innocent bystanders. It had a merciless character of its own.

The locals were hiding wherever they could. They had been systematically frozen, crushed, soaked, scolded, and electrified. Some of them were convinced that it was the end of days.

Others knew that it was magic. They could smell and taste it, but despite their own magical abilities, they could do little about it except wait for the calm after the storm. And then the storm came. Battering winds of over one hundred miles an hour. Freezing, bone-shattering winds that ripped apart anything that wasn't firmly held down. Malvern was getting a good old lashing.

Then the straggling remains of their army returned. One regiment ceased to exist, and the rest of the army were physically and emotionally spent. Sleep was the only thing on the agenda.

They couldn't believe the weather-induced destruction that lay before them. Ten miles away, the weather was happy in its placidity.

Thomas was put into one of the few dry hospital rooms and left to start his recovery. A junior wizard was left to protect him, and then the whole town went to sleep. At that stage, anyone could have invaded them, and no one would have murmured.

On a barn door, some verses were left:

No one had seen such snow,
That the gods agreed to bestow,
Or the troubled winds that blow,
Faster than the defeated cross-bow.

The sun will make you blind,
But it is just a state of mind,
Don't give in to the daily grind,
Never, but never leave him behind.

58

Gloucester Bridge

Major Clutterbuck felt guilty. He was there to scout the Gloucester toll bridge. The population were leaving the city, and his men were destroying anything valuable that had been left behind. He wasn't sure who suffered the most: the victims of a burnt-earth strategy or those enforcing it. He was being stupid. It was the victims. It was always the innocent victims.

But the locals didn't want their bridge destroyed. It had taken a lot of time, effort, and money to get it built. Without it, you had to use a ferry or travel an extra forty miles. Both options were fraught with danger. Some of the locals were willing to fight for their bridge but not against the Gloucestershire Regiment.

Major Clutterbuck tried to think of an easy way of demolishing it. He considered using heavily laden barges to batter it to pieces. In the end, he decided it was going to take hard labour with axes, and, as he pondered, he felt an axe crush his spine and enter his heart. He dropped dead with serious surprise written all over his face.

Major Clutterbuck wasn't the only one who was surprised when two or three thousand Slimies climbed out of the river and immediately engaged the shocked regiment. A lot of the brave Glosters were cut down while they were trying to retrieve their weapons. The regiment was heavily outnumbered and was forced to retreat.

The Slimies had crossed the Severn, which made the fortifications at Upton pointless. The Regiment stayed in the Gloucester area to monitor the Slimenest activities. It looked like it was only an advance guard. They sent riders to Malvern to update Lord Malander.

Lord Malander's first reaction was to take a large force and re-take the Gloucester bridge, but what was the point when the Slimies could walk along the river bed. Judgement day was getting nearer.

He ordered the Gloucestershire Regiment to return to Malvern, and he called yet another meeting of the War Council.

A member of the Worcestershire regiment found the following note:

> *The Slimenest cry will make you shiver,*
> *As you reach towards the arrow's quiver,*
> *Now they walk under the river,*
> *It's time for the master to deliver.*

59

A Great Loss

The urgent meeting of the War Council consisted of:
- Lord Malander, Commander-in-Chief
- Abbott Frogmore, Head of Prophecy Research and Planning
- Major Dragondale, Commander Archery
- Major Mainstay, Deputy Commander
- Lady Malander, Commander Mystical Arts
- Major Bandolier, Commander Cavalry
- Major Hogsflesh, Commander Intelligence
- Major Lambskin, Commander Infantry
- Fay Mellondrop, Quartermaster General.

Lord Malander, 'I can't believe that we have lost Lindsey Clutterbuck. He was a great friend, a great talent and the best engineer I have ever known.'

Major Hogsflesh, 'He was a true gentleman, one of the people.'

Lady Malander, 'I will miss his fatherly smile. He was a font of great kindness.'

Lord Malander, 'We could go on all day but to put it bluntly, we are losing:
- Our delaying tactics have ceased to be effective as they have a new, cunning leader who knows how to mould

- an army
- The Slimies have crossed the Severn at Gloucester. We now know that they can cross it whenever they want
- Their magical abilities are beyond ours
- Thomas is in some sort of magically induced coma.'

Whilst Lord Malander was listing the recent disasters, a courier rushed in and said, 'My Lord, I have urgent correspondence from Earl Winterdom, Lieutenant-General Worcestershire.'

Lord Malander opened it with some trepidation. It said that the Slimies had broken through the northern defensive line and that there were no forces to protect the locals who were being decimated. He was also worried that they might outflank his troops and that he was awaiting orders.

It contained a map showing the Slimie break-through in Eastern Lincolnshire. Clearly, that also meant that the whole of Norfolk was lost.

Lord Malander, 'That wasn't expected. It must mean that their forces in the South-East have been substantially reduced.'

Abbott Frogmore, 'You must realise that territory means nothing to them. They want souls, not acres. They want new blood.'

Lord Malander, 'This means that the Slimies have broken through at both extremes of our defensive line. The big question is: can we hold Malvern? If we don't think we can, we need to retreat to another defensive line.'

Abbott Frogmore, 'That would probably mean losing Wales and most of the Midlands.'

Lord Malander, 'That's true, but your previous point is still valid. It's really about killing Slimies and saving lives. I was wrong. When Thomas put those Slimies asleep, we should have killed every one of them.'

Lady Malander, 'But we might have lost Thomas.'

Lord Malander, 'But we still might.' He called the courier over and gave him a note. He wrote the following — *take whatever forces you need and kill every Slimie you find, Show no mercy.*

Major Bandolier, 'It's all very simple. It's kill or be killed.'

Lord Malander, 'How big is the Slimenest army in Gloucester?'

Major Hogsflesh, 'This is always difficult, but I would say one hundred and twenty thousand.'

Major Dragondale, 'I suspect that it is nearer to one hundred thousand.'

Major Hogsflesh, 'Forever the optimist.'

Major Dragondale, 'Better than being an old perv.'

Lord Malander wondered if there was a story there. There was, she caught him spying on her in the shower.

Lord Malander, 'I guess that if we had to, we could rustle up half that number.'

Abbott Frogmore, 'However, we could take some troops from either line. The Malvern forces could line up against them, and the south-western forces could attack their rear.'

Lord Malander, 'That sounds like a plan, but it must be a Slimie killing field.'

Abbott Frogmore, 'I will work on the plan.'

Lord Malander, 'In the meantime, we might as well carry on with the defence of Malvern.'

Earl Winterdom found the following note:

> *They charged through the gap;*
> *With lightening and thunderclap,*
> *Time to restructure the map,*
> *Or your chances of survival are crap.*

60

A Magical Recovery

Lady Malander was called to Thomas's bed. It wasn't looking good. He was covered in sweat and shaking. His eyes had withdrawn, and his tongue was covered in pus-filled boils. He was struggling to breathe, making strange gurgling sounds. Some would call it the death rattle. Lady Malander's maid was preparing the death shroud.

Lady Malander held his hand, thinking that it might be the last hand he ever held. What a waste of a great talent. What a tragedy for their cause. Without him, they practically had no magical defence.

Then a robin flew into the room and dropped a red lingonberry onto Lady Malander's hand. Lady Malander was quite shocked and even more shocked when the robin winked at her. A few minutes later, it returned with another berry and then another until she had at least thirty.

She wasn't sure what she was supposed to do with them. Should she make a soup or a paste? Then the robin grabbed one from her hand and pushed it between Thomas's lips. Lady Malander got the idea, and the Robin encouraged her to force-feed him. After ten, he started to show signs of recovery. The sweating and the shaking stopped, and his breathing improved.

After another ten berries, Thomas sat up and said, 'What's for tea?' Lady Malander almost collapsed from astonishment and joy.

Lady Malander, 'But you were almost dead?'

Thomas, 'My sister always knows what to do?'

Lady Malander, 'Your sister?'

Thomas, 'Yes, my sister, Robin.'

Lady Malander, 'Do you call that robin your sister?'

Thomas, 'I'm not sure what you mean.'

Lady Malander, 'Well, a robin fed you berries.'

Thomas, 'That's right. That was my sister called Robin.'

Lady Malander, 'Is she a robin.'

Thomas, 'Of course not. She is human like you or me. She just decided to come in the form of a robin.'

Lady Malander, 'I've heard about it but never seen it in action. Well, apart from your sister, do you know others with magical powers?'

Thomas, 'Lots.'

Lady Malander, 'Why didn't you tell me before?'

Thomas, 'Don't you know lots of other people with the eye?'

Lady Malander, 'Not that many. Would they help?'

Thomas, 'I'm sure they would if you asked.'

Lady Malander, 'I will get you some food, rest, and we will talk about this later.'

Robin, the robin, sat on Thomas's shoulder with a note in her beak:

> *Would the world be saved by a bird?*
> *Surely that would seem absurd,*
> *But not a doctor was conferred,*
> *In this story, where death was deferred.*

61

Up North

Earl Winterdom wasn't known for his finesse. The training at Malvern had made a big impact on him, but you can't give a man what he hasn't got. And he didn't have a tactical brain. He wasn't even a strategist. He wasn't even a great communicator, but he was brave, and he was popular with his men.

He decided to take all the men he could find and just attack the Slimenest. It would be one giant melee. A clash of two armies battering each other until a winner was declared. Not that there was ever a winner: the victor was the one that lost the least or was still left standing. Both sides just wanted to kill.

The two armies lined up in no specific order facing each other in a flat field outside Grantham. Neither side had given any thought to the lay of the land or had even tried to take advantage of the natural features. Earl Winterdom had kept the Worcestershire and Oxfordshire regiments back as a reserve. That proved that the training had been of some benefit.

Nearly half a million individuals were on the field. It was easily the largest battle that had ever taken place on the soil of Grand Britannica. And it looked like it was probably going to be one of the bloodiest. For the humans, the problem was that the Slimenest were generally stronger and more aggressive, but the humans were fighting for their families.

Both sides were shouting and screaming at each other, but

they were waiting for the signal to start. Then the arrows started flying, thousands of them from both sides. The humans had the benefit of shields and for the more prosperous thick leather jerkins and pantaloons. The Slimenest had nothing, just their nudity.

Then the Slimies charged, partly to avoid the avalanche of arrows and partly because it was what they did. It was time for hand-to-hand fighting. The humans linked shields and initially used pikemen to keep the Slimies back. Some of the Slimies deliberately impaled themselves on the pikes to make them ineffective. The human line held, but it would eventually fail as the Slimies threw more and more numbers against specific points.

Human crossbowmen came into their own. They were far more suited to close combat fighting. Thousands of bolts punctured the Slimie bodies, ripping away vital organs as they went. But the humans did not have it their own way. The taller Slimies used scythes to remove human heads. It was hard to look forward and upwards at the same time. And you had to look downwards as the ground was gradually being reconstituted into a quagmire. The trampling of feet and the concentration of human and Slimie body parts had made the already wet ground very slippery. And the Slimies weren't called Slimies for no reason.

Earl Winterdom ordered the bugler to play a specific note, and to a man, nearly two hundred thousand human troops moved backwards three steps. This surprised the opposition. Some thought it was a retreat and were disappointed. Some fell over and struggled to get up. Some were shot by crossbowmen. New pikes were delivered, and the fighting continued.

It was a competition of strength and determination, and eventually, the Slimies would out-strength them. In the meantime, the slashing and the stabbing continued. Heads were sliced off, guts were ripped out, and limbs were left dangling. Numbers on both sides were being decimated. Bodies were not designed to cope with steel incursions.

Earl Winterdom ordered the bugler to play a specific note again, and the backwards move was repeated to much the same effect. But this time, he had ordered a firing of Tanylip arrows. And this was the more refined sort of Tanylip. The Slimies stopped in mid-flight and began itching. And then itching some more. Whilst they were itching, they were being killed.

The battle-ground became an itch-fest. Over a hundred thousand Slimies gave up fighting and just itched. They were almost itching themselves to death. And if the itching didn't kill them, the humans did. He ordered his men not to show any mercy, and they didn't. The battle was a huge success for humankind, and his best two regiments weren't even used, much to their displeasure.

The less experienced county units were allowed to go home, but the best, were ordered to Malvern. Earl Winterdom was now the greatest hero ever, putting Lord Malander well into the shade. The Earl picked up a note which said:

> *Bring them on, let them attack,*
> *Now is the time for some payback,*
> *Avoid the thrusts and the flack,*
> *It will be the Slimies day, most black.*

62

Everything had Changed

Earl Winterdom's great victory at the Battle of Grantham Marshes, or as the soldiers called it 'The Itchy battle', changed the whole nature of the battle against the Slimenest. The only Slimie force left in the field was the one in Gloucester.

As Lord Malander said before,' What a difference a day makes.'

And to make it even better the humans had two forces coming to Malvern's aid. Did the Slimenest realise how precarious their position had suddenly become?

Did the Slimenest army in Gloucester know about their new, improved Tanylip weapon?

Lord Malander sent Majors Dragondale and Bandolier and every soldier they had that could ride a horse and fire an arrow to Gloucester. The infantry followed. When they got to Gloucester, they found that the Slimenest were withdrawing.

The mounted archers immediately attacked with the Tanylip infused arrows and watched in amazement as the Slimes ripped themselves to pieces. They pressed their attack, but the Slimies were fleeing as fast as they could. About a thousand mounted archers pursued them but kept their distance.

Lord Malander ordered the following:
- All regular Malvern forces except First Welland and First Colwall to depart for south-east England

- Northern forces under Earl Winterdom to head for London
- All south-west forces to pursue Slimenest forces
- Eliminate any Slimenest pockets found on the way
- Issue all remaining Tanylip stocks for the journey
- Magical forces to attend

Lord Malander was looking forward to being at the demise of the Slimenest. Thomas was looking forward to seeing more of England. Lady Malander was looking forward to spending more time with her husband.

Major Hogflesh's scouts were tracking the Slimenest all the way. And the mounted archers were staying close to the fleeing Slimies. Both groups had strict instructions not to kill all of the Slimies as Lord Malander wanted to obtain information regarding their origin.

He wanted to consult with Abbott Frogmore, but he had gone missing.

63

The Long Trek

There wasn't much to report regarding what became known as the long trek. Most inhabitants barely made a journey of twenty or thirty miles in their lifetime. It proved to be a good thing. It brought people from different towns and counties together to focus on a common purpose. There was great excitement that they were heading towards the final hurdle. Victory was in sight.

And victory meant that they could return to normality. They could return to the drudgery of their normal lives. Ploughmen could be ploughmen again. Blacksmiths could be blacksmiths, and stories would be told of their great adventure and how they single-handedly killed fifty Slimies, or was it sixty?

Slimies were regularly being doused with Tanylip as they progressed through Oxfordshire, Wiltshire, Berkshire, and Surrey. The humans had no idea where they were going, but the Slimies did. The dwindling numbers of Slimies led, and the humans followed. The Northern forces joined Lord Malander at Reading. The South-Western troops were about thirty miles behind.

What was depressing was the complete lack of human life in the towns and villages they passed through. In fact, a complete lack of wildlife. Everything had been consumed by the Slimenest horde. Much of the South would have to be re-populated. Rumour was that London had held out, but nobody really knew.

Reading itself was a ghost town.

At first, it was assumed that the Slimenest were heading towards London, but gradually it became obvious that they were heading south. Major Hogsflesh was trying to predict their final destination, but the remaining twenty or thirty thousand Slimies were too spread out to be specific. In the end, he thought Brighton looked to be the best bet.

The Slimies camped overnight in Cuckfield, oblivious to the fact that over one hundred thousand troops were tracking them. Lord Malander ordered the death of another twenty thousand Slimies leaving ten thousand to continue. This was achieved without the loss of a single human. It wasn't particularly honourable, but honour had never been a relevant aspect in this war.

The Slimies had left early, surprising their human bloodhounds. Major Hogsflesh was embarrassed that they got away unnoticed, but he soon tracked them down through Haywards Heath and Burgess Hill and then through Ditchling Common.

The Slimies then climbed the narrow winding track to the top of the Beacon, and then they marched along the Downs to Devil's Dyke, the highest point in East Sussex. There was no doubt that this was a beautiful but slightly eerie spot where the wind howled, and the weather could change whilst drinking a small glass of the local brew.

Then it happened.

A verse floated down:

> *It was a journey too far to walk,*
> *Too much discussion and little talk,*
> *To the green hills made of chalk,*

Once there, one could only baulk.

It was the end of the line,
For some, it was a chance to shine,
For others, they had seen the sign,
Now it was much more than a shrine.

64

The End

A giant Slimie stood at the entrance to a cave in the side of the Dyke that seemed to open onto infinity. Inside the cave, you could see galaxies full of stars and whirling clouds of cosmic dust. The multitude of colours was mesmerising and enticing, eager to suck you in.

Your normal standard size Slimies were disappearing one by one as they jumped into the nothingness. The giant looked on, disinterested in the human spectators that were gawping at the two spectacles. Most Slimies were pretty nasty looking things, but this one was particularly ugly.

They were not unlike giant, vertical slugs but with four legs and two arms. There was no head as such. Their light blue bodies just contained a large slit for a mouth that was full of razor-like teeth. Their eyes were small and beady. There were no discernible ears or hair. Their bodies were smooth, shiny, and cold and typically between seven and eight feet tall.

Some of the Slimies had darker blue bodies, and there was a suggestion that they were more senior, or perhaps just older. There were no genitalia, but there was an aperture for disposing of waste material which they seemed to have no control over. When the need arose, they had a shit.

The giant Slimie differed in that it was wearing a cloak and held an ornate staff in its hand. It appeared to show no interest in the events that were unfurling, but then it had always been difficult to superimpose human expressions onto a slug. The Slimies weren't really slimy until you cut them open, and then a foul-smelling, mud-like ooze erupted. And if you got it on your body, it stung. It was almost impossible to remove from clothing.

As the Slimies jumped into the cosmic opening, they showed no emotion. You couldn't see what was happening to them; they just disappeared.

Lord Malander ordered his troops forward, but the Slimie Boss waved his wand, and the entire human assembly simply froze. Everyone was paralysed except one: Thomas walked forward.

Galattermous, 'So, Merlin, you show yourself.'

Thomas, 'And why do you call me Merlin?'

Galattermous, 'That was what you called yourself the last time we met. And I'm Galattermous.'

Thomas, 'But we have never met before.'

Galattermous, 'Why do you speak in riddles? We have crossed swords on many occasions.'

Thomas, 'I'm sure that I would remember you. And what have you done to my friends?'

Galattermous, 'A simple paralysis spell. That should take you seconds to undo.'

Thomas, 'What are you doing here?'

Galattermous, 'The same as usual, collecting souls for my incantations. It's a shame that your people had to die, but their suffering will keep me alive for decades. And I can sell the excess souls for a tidy profit. This has been a very successful exercise with so little resistance. Anyway, it's time to go.'

Thomas, 'I will be ready for you next time.'

Galattermous, 'You usually are, but I've just worked it out.

You are a boy. You are not Merlin yet. I could easily kill you and save myself a lot of trouble, but then life would be rather boring.'

Galattermous, the Slimies and the magically created cosmic portal all disappeared, and the paralysis spell was broken.

Lord Malander, 'What just happened? Who is Galattermous?'

Lady Malander, 'So you are the Merlin of legend?'

Thomas, 'How can I be a legend if I'm still a boy?'

Lady Malander, 'Magic has no time for time and space.'

Thomas, 'I ascertained that Galattermous is an evil sorcerer that has lived for centuries by eating human souls. They have sustained him and other evil magical entities since time immemorial. Apparently, I have or will fight him many times, but I have never defeated him.'

Lord Malander, 'So what actually happens to these souls?'

Thomas, 'He absorbs their life essence, thereby terminating that soul forever. It ceases to exist. The wheel of time will not turn for them any more.'

Lord Malander, 'How can we avenge them?'

Thomas, 'I've no idea.'

Lady Malander, 'I think that we might as well start calling you Merlin.'

Merlin, 'That's fine with me.'

Laying in the grass, there was a verse:

> *The clues were there, but still, we won,*
> *Merlin lives, but things are far from done,*
> *Life goes on, full of laughter and fun,*
> *So it's time for a brief period in the sun.*

65

Home Again

The journey home was joyous. There was singing and laughing and at every opportunity, some dancing. Camps became parties. The war was over; the danger was gone. Men started going home of their own accord as they had done their bit.

Some were returning to a happy family life. Others were going to an empty house with terrible memories. And it was the memories that were now going to do the most harm. Some would be scarred for life. Some would spend the nights in bed with nightmares. For some, the demons of the nights became their friends.

Now the fields needed attention, and their wives too. There was, without doubt, going to be a population explosion as love was in the air. Lady Malander was looking forward to her first one, and hopefully some more.

Lord Malander knew that there was going to be a mountain of work as so much had been ignored, but at least the killing had stopped.

Thomas or Merlin wondered what was in store for him now. Who was going to feed him? Would there still be a market for his services? Everything was going to change again.

And then everything changed: Merlin appeared.

Book 2

1

Another Day

Merlin woke up with a stinking headache. It was quite normal after time travel. He had often pondered that it was the way the brain coped with the misuse of time and space. It was one of the downsides of chasing Galattermous.

Merlin knew that a mixture of Elderberry, Spanish onion and crushed saffron would soon cure his head, but he preferred a cup of hot black coffee. He liked it as hot as possible so that the tongue hurt when you drank it. It made you feel alive. And he was grateful that he was, as this time his life had been on a very thin thread.

The headquarters of the Malander Society was a well-kept secret. But for hundreds of years, it had been based in Malvern in Worcestershire. It had been there well before recorded history, and for the last few hundred years, it had used the same building: Little Malvern Court, a fourteenth-century prior's hall.

It was a stunningly beautiful spot with its giant lime tree and yew hedge. In the garden, there were some very impressive cedar trees planted from seeds brought back from the Holy Land, and there was a chain of lakes that were originally fish ponds for the monks that lived in the property. And the views over the Severn Valley were simply magnificent.

Of course, they weren't monks in the building. They were magicians who needed cover during the Christian suppression of anything magical. Magic was still alive, but it had suffered serious repression since the dawn of Christianity which used a lot of mystical symbolism in its rituals. It was the old story: the best way to defeat a culture was to willingly absorb it with kindness and then cut its throat when it least expected it.

Merlin remembered how Christian hoodlums had destroyed the great libraries of the ancient world. He remembered how they demolished stunning architecture and great art. Their vandalism seemed to have been forgotten, and the opposite happened: they were now seen as the guardians of great antiquity. The Christians had re-written history, but their time would come. Merlin knew that what goes around comes around.

Anyway, history had been changed a few times before Merlin had corrected things. Although the correction had not restored the correct originality. That was almost impossible as little changes at crucial points in history can have devastating effects. He remembered when Galattermous killed George Washington's childhood nurse, which resulted in the American War of Independence never happening, resulting in the British Empire controlling half of the globe.

When he tried to correct things, he saved the nurse but gave George Washington the measles. George didn't die, and he ended up becoming a member of the British Parliament. On his third attempt, he almost restored things as they should have been, except that the constitution had been changed to allow Americans to bear arms.

Merlin realised then that the 'correct version' was just an illusion. Nothing was permanent or fixed in history. He now knew that many of the major wars were caused by Galattermous's desire for souls. Both the World Wars were of his doing. Merlin knew that he could go back and stop them from happening, but the consequences of that would be mind-boggling. He drank his coffee, knowing that reminiscing achieved nothing. He had a job to do before this reality was lost forever. Merlin never saw the verse on the door:

The sun sets on Little Malvern Court,
With a giant lime tree as your escort,
It hides the battles that have been fought,
From the Somme to Agincourt.

2

We Meet Again

Merlin knew that Galattermous was organising two further attacks. One was going to be a few years after the Slimie invasion, and the other was going to be in the eighteenth century in Spain.

Galattermous planned to eliminate all humans in Grand Britannica and then use that island as a base to extract souls from all over the world. Merlin had never really understood where the demand for souls was coming from. An ancient book he read suggested two things. They were needed by demons so that they could enter Heaven, and alternatively, the damned wanted them so they could bluff their way into the same place. He had never seen any proof of this. Nevertheless, Galattermous seemed to have a ready market.

Merlin wasn't sure why Galattermous planned to attack Spain. It might just be a soul raid. Anyway, he decided that his younger self would look after the attack in Britain and he would handle Spain. But what would happen if his younger self was killed? But then he couldn't have been because he was still alive. But then he couldn't remember his youth either. He would need to investigate that later.

He returned to Grand Britannica at the exact time he left, which meant that he had never left as far as the locals were concerned. He tracked down himself for a chat.

Merlin, 'How are you today?'

Thomas Merlin, 'I'm fine, but still confused by this whole Merlin thing.'

Merlin, 'In what way are you confused?'

Thomas Merlin, 'Well, if you were me, then you would remember all of this. You could tell me what happens next.'

Merlin, 'You are definitely me but not the actual me.'

Thomas Merlin, 'Brilliant. That clarifies everything.'

Merlin, 'I see what you mean. So far, you have only experienced a linear history; you are born, you live, and you die. But history is not fixed. There have been many different versions, and there will probably be many more.

'I suspect that I had the childhood I remember, but then history was changed, but my memories stayed the same. Normally they would change, but my time-hopping may exclude me from that process.'

Thomas Merlin, 'So we are the same person, but have different pasts.'

Merlin, 'I know that it is confusing.'

Thomas Merlin, 'So will we have this conversation again in the future when I'm you?'

Merlin, 'I guess so.'

Thomas Merlin, 'So then I will know the future?'

Merlin, 'That makes sense.'

Thomas Merlin, 'So what if I killed my younger self then?'

Merlin, 'That's what they call a paradox.'

Thomas Merlin, 'Do you want to meet my parents, as they must be your parents as well?'

Merlin, 'I better not, as they will be different from how I remember them.'

Thomas Merlin, 'Are you going to train me?'

Merlin, 'Just a little, but somehow we know how to do things without training.'

Thomas Merlin, 'Can I time travel?'

Merlin, 'Yes, but you will make mistakes.'

Thomas Merlin, 'But surely I will make the same mistakes as you?'

Merlin, 'Possibly not, as this conversation has already changed the future.'

Thomas Merlin, 'I can't say that I'm less confused than I was.'

Merlin, 'Nor I.'

Nearby was a note with a verse:

> *How can two Merlins meet,*
> *Surely that had to be a cheat,*
> *Or was it just another deceit,*
> *That the circle of life can't complete.*

3

To the Manor

Merlin sat down with Lord and Lady Malander and Thomas Merlin, who had more or less been adopted by his Lordship.
Lady Malander, 'I still can't get my head around the fact that you are the older version of our Merlin. It doesn't really make sense.'
Merlin, 'I understand that, my Lady. I've been discussing this with young Merlin, and it is a paradox within a paradox. But I'm really here to warn you.'
Lord Malander, 'Warn us. We have had a great victory. We need time to recuperate.'
Merlin, 'You will get some time but not a lot. The enemy is on the move, and unfortunately, you are going to be the target again.'
Lord Malander, 'Why us?'
Merlin, 'I don't know how to say this without being rude.'
Lord Malander, 'Just say it.'
Merlin, 'Your level of development is quite primitive.'
Lord Malander, 'How dare you. We are not savages.'
Merlin pulled out a few items from his holdall. He placed on a table a cigarette lighter, a pocket calculator and a pen.
Merlin, 'These are simple everyday items that will be used in the future.' He took the lighter and made fire. There was a shock in the room. It was the best magic they had ever seen. He

handed it to his lordship, who played with it with great enthusiasm.

He then turned on the calculator and asked them to request a summation. The onlookers were interested but not too excited, but the pen was regarded as sheer brilliance. Lady Malander started drawing pictures, and then they all wanted a go.

Merlin, 'These are very simple technologies. In the future, men will fly and ride in horseless carriages. They will have terrible technologies that can kill thousands of people in one go. And men will land on the moon.'

Lord Malander, 'I wouldn't believe anyone but you. So can you give us these things to help defend ourselves?'

Merlin, 'I can't. I'm not allowed to. Time itself stops me, but I can show you how to improve your current technology. I've brought a series of pictures and photographs to help.

'The first picture is a sword made of steel. I can show your blacksmiths how to turn iron into a much harder material. Your weapons will be much stronger.'

Lord Malander, 'Thank you, Merlin, that would be very helpful.'

Merlin, 'The second picture is chain mail. It is a type of coat consisting of small metal rings linked together in a pattern to form a mesh.' The picture was a typical Norman soldier.

Lord Malander, 'What's that on his head?'

Merlin, 'It's a protective helmet.'

Lord Malander, 'But that is so obvious. Why didn't we think of that?'

Merlin, 'I agree with you. It's hard to explain why no one had thought of it earlier. I've also brought some gunpowder with me. Let's go outside.' They all followed him.

He poured some of the gunpowder on the grass and told

everyone to stand back. He stuck a long piece of gauze in the middle of it to make a fuse and set fire to it. It caused one of the biggest explosions ever seen in Grand Britannica. There was a mixture of shock and admiration.

He then took a short metal tube and put both a small metal ball and some gunpowder in it. He used the gauze again to cause a mini-explosion, but they were shocked to see the metal ball fly out of the tube at a tremendous rate of speed and bury itself in a nearby oak.

Lord Malander, 'That could easily kill someone.'

Merlin, 'That's the general idea.' They went back inside, and he showed them a picture of a gun and a cannon.'

Lord Malander, 'How do we make all these things?'

Merlin, 'I can show your engineering team.'

Lord Malander, 'Thank you, Merlin.'

Merlin, 'This is going to shock you. I'm going to show you some moving pictures of men fighting. It may give you some ideas.'

Merlin took his smartphone and showed a variety of films showing early fighting techniques. It included a lot of Roman manoeuvres. The audience was shocked, thrilled, and mystified. Lord Malander even checked the back of the phone to make sure there were no little people anywhere. They accepted it all as magic because it was.

Lord Malander, 'This is all very interesting, but I have to be honest. We simply don't have the funds to continue much longer. The treasury is almost empty.'

Merlin, 'Leave that to me.'

The two Merlins spent time together, and then the older one skipped off to Spain.

Neither of them spotted the verse:

What about the gun and the pen?
Who has killed the most, now and then,
The how, the what and the when,
Now duplicated in two wise men.

4

Bullion

Lord Malander heard a large bump in the night. Well, more of a crash. When he investigated, there was the largest stack of gold he had ever seen sitting in the entrance hall. He had never seen it in the shape of bricks before. Merlin said that he would solve the financing problem, and he did. However, he wasn't sure where he was going to store it.

It was time to call a meeting of his military command which now consisted of himself and:
- Major Mainstay, Deputy Commander
- Abbott Frogmore, Head of Prophecy Research and Planning
- Major Dragondale, Commander Archery
- Lady Malander, Commander Mystical Arts
- Major Bandolier, Commander Cavalry
- Major Hogsflesh, Commander Intelligence
- Major Lambskin, Commander Malvern Infantry
- Major Staniforth, Commander Engineering
- Fay Mellondrop, Quartermaster General
- Colonel Winterdom, Worcestershire Regiment
- Colonel Mannering, Oxfordshire Regiment
- Colonel Walsh, Gloucestershire Regiment
- Merlin

They all sat around a large round table. It was a table that they came a lot to.

Replacements had been found for the Engineering role and the Gloucestershire Regiment, and Merlin had been invited for the first time. The three colonels were still invited as they had earned their place, and the other county forces weren't professional enough to be represented yet.

Lord Malander, 'Welcome my victorious comrades in arms. I need to thank you all for your dedication, hard work, and loyalty. It was a close-run thing, but we did it. We need to remember and toast those we lost, but as we have said several times, "life goes on".

'I want to commend Colonel Winterdom for his brilliant victory and thank young Merlin for his timely interventions. You would now think that it is a time for peace and we will have some, but at the same time, we need to plan for war. I have learnt that we are likely to suffer another attack by Galattermous.'

Major Hogsflesh, 'How do you know?'

Lord Malander, 'We received a visitation from Merlin, not this one, but an older version of himself.'

There was an outbreak of disbelief. They weren't challenging his lordship, but it just seemed too unlikely. To be honest, it was just another unlikely event piled up on to an enormous pile of unlikely events.

Lord Malander took the lighter and lit it. The looks of astonishment in the room were way beyond funny. Eyes bulged out of their sockets, two majors jumped back in terror, and there was a considerable amount of swearing. Things calmed down, and they all took turns playing with it. It wouldn't be long before the fuel would run out.

The calculator didn't generate much interest except for the

plastic material it was made of and the green light display. But the pen went down really well. Everyone wanted to keep it, but Lady Malander made sure that it was hers.

Most started to believe that a Merlin from the future visited them and warned them of the coming danger. Lord Malander then laid the pictures and photographs out on the table. It was almost too many shocks in one day for some of them, but Major Staniforth was fascinated. He had already started thinking about the manufacturing process.

Lord Malander, 'I think that most of you now believe that we were visited and consequently that there is a real threat on the horizon. I need to point out that Merlin plans to return to assist in the making of the following:

- Chain mail
- Helmets
- Gunpowder
- Guns
- Steel.

'In addition, we have received funds that will be used to renovate our society. We will re-build. We will develop the technologies that we have listed above, and we will not disband. We have the monies to fund a standing army and indeed to develop it further.'

The meeting attendees stood up and clapped, and then dinner was brought in. Some said that it was the best dinner ever.

A verse was found on a plate:

> *At the successful military meeting,*
> *There was no chance of them retreating,*
> *They were gearing up to ensure competing,*
> *Any enemy would get a good beating.*

5

The Plans Unfold

Lord Malander, 'So James, what do you think of these new revolutionary ideas?'

Major Staniforth, 'To be honest, I'm excited. I plan to make you a chain-mail suit and a helmet.'

Lord Malander, 'That would be excellent, although I'm not sure if I can face the common soldier. We are in this together. Why should wealth buy me an advantage?'

Major Staniforth, 'I can see where you are coming from, but if we perfect the process, then we can gradually share this technology with others. Certainly, if we can get the material, then everyone should get a helmet.'

Lord Malander, 'That's good.'

Major Staniforth, 'Merlin left plans to manufacture gunpowder. I'm still trying to get sulphur and potassium nitrate. Carbon is everywhere. When I get it, I will need more men to produce the guns. And did you want me to manufacture a cannon?'

Lord Malander, 'Get as many men as you need, and yes, please make me a cannon. Use this opportunity to express yourself.'

Major Staniforth, 'Thank you, my Lord.'

Lord Malander, 'Good luck, can you send in our military friends on the way out, please.'

Majors Mainstay, Dragondale, Bandolier and Lambskin, and Colonels Winterdom, Mannering, and Walsh entered the room. Lord Malander offered them seats, and drinks were organised.

Lord Malander, 'Welcome all. I thought that we should get together to discuss the structure of our military operation. We now have the entire country to defend, and we are introducing new technology. The gun is going to change everything.

'Let me throw out some suggestions first, and then we can discuss:

1. The country should be divided into the following regions:
   - North
   - Midlands
   - South-East
   - South-West
   - Wales
2. Each region should have a Governor with a military command
3. Each region should have three full time, professional regiments
4. Malvern would remain as the military HQ with ten full time, professional regiments
5. Of the three regiments in each region, two would be mobile
6. A castle will be established in each region
7. Guns will gradually replace bows assuming they work
8. An artillery regiment will be established assuming that cannons work

'Over to you?'

Major Lambskin, 'What about Scotland?'

Lord Malander, 'During the Slimie campaign, we had no contact with Scotland at all. Perhaps we should include them?'

Colonel Winterdom, 'I suggest we leave them for now as we have enough to do.'

Lord Malander, 'Let's run with that for now.'

Major Dragondale, 'To me, the regions look very large and the resources quite limited.'

Lord Malander, 'We still have the militia, but we are limited by what we can afford, but we could increase the numbers if that were what was required.'

Major Bandolier, 'Should we go with the Lord's suggestion and then review later?'

Colonel Walsh, 'The problem here is the training period. It takes time to recruit and train a whole regiment. And we lost a lot of people to the Slimies.'

Colonel Winterdom, 'Changing the subject, who is going to allocate the posts?'

Lord Malander, 'I think Major Tindall should continue to command the Malvern Forces, but the rest is up for grabs.'

Colonel Winterdom, 'I would like the northern region so that I could go home.'

Lord Malander, 'I'm happy with that if everyone else is.' No one objected.

Lord Malander, 'Does anyone want the other regions?'

Major Dragondale wanted the South-East, Major Bandolier wanted the Midlands, Major Mainstay wanted Wales, Colonel Winterdom wanted the North, and Colonel Mannering wanted the South-West. It all worked out rather well.

The Discussion wandered on, but most of Lord Malander's suggestions were accepted.

No one saw the verse under the door:

What's in a plan?
Said the solider to the gentleman,
It's where regional success began,
Sometime in my lifespan.

6

Even More Plans

Lord and Lady Malander, Abbott Frogmore and Merlin got together to agree on the magical way forward.

Lord Malander, 'Just to update the Abbott, the adult version of Merlin visited us to explain that Galattermous is planning two attacks: one against us in the near future and one against Spain in many years to come. He is going to tackle the Spanish incursion, but he will visit us again later. Don't worry about the time paradoxes; we have been through all of that.'

Abbott Frogmore, 'Fascinating. I must admit I'm very nervous about his motives. Are we sure we can trust him?'

Lord Malander, 'Are you sure that you can trust anyone? Anyway, you've seen the gadgets and the pictures. He also gave us a demonstration of gunpowder and showed us images of moving people carrying out different military formations. We need to upgrade our military to cope with a potentially stronger foe.'

Abbott Frogmore, 'Why didn't he just give us better weapons? And is he as strong as he says he is?'

Lord Malander, 'Apparently that would be against the rules of time travel, and I'm led to believe that he is very strong.'

Abbott Frogmore, 'That doesn't sound that rational.'

Lord Malander, 'It's very hard for us to judge.'

Thomas Merlin, 'I suspect that is true as it would have made his job a lot easier.'

Abbott Frogmore, 'But he left those gadgets and gunpowder behind. However, mark my words, Merlin could be trouble, and I'm not pointing my finger at you, Thomas.'

Lord Malander, 'I would agree, but I guess that technically they are not weapons, and gunpowder is OK because the constituent parts are well within our current capability. I also understand your concerns regarding Merlin. We know so little about him.'

Abbott Frogmore, 'Perhaps Merlin and Galattermous are working together?'

Thomas Merlin, 'That is nonsense.'

Lord Malander, 'Anyway, they are the parameters that we have to work with. What are our magical plans?'

Lady Malander, 'Thomas Merlin has recruited his sister and has identified at least twenty other natural magicians. Give us a few weeks, and we will have quite a formidable force.'

Lord Malander, 'Excellent, but what are our plans?'

Abbott Frogmore, 'Can I butt in? We don't really have a military plan yet, so it's going to be difficult to agree on a magical plan.'

Lady Malander, 'Thank you, dear Abbott.'

Abbott Frogmore, 'You are welcome, my Lady.'

Lord Malander, 'Merlin, what are your views?'

Thomas Merlin, 'I would recommend the following:
- That we create a network of ley lines so that magical energy can flow to where it is needed
- That we have a magical team supporting each region and a core team at Malvern
- That we create a magical monitoring team that will identify any anomalies like the one in the South Downs

- That we organise a witch hunt
- That we develop amulets for our troops that will help them resist incantations and enchantments
- That we build a relationship with the wild folk.'

Lord Malander, 'Do you agree, my love?'

Lady Malander, 'I believe I do.' She knew that she was out of her depth from a magical perspective.

Lord Malander, 'What do you think, Abbott?'

Abbott Frogmore, 'Sounds super to me.' He acted like he was totally out of his depth. But that wasn't the case.

Lord Malander, 'Do you have any developments regarding the Prophecy?'

Abbott Frogmore, 'I've come to the conclusion that it is more of a history than a prophecy, especially as we tend to get the verse after the event.'

Lord Malander, 'Merlin, what do you think?'

Thomas Merlin, 'It's not the content that intrigues me but the author. Who is writing the verses?'

Lord Malander, 'Do you have any ideas, Abbott?'

Abbott Frogmore, 'Sorry my Lord, it's a total mystery, but I can say that there are at least twenty different styles. Some verses are childish or certainly naïve. Others are quite profound and show intense intelligence. Some of the early ones were prophetic. The later ones are more historic.'

Lady Malander, 'That's not my view.'

Abbott Frogmore, 'We are wasting our time even looking at them, although they are rather amusing.'

The mystery writer struck again:

Is it a prophecy or a prediction?
Merlin's forecasts lead to contradiction,
Is it an addiction or an affliction?
His foresight may just be fiction.

The friar's insight may be benediction,
Foretelling can lead to malediction,
So is history just dereliction?
Or is it time for some conviction?

7

Ley Lines

Thomas Merlin spent a few weeks working out his system of ley lines. They were going to be invisible conduits of magical or physical energy that was dragged from the Earth and made available to knowledgeable practitioners of the mystic arts.

He sent men out throughout Grand Britannica to build henges. These were normally circular stone or wood constructs that simply collected energy and fed the grid. It took Merlin some time to work out the best locations as there were no maps to assist, but somehow, he knew where they should go. He had to learn the skill of thought transfer so that the workers would know the exact location of the construction. When the workers found the place, they could mentally converse with Merlin to get his approval. It didn't always work.

The biggest source of this energy was the Malvern Hills. They became the centre point for every ley line in the country. Other centres also had ley lines emanating from them, and where ley lines crossed, there was a considerable build-up of energy. Key points included Glastonbury, Chanctonbury, Puzzlewood, Cheddar, Elva Hill, Cadair Udris, St Fillan and almost every peak in every county.

Lady Malander started work on the construction of the magical amulets that would ward off evil magic. Merlin and his new recruits would actually do the hard work of magicising them.

Merlin's sister, Robin, was particularly gifted in this type of magic, as was her black cat, Herbert. To be honest, he wasn't really a cat. He was a young magician who transformed himself into a cat, and absolutely no one had been able to restore him. In fact, Herbert had reached the stage where he preferred being feline.

The construction of the citadel on the hills was almost complete. It was partly a home but mostly a defensive structure with some seriously thick walls. It could sleep two thousand soldiers, had stables, meeting rooms, kitchens, a hospital complex, storage facilities, an armoury and so on. Water was not a problem as it literally flowed out of the side of the hills.

Lady Malander was excited that it contained Grand Britannica's first magical services centre with an extensive and growing library, a herbarium, an observatory, academy buildings and most important of all, a monitoring centre. This was designed to provide an early warning of any magical threats. It also contained the start and end of numerous ley lines.

The citadel, which was built into Summer Hill, was designed for both physical and magical defence. Catapults captured from the Slimies had been converted to work within the complex against attackers. Smaller castles had been established above the citadel and on each side of the Wyche Cutting. Smaller defensive installations were installed on most of the individual hills. Lookout posts were placed at regular points on each side of the hills. Larger fortifications were built at the ends of the hill line.

The citadel itself was a beautiful multi-towered edifice. Its white, iridescent steeples looked majestic against the sides of the grass-covered volcanic ridge. It had that unique combination of military strength and a netherworld romantic quality. The locals were in awe of it but at the same time were proud to be associated with it, and it gave a lot of them a very good living.

Further innovations were being developed: horse-driven carts, saddles, spurs, tourniquets, slit windows for archers, roof tiles, different types of swords and pencils. It was amazing what humanity could do when it was on a war footing, and cash was not a problem. One innovation led to another. Pencils led to a huge increase in written orders for the military, and sketching became an important pastime. Saddles and stirrups dramatically improved the performance of mounted archers, which led to an increased demand for horses which in turn led to an increased demand for hay. So farming practices had to improve to meet the demand.

The days were good, and the general mood of the Malvern community was very good, if not seriously happy. That was going to change.

The stonemason found the verse when he laid the final stone:

>*Strong enough, the citadel on the hill,*
>*Beauty cut from rocks with great skill,*
>*Will, it be the guardian of free-will,*
>*Or much worse, humanity's poison-pill?*

>*The start and end of any line,*
>*Mystic energy does define,*
>*Follows the Malvern Hills chine,*
>*Forcing celestial bodies to align.*

>*Magic flows have no confine,*
>*Mostly safe and quite benign,*
>*But some quite sour and malign.*
>*Giving mankind a needed lifeline.*

8

The Witch Hunt

Lord Malander, 'So what is a witch?'

Lady Malander, 'Someone who practices the dark arts.'

Lord Malander, 'It seems to me that historically the main criteria were age, sex and appearance.'

Lady Malander, 'What are you saying?'

Lord Malander, 'Well, every person who has been punished as far as my memory is concerned has been an ugly, old woman. The older and uglier they are, the more likely that they would be accused of witchcraft. And to make it worse, if they carry out any healing activities, they are definitely doomed.'

Lady Malander, 'You are right, but there are witches out there. They even attacked Malvern whilst we were away.'

Lord Malander, 'I'm not disputing that there are witches out there. I just don't want to see innocent old ladies burnt on my watch. I'm not having it.'

Lady Malander, 'So what are you suggesting?'

Lord Malander, 'I'm suggesting that we need a more scientific approach to detection and a more just approach to punishment.'

Lady Malander, 'I can see where you are coming from, but when we identify a true witch, someone who supports Galattermous, what are we going to do with him or her? They are dangerous, potentially deadly.'

Lord Malander, 'Is there any way of stripping the witch of its powers?'

Lady Malander, 'I will go and get Thomas, as he might have some ideas.'

Thomas entered the Malanders' new lounge in the Citadel.

Lord Malander, 'Thomas, good morning to you.'

Thomas Merlin, 'And a good day to my two most favourite people in the Universe.'

Lady Malander, 'Morning Thomas, we have been discussing witches. How can we identify them, and what do we do with them once we have them in custody?'

Thomas Merlin, 'I can produce a spell that will identify every witch and mark them.'

Lord Malander, 'Mark them?'

Thomas Merlin, 'Yes, we could turn them orange or any colour you like, or any other way you want them identified. The only downside is that it will pick up actual witches and those who have witching talents. It will cause a lot of anguish for a few individuals.'

Lady Malander, 'I would say that it's unfortunate but a relatively small price to pay.'

Lord Malander, 'I agree.'

Thomas Merlin, 'Shall I colour their heads?'

Lord Malander, 'I think so.'

Thomas Merlin, 'What colour?'

Lady Malander, 'Orange works for me.'

Thomas Merlin, 'Orange it is. The second question is, what should we do with them? There are quite a few issues here.

'As soon as they turn orange, they will know that the game is up. There is every chance that they will turn nasty.'

Lord Malander, 'What are they likely to do?'

Thomas Merlin, 'It's very hard to tell. Some will flee or go into hiding. Others will join their coven. Some will take revenge on whoever suits them, possibly us.'

Lady Malander, 'So we need to be prepared for that.'

Thomas Merlin, 'We are much better protected than when the witches last attacked Malvern.'

Lord Malander, 'Fair enough. How many witches do you think there are in the country?'

Thomas Merlin, 'I would say between twenty and thirty thousand.'

Lady Malander, 'You must be joking.'

Thomas Merlin, 'Possibly, I might have under-estimated the numbers.'

Lord Malander, 'We don't have the facilities to imprison that number or even half that number.'

Thomas Merlin, 'I don't think you would be able to imprison them. When you corner them, they will fight. They will probably die fighting, and sadly they will take innocent people with them.'

Lord Malander, 'Why would they do that?'

Thomas Merlin, 'It's partly their evil nature and partly self-defence. They know that historically they were burnt alive, so you might as well die fighting.'

Lord Malander, 'Could we turn them?'

Thomas Merlin, 'What do you want to turn them into?'

Lord Malander, 'That wasn't what I was thinking. I was wondering if we could turn them away from the dark side.'

Thomas Merlin, 'It's unlikely as that's the very essence of what they are. We could try, but it is likely to be a very time-consuming and dangerous process.'

Lord Malander, 'But I like your other idea. Let's change them into sheep.'

Thomas Merlin, 'That would work. They would still be witches, but I'm pretty sure that their powers would be neutralised.'

Lady Malander, 'Orange sheep would allow us to identify

them.'

Thomas Merlin, 'What about the innocents? They would become orange sheep as well.'

Lord Malander, 'If someone vouched for them, could they be changed back on an individual basis?'

Thomas Merlin, 'I could do that.'

Lady Malander, 'So our plan is to convert all existing witches and those with inert witchery skills into orange sheep, and those who can be vouched for will be restored to human form?'

Thomas Merlin, 'That sounds good to me. When do you want me to do it?'

Lord Malander, 'It would take at least three weeks to inform each county leader.'

Lady Malander, 'That is too long as the witches are too big a threat.'

Thomas, 'That is fine with me.'

Lady Malander, 'We need to warn people in advance; otherwise, it will be too much of a shock.'

Lord Malander, 'I agree with you, but the risk is too great. Let's do it today and sort the problem out tomorrow. I will send messengers out now.'

That night the deed was done.

Attached to an orange sheep was the following verse:

> *Which witch was affront?*
> *It's time to catch and confront,*
> *The growing evil in the forefront,*
> *Needs culling to be blunt,*
> *Is now an orange, sheepish stunt.*

9

The Return

Today was an exciting day; Merlin had returned. Lord and Lady Malander gave Merlin a tour of the Malvern complex. Thomas Merlin tagged along. Mentally he regarded Merlin as an uncle rather than an older version of himself.

Sadly, Merlin brought bad news. It was almost definite that Galattermous would launch an attack on them this year. He had no idea how the attack would manifest itself, but it was coming in the near future.

Lord Malander sent messengers out to the regions to collect the attendees for an emergency Council of War. The regional structure was tending to slow things down because of communication delays.

The meeting consisted of the following:
- Lord Malander, Commander-in-Chief
- Lady Malander, Commander Mystical Arts
- Commander General Lambskin, Malvern
- Deputy Commander Walsh, Malvern
- Governor Commander Winterdom, Northern Region
- Governor Commander Mannering, South-West
- Governor Commander Mainstay, Wales
- Governor Commander Dragondale, South-East
- Governor Commander Bandolier, Midlands
- Abbott Frogmore, Planning

- Major Hogsflesh, Commander Intelligence
- Major Staniforth, Commander Engineering
- Fay Mellondrop, Quartermaster General
- Merlin
- Thomas.

Lord Malander did the introductions. Merlin appeared to be impressed with the assembled team, but it was difficult due to the noise outside. Thirteen orange sheep had been rounded up in Malvern. Lord Malander sent his aide to sort things out.

Lord Malander, 'Merlin brings bad news. Galattermous is on the move. We can expect another incursion this year.'

Commander General Lambskin, 'But that only gives us seven months at best to prepare.'

Merlin, 'Probably less.'

Lord Malander, 'How did Spain go?'

Merlin, 'It's touch and go at the moment. To be honest, I need a break from it.'

Major Hogsflesh, 'Aren't you needed there?'

Merlin, 'That's one of the upsides of time travel. I will be here for a few weeks, and then I will go back. I will arrive one minute after I left.'

Major Hogsflesh, 'Sounds like a neat trick to me.'

Lord Malander, 'We need to update Merlin on our progress. I will start first:
- The citadel is complete
- We have built numerous other fortifications throughout the hills
- We have divided the country into five regions with Governor Commanders
- Each region is creating three regiments, and a magical

services team and castles are in progress
- The Malvern forces of ten regiments are now full time and paid.

'They are the key points. Any questions?'
Merlin, 'How do you communicate with the regions?'
Lord Malander, 'That's still very slow and difficult.'
Merlin, 'I have some ideas. I will come back to you on that.'
Lord Malander, 'Thank you. My love, do you want to update Merlin next?'
Lady Malander, 'Of course. Thomas should take most of the credit, but we have done the following:
- Built henges and a network of ley lines
- Produced thousands of amulets
- Established a magical services centre with a library
- Carried out a witch hunt
- Recruited fifty-plus gifted magicians.

'The progress has been astonishing.'
Merlin, 'Believe me, you are going to need all of the help you can get. By the way, how many witches did you find?'
Thomas Merlin, 'Assuming that my spell is correct, over eighty thousand.'
Merlin, 'I'm not surprised, Galattermous has been steadily building up his forces for centuries.'
Lord Malander, 'I can't believe that it's eighty thousand.'
Lady Malander, 'We had our fair share here.'
Merlin, 'What have you done with them?'
Thomas Merlin, 'I transformed them into orange sheep.'
Merlin, 'Then what?'
Thomas Merlin, 'I guess what will happen to them will be

whatever happens to sheep.'

Merlin, 'So we are going to eat them? That's fine with me. Changing the subject, I'm happy to run some training courses for your new recruits.'

Lady Malander, 'That would be most appreciated.'

Lord Malander, 'Tindell, do you want to cover your area now.'

Commander General Lambskin, 'Yes, Sir. Our position is as follows:

- The Citadel and the surrounding area are reasonably secure
- There are about two thousand troops protecting the complex and ten regiments acting as a standing army
- Eight of the regiments are mounted
- There are an additional twenty thousand militia in the local area
- We are ready to take onboard guns and cannons when available
- An artillery regiment is being formed, which will be partly mobile using our new wagons.

'Any questions?'

Merlin, 'Do you have enough stocks of arrows?'

Commander General Lambskin, 'We are well-stocked, my Lord. We can rely on Fay to deliver whatever we need.'

Merlin, 'And what about helmets?'

Commander General Lambskin, 'Early versions were delivered, but they are being re-worked. It is my intention that every soldier should receive one.'

Merlin, 'Excellent. And are you carrying out marching exercises?'

Commander General Lambskin, 'To a limited extent.'

Merlin, 'Would you like some assistance in this area?'

Commander General Lambskin, 'It would be most welcome.'

Merlin, 'Let's fix some days later.'

Lord Malander, 'Commander Winterdom, I think that you are going to cover the regional updates?'

Commander Winterdom, 'That's correct, my Lord. Firstly there are five regions with a Commander and three regiments, two of which are mounted. We have all taken elements of the three-county regiments and used them as the backbone of the new regiments. Tough professional training has been provided.

Recruitment has been relatively easy as the positions are paid and full time. Magical services units are also being created. Castle development is slow due to the lack of trained labour.'

Merlin, 'Excellent, but what would you say is your biggest problem?'

Commander Winterdom, 'I'm not sure if my fellow commanders would agree, but I would say communications. How do we contact each other? Messengers take days.'

Governor Commander Dragondale, 'There is a system of hilltop bonfires which are lit when there is a crisis, but they are only useful on clear days.'

Merlin, 'I have some ideas which I will discuss later. What is morale like?'

Governor Commander Winterdom, 'Very good. They get fed every day, a uniform, a warm bed, money, and a tot of rum. It's a very desirable occupation.'

Merlin, 'But will they fight?'

Governor Commander Winterdom, 'There is absolutely no doubt of that.'

Merlin, 'Well done.'

Lord Malander, 'My dear Abbott, do you have anything to say?'

Abbott Frogmore, 'Of course I do, have you ever known me to be quiet?'

Lord Malander, 'That's true.'

Abbott Frogmore, 'I'm responsible for planning, and I can give you lots of "don't knows":

- I don't really know who we are fighting
- Or when we will be fighting
- Or where we will be fighting
- Or their numbers and capability.

'It makes planning really difficult.

'We can put about twenty-six regiments on the field, about sixty-five thousand men. With the militia, we could possibly double or even treble that. Is it enough?'

Merlin, 'That is the problem with planning. Generally, you start off with a serious lack of information and later, you have too much. You can only do your best.'

Abbott Frogmore, 'Do you not have any wise words?'

Merlin, 'Words are not wise in themselves, but they can be wielded brilliantly by the best of men. All I can say is that few plans survive contact with the enemy, but the man who plans knows where he is going.'

Abbott Frogmore, 'Thank you, Merlin.'

Lord Malander, 'Major Hogsflesh.'

Major Hogsflesh, 'I can only agree with my dear drinking buddy, the Abbott. I have scouts and contacts throughout the country but with little to do.'

Merlin, 'Your time will come, believe me. It will come when

you least expect it.'

Lord Malander, 'Major Staniforth, I think it is your turn.'

Major Staniforth, 'I have got so much to ask Merlin, but here is my update:
- We have produced some early batches of steel, but I could do with more help regarding purity and the manufacturing process
- We have got lots of gunpowder, and we have had a few mishaps, as you would expect. I need help with gun design. But we fired a variety of balls of differing sizes
- We have designed saddles, stirrups, wagons, new types of sword and dagger, bandages etc. We can't stop ourselves from inventing new things. Somehow it seems that we are now allowed to, although no one stopped us in the past.

'I would be very grateful if I could have a few days of your time.'

Merlin, 'You shall have them, my enthusiastic friend.'

Major Staniforth, 'Thank you so much.'

Lord Malander, 'Fay, what do you have to add?'

Fay Mellondrop, 'I would just like to thank Mr Merlin for sparing the time to help us.'

Merlin, 'I'm pleased to help; we are all in this together. Is there anything you need?'

Fay Mellondrop, 'I would like to know if there are any other ways of storing fresh food.'

Merlin. 'I'm sure that I can help you there.

'I would like to say that I'm very impressed with your efforts. They may be enough, or they may not be. Soon you will be tested, possibly to breaking point.

'Thomas will look after my diary. Book dates and use me.

I'm here to help.'

There was a spontaneous round of clapping and a round of mead, and on a cup was found the following:

> *When will the magic return?*
> *We all have so much to learn,*
> *Engineering problems concern,*
> *For his arrival, we all earnestly yearn.*
>
> *No rest, no patience, no time to adjourn,*
> *Delays and failures we do spurn,*
> *Merlin's enemies we will burn,*
> *His pride in us, we must earn.*

10

No Warning

There was no warning. They were taught to expect the unexpected. But they didn't expect an invasion from underground in the early morning. The slaughter was quiet and efficient, and hundreds died in their bed with slit throats. Most of the guards were ineffective as they were outward-looking. The Citadel had almost fallen.

The supporting castles received the same treatment. The invaders didn't smash through the floor. They somehow melted it so that their approach was silent. They were the silent killers of the night. The silent massacre continued. A chemical was used to silence the horses in the stables, and then they were murdered in their thousands along with their riders.

The Magical Monitoring Centre picked up nothing because magic wasn't being used. But both the Merlins felt that something was wrong, but that wasn't that unusual. Merlin was worried enough to get dressed. Thomas Merlin knocked on Lord and Lady Malander's door. Lady Malander answered the door in her nightdress, which was almost too much for the virginal Thomas.

Thomas explained that he had a strong feeling that something was wrong. Lord Malander was not the sort to be disturbed by a feeling, but when the middle of the room started sinking, and he could hear movement below, he reacted. All three of them fled to the Magical Wing after locking the door. Merlin was there waiting for them.

Merlin, 'We are being attacked by Galattermous's spawn from underground. I fear that we might be too late to save the Citadel.'

Lord Malander, 'Nonsense, sound the alarms.' This in itself saved many lives as the murderers were caught in the act.

The guard was called out, and the real battle began. The enemy had the ground floors and were protecting their incursions, but they couldn't get a large enough force into the building because of size restrictions. The outlying regiments didn't rush in. They prepared for battle and approached in formation, which was fortunate as the enemy had laid traps.

Most of the traps were easily dealt with as they were rather primitive, but they got their first glimpse of the enemy. They looked fierce and were indeed fierce: cold-hearted killers. One of the soldiers called out, 'Kill the leggers.' And that became their name.

Commander General Lambskin woke up just in time to see the enemy. He had the ability to jump straight into action after a deep sleep, but it didn't save him. Two of the leggers grabbed him firmly and used their proboscis to suck his blood. Others joined in the feeding frenzy and pumped chemicals into his body which dissolved the soft tissues so that they could be sucked up. It wasn't long before the bravest of the brave was a dry, emasculated husk.

Abbott Frogmore locked himself into one of the towers, but he knew he was safe. It was a chance to grab a few hours of sleep.

A young magician called Rachel managed to find a room with a thick wooden door that was held in place by sturdy iron bolts. She felt reasonably safe, but there were mind-piercing scratching sounds coming from the other side. And the smell of acid was particularly strong. A fluid of some sort was seeping under the door and causing smoke to rise.

Lord Malander and a few guards were protecting the magical centre, but spells had been cast, and things were pretty secure. From their balcony, they could see the regular troops approaching in every direction. Lord Malander was proud of their organisation and discipline. He could also see that the hilltop fires had been lit. Additional help would be on its way.

As they watched, a flying creature swooped down and took one of the guards away. He had no chance. This was followed by thousands of the creatures attacking the regiments coming to their rescue. The troops dived for cover, but many were lost. The archers retaliated, but they weren't experienced at firing directly upwards. The returning arrows were a hazard in themselves.

When one of the flying creatures caught a trooper, it took it away, presumably to feed on it. Although this thinned out the soldiers, it also saved many others as the creatures didn't return. The archers learnt that fighting in formation was the answer as the winged enemy struggled against a massed volley.

Rachel could see that the sturdy old door was gradually dissolving, and she looked to clamber out of the window, but the height put her off. Anyway, as she looked out of the window, she was almost skewered by a giant mosquito. She thought to herself, 'We had just heard from the military how secure the place was, and now I'm being attacked from all directions.' She decided that if she got out of this alive, she was going to really live.

All of the window shutters in the citadel were closed, which made the rooms very dark. Lord Malander was also in the dark. It was hard to figure out a strategy when you had no idea what was going on. But then Merlin came to the rescue. He created a viewing portal, almost an X-Ray scanner.

One view showed thousands of massacred soldiers and horses with giant, eight-legged spiders sucking out their internal fluids. Another showed Rachel under attack. Then they saw the regiments fighting off giant sand-flies, or were they mosquitoes? Some of the troopers had reached the citadel and were attacking the feeding leggers. Wherever they looked, the enemy was feeding.

And this is what saved the Citadel. The enemy attack was immensely successful, but their troops lacked discipline. Their desire to consume their prey was too great. Nevertheless, the battle raged on as a series of individual encounters. A single human was no match for a legger, but groups would win. The enemy was particularly susceptible when they were feeding as they became entrenched in the human body.

Merlin mentally directed troops to one of the towers to save Rachel, who was immensely grateful. Further troops arrived, and the slaughter of the leggers was relentless. Most had fed to the point of over-indulgence. There was no way they could fight, and death didn't seem to trouble them.

They weren't true spiders in that they had four legs and four arms with a nasty-looking set of mandibles and suckers. These arachnids were not consistent in the number of eyes they had. Their mouths dripped an acid-like compound. There were no teeth. Some were quite hairy, while others were multi-coloured.

Eventually, every living legger was exterminated. Lord and Lady Malander surveyed the scene. There were over two hundred incursions through the floor. Over three thousand legger and four hundred mossie bodies were removed. Nearly three thousand troopers were killed and a similar number of civilians,

The loss of Commander General Lambskin was a huge blow.

He had been the backbone of the army and a great and loyal friend. At least he had died fighting, but what a horrible death.

Then they discovered that Fay Mellondrop, the Quarter Master General, was missing. Eventually, they found her body in the Suckley Hills. Eggs had been planted in her paralysed body. She died as they were taking her back to the citadel. Her body was quickly burnt as eggs were hatching.

They then started a search for other victims of the mossies. It had not been a good few days.

On one of the dead bodies was found a note containing the following:

> *It's a very angry spider,*
> *That was trying to get insider,*
> *Death has always been the great divider,*
> *And a very poor provider.*
>
> *Those safe and sound in the citadel,*
> *Were surprised when it nearly fell,*
> *To the arachnid's acidic smell,*
> *And the sounding of the funeral knell.*
>
> *The leggers had a guilty theme,*
> *As they attacked our bloodstream,*
> *Suckers were caught in midstream,*
> *Like light from a starry moonbeam.*
>
> *Great losses to the team,*
> *For those held in great esteem,*
> *It was a nightmare, not a dream,*
> *But mankind just won supreme.*

11

And So it Begins

The clean-up was a very demoralising affair. It was a massive job, just removing the dead. The enemy and the horses were burnt, and the humans were buried. Services were held, but there were too many to grieve properly.

The Malvern Hills had seen their share of death and destruction, but this was another blow to this happy and majestic land. But the sun still shone, and the rivers still flowed, and life went on. However, there were still dangers. The giant mossies still attacked, causing groups of armed archers to be stationed throughout the complex. The old and the young were particularly susceptible to these evil kidnappers.

Some of the mossies were relatively small, which suggested that eggs were hatching from the unwilling victim's bodies. Parties were sent out to track the hosts down. Not a single one of them was saved, and it soon became normal practice to put them out of their misery when they were found. The junior magicians ended up being good trackers.

The holes in the citadel's floor were covered in newly manufactured steel plate. Then they decided that certain floors in the building should be completely covered. This caused a crisis as steel was now in great demand. Fortunately, Merlin helped them improve their output, but for the first time, their land experienced a factory and a particularly nasty and noisy one. They wondered if they would ever experience peace again.

Anyway, the war had begun. A new Citadel Guard was needed. A new Commander-General and a new Quartermaster General were also required. But where was the enemy? Troops crawled down the stinking, fetid tunnels created by the leggers. They went on for about four miles in several different directions. It was, without a doubt, an amazing piece of engineering. There were no supports, just bodily fluids holding the tunnels up. No wonder they were hungry when they got to the citadel.

When they got to the other ends, they found giant webs with hundreds of emancipated human bodies held in suspension. They had been sucked dry. If you touched them, their skin collapsed to expose their skeletons. On the ground nearby, there were millions of tiny spider-like creatures: their offspring who had been gorging on the innocent victims.

Teams were set up to burn the baby leggers, human remains and the webs. It was a particularly unpleasant and nauseating task, and the teams had to be replaced regularly. The mission of finding every tiny legger was going to be almost impossible, but it was assumed that they could all grow into the monsters that were fighting in the citadel.

Magical assistance was requested, but Merlin explained that there were limits on magical use. It had to be saved for more important tasks. Human magical batteries had to be restored as he was expecting further attacks.

Both Lord and Lady Malander were somewhat depressed as their citadel and home had failed the first test. It was generally agreed that no one could have predicted an attack from underground, but nevertheless, it was a failure. Statistically, one could argue that it was a draw, but Galattermous was just after souls, and he got them, including some of their close friends.

So, all they could do now was to prepare and wait for the next attack.

12

And So it Continues

And the next attack came around dawn. Giant aggressive snakes, or perhaps they were worms, burst through the legger tunnels and then through the steel sheeting. They had both poisonous fangs and rows of snarling teeth. The Citadel buildings shook as they burst free.

They consumed anything edible in their path, animal, vegetable or human. They were fast and almost invulnerable. Arrows just bounced off their thick hide. There were twenty of them ripping the buildings apart and smashing through walls. There was no way the Citadel could stand this sort of damage.

The magical team tried shrinking them but failed. They tried converting them into onions but failed. They tried making them go to sleep but failed. Merlin said that they were not of magic but magically protected, and they could only be defeated by non-magical means. They had recently perfected the cannon technology, and here was their chance to test it.

Commander Staniforth got his four cannons prepared and loaded in the square. Several of his men then dragged some dead horses into the central area to act as bait, and then they waited. It wasn't a long wait, but it was typical. You wait for one worm, and three come at the same time. There was so much killer worm in the courtyard that it was impossible to miss. All four cannons blasted away. They were quickly reloaded and used again.

It was soon discovered that the killer worms easily survived the loss of half of their bodies. But the same couldn't be said of Commander Staniforth. His head was ripped off, and there was no doubt that he stopped functioning. He would have been proud of his men who kept firing and reloading until the cannons were red hot. They succeeded as all three worms were dying, although they didn't know it.

The other worms were still causing devastation. The cannons ceased to be an option as there was no more ammunition. Lord Malander decided that the only option was poison, but no one knew where the stocks were being kept since Fay's untimely death.

Fortunately, Thomas felt that he could convert bags of hay into cyanide. It took him some time to understand what cyanide was so that he could magically transmute the hay. It was tested on an unlucky rat and proved successful. They didn't know how much would be needed to kill a killer worm.

Once again, dead horses were used as bait, but this time they were stuffed with poison. The first worm to discover the horse-meat feast scoffed away and then exploded. Great chunks of dead worm went flying everywhere, becoming food for other worms, which then exploded in turn. The domino effect was quite amazing. The worm threat was over, but the public health problem had just started as the carcasses were enormous. Strangely the problem was solved when someone ate a bit of a dead worm. They turned out to be delicious.

Merlin was worried that worm bodies might be poisonous, but he couldn't detect a problem, and by then, most of the community had sampled a slice.

Lord Malander and Merlin were both very upset over the loss of Commander Staniforth. His enthusiasm and inventive genius would be sorely missed. The cannons had been proved in action and were named after him.

About eight hundred humans lost their life, mostly employees of the Citadel and a few guardsmen. A safe and well-paid job had suddenly become a death sentence.

Lord Malander wanted a staff meeting, but he was exhausted, and he knew that the others would be too.

Stuck on some worm meat, there was a verse:

> *It was the night of the worm,*
> *It was enough to make you squirm,*
> *Killing the strong, but mostly the infirm,*
> *But man survived in the short-term.*

13

And Some More

Builders were re-enforcing the Citadel as parts of it were structurally unsound. Thicker steel covers were put over the wormholes after removing the bodies, which was a daunting task. Their hole entrances were also blocked, and in three cases, they were flooded. In some ways, it was a bit pointless as the enemy could easily build new tunnels. But it made people feel safer.

Mossies were still a problem, and young leggers were quite irritating. Work parties were still being sent out to eliminate them, but the big question was: what is coming next? Merlin made no secret of the enemy's intentions. Galattermous had always favoured a war of attrition. He used to argue that a stressed enemy provided better quality souls.

Most of the residents of the citadel were too scared to sleep. It had proved to be a dangerous hobby. Some of them locked themselves in cellars. Others stayed out in the countryside, but nowhere was safe.

They were right to be frightened as the next attack was fear itself. The citizens and military were plagued with some of the most terrifying nightmares imaginable. So terrifying that the sleepers shook with fear. And they then found that they couldn't wake up. Then the terror level increased so that it was almost unbearable.

The weaker souls had heart attacks and died. At least their

misery had ended. Others smashed their heads against walls. Some slit their throats. The nightmare demanded satisfaction. It demanded your death. Somehow you wanted to comply. People started throwing themselves off the rampart walls. Soldiers stabbed each other to death.

The Magical Team, although suffering themselves, started building protective walls. There was a warning, but things moved too quickly for it to be of any great value. Soon hypnotic spells were putting people into a much deeper sleep where nightmares could not penetrate. Slowly the counter-magic magic worked, but it had cost at least four hundred lives.

Then, while everyone was in a very deep sleep, almost a coma, the Citadel started to flood. The waters rose and rose until the ground floor was flooded. What was strange was that none of the water escaped. If you opened a window, none of the water poured out. It didn't seem natural, and that was because it wasn't natural.

People were drowning in their beds. The water started flooding the second floor. Some people escaped, but most died in their sleep, oblivious to their own deaths. The Magical Team knew nothing about it until their rooms started to flood.

Knowing the danger, they released the population from their comas, and they started to have extreme nightmares again. Some preferred to drown rather than face that again. The magicians managed to stop the water from rising, but then it turned to ice. This was solid, rigid ice that was almost unbreakable. Those trapped in it simply died.

Merlin, 'Galattermous is one step ahead of us all of the time.'

Thomas, 'Can't we track him down?'

Merlin, 'We could try, but he could be anywhere, even in a different time or dimension.'

Thomas, 'What are you going to do?'

Merlin, 'What are you going to do?'

Thomas, 'What do you mean?'

Merlin, 'You can't assume that I have any better ideas than you.'

Thomas, 'You are more experienced than me.'

Merlin, 'But you have the benefit of youth.'

Thomas, 'I'm not sure if that is a benefit.'

Merlin, 'Let's stand back and be rational. What is the problem?'

Thomas, 'The citadel is full of ice, and the nightmares are killing people again.'

Merlin, 'What is the most critical problem?'

Thomas, 'The nightmares.'

Merlin, 'So put them back into a coma.'

Thomas, 'But some might drown.'

Merlin, 'That can't be helped.' Thomas put everyone back into a coma.

Thomas, 'What about the ice?'

Merlin, 'What's the best way of getting rid of the ice?'

Thomas, 'Melt it.'

Merlin, 'Go on then.'

Thomas, 'But there will be floods.'

Merlin, 'That's our next challenge.' Thomas melted the ice.

Thomas, 'So what do I do with the water.'

Merlin, 'What's the best way of getting rid of water?'

Thomas, 'Evaporation, drainage, drinking, pouring it away, but it's not going away of its own accord.'

Merlin, 'Then you need to help it.'

Thomas, 'Where could I put it.'

Merlin, 'You need to think it through. I would magic some

taps and pour the water down into the tunnels. We have done it already to some of the tunnels.'

Thomas, 'Why didn't you tell me ages ago?'

Merlin, 'Because you have got to learn.'

Thomas magicked the water away into the tunnels, and the problem was solved, but not until nearly five hundred people had died.

When the locals woke up, they couldn't believe what had happened to them. As far as the survivors were concerned, it was one of the best night's sleeps they had ever had.

There was lots of work to do regarding the flood damage, and sadly more burials.

Lord Malander chatted with Abbott Frogmore and Merlin. He wondered if they should evacuate the citadel. Merlin couldn't see much point as people would be just as vulnerable elsewhere. Lord Malander could not see how the attrition rate could continue. The Abbott suggested that they were all doomed and that perhaps we should just accept our fate.

Lord Malander was beginning to find the Abbott a bit negative, but his sensitive soul was probably being worn down by the recent events.

The following note was found floating in the water:

> *My people, please be aware,*
> *It's only a terrifying nightmare,*
> *There is nothing to fear but despair,*
> *So no point in going anywhere.*
>
> *But it is best to beware,*
> *That life is for those who dare,*
> *Although it may seem like a prayer,*

Good wishes are for those who care.
Some would say that was unfair,
Especially if they have been nowhere,
But it is more than some can bear,
The horrors of the nightmare.

Who would think it could flood?
The Citadel made of stone and mud,
Killing commoners and those of blue blood,
And even horses out to stud.

14

A Little Less

People were starting to leave the citadel. For the average man and woman, it wasn't safe. But that was also true for the military it wasn't safe, but as Merlin said previously, nowhere was safe.

Soon the number of leavers was large enough to form migrant convoys, but nowhere was safe. And to prove the point, some of the castle outriders discovered piles of corpses, mutilated to the point of unrecognisability. They had clearly suffered. It wasn't clear who the villains were, but it was obvious that they were ruthless, merciless bastards.

This discovery stopped further people from leaving the citadel. Lord Malander was reluctant to weaken the other regions, but in the end, he requested a regiment from Wales and the Midlands. The additional five thousand men and horses would be vital if the defence of Malvern was going to continue.

Lord Malander also made the following appointments:
- Commander-General Mainstay, Malvern
- Major Copson, Commander Engineering
- Alice Marshall, Quartermaster General

The two remaining Welsh regiments were moved forward to Herefordshire to act as a fighting defence if needed.

With Merlin's guidance, both cannons and firearms were being produced on a production line. It was fortunate that all of the raw materials were available reasonably locally. The newly formed artillery regiment was proving to be extremely successful. Some of the archery squadrons were being reformed as musketeers, but most of them kept their bows just in case.

Cannons were being distributed to key parts of the citadel, including some internal areas, just in case another underground attack was carried out. Huge quantities of gunpowder had been produced, so it was decided to create small dumps with long fuses in strategic places outside of the fortifications.

The Magical Services Team created a series of viewers in an effort to search for the next incursion. It was hard to tell how far the viewers were actually seeing as it was a fairly new development. And any attempt at fine detail was impossible. One of them picked up a flaming vehicle of some sort. Then a second flaming carriage was spotted. They were probably still a long way off, but it was soon recognised that the next threat was going to be fire.

Lord Malander ordered access to be made to the flooded tunnels, which would provide an ample supply of water. Buckets and containers were found to store water in locations all around the citadel. Fire wardens were appointed. Burnable materials were locked away in reasonably secure rooms. The straw roofs of some of the cottages were removed.

Lord Malander then sent out a search party to track down the fiery fiends. Major Hogsflesh decided to go himself. What they found was seriously worrying. There were four carriages being pulled by cows. Each carriage contained catapults with burning materials on them as well as boulders. These were two or three degrees more sophisticated than anything the Slimies had produced. The drivers appeared to be semi-transparent beetles.

When the search party got nearer, they were astounded by

just how big the carriages were. The wheels were twelve foot high and just crashed over anything in their way. They then realised that they weren't cows but a type of giant buffalo.

Then they heard stamping, and the ground trembled slightly. And as they waited, they could see thousands, possibly hundreds of thousands of marching troops. It was hard to figure out what they were as they wore long black coats and black headgear with a red ribbon. Their marching was impeccable, but it didn't look right. Their gait wasn't human.

Major Hogsflesh felt his skin crawl. There was something wrong and alien about these troops. He hatched a plan to capture one but then decided that it was far too risky. It was more important to report back. He left some scouts behind to monitor the situation and do the maths.

When he returned, Major Hogsflesh updated his boss. A decision was needed on whether to flee or fight. In the end, it was decided to fight, but the civilians were evacuated to Wales. He insisted that his pregnant wife should go as well. She was totally opposed to the idea, but the Chief Elder ordered her to obey, and she did. She worried that it might be the last time she saw her husband alive, but then that was probably true of most of the women.

The enemy moved at speed, but it still took them two days to get in position in front of the Citadel. They destroyed much of Malvern in the process. Lord Malander surveyed the scene. In front of them were four hundred catapults and probably One hundred and twenty thousand troops, although some of the scouts thought that there were more. Lord Malander pondered whether they would find their way onto the hills.

Lord Malander sent out scouts to the regions, appraising them of the situation. They were outnumbered five to one, possibly more, and that assistance was required. They were not to come if they were under threat.

Commander-General Mainstay provided his lord with roll-call data. There were forty-six thousand, four hundred and nine troops, including militiamen defending the citadel. A further seventeen thousand and sixteen soldiers were guarding the hills. There were now thirty-six canons in place and just over two thousand men with muskets. Gunpowder, ammunition, and arrows were in plentiful supply. He also had some rockets, but he had no idea what they were for. Water stations were on full alert.

Merlin got his team together and gave each magician a personal task. He explained that they had a key role to play. The tasks varied from fire watching to blinding the enemy soldiers, from causing the catapults to fail to stampeding the buffalos, from mirages to deflecting cannonballs, from spreading despair amongst the enemy to countering any opposing magic.

The game was on.

The following was on one of the catapults:

Few praise the skill of a scout,
As he checks the enemy's layout,
Surely there can be no doubt,
That no army should be without.

As he hides in the enemy's redoubt,
Or waits patiently in his look-out,
Looking for a chance to use his clout,
Always silently, he has to hold out.

15

Virgins at Work

Thomas had spent a fair amount of time training a young, very talented magician called Rachel, who had experienced a very sheltered background until then. She was eighteen with auburn hair, large brown eyes, and legs to die for. Not that Thomas had seen her legs, but he knew that they would be gorgeous. He had seen a fair amount of her cleavage as her tops had gone from demure to brazen.

She knew that he was looking at her breasts and revelled in it. He was the first man to take a shine to her, except for an old tramp. Thomas tried to hide the fact that he had been ogling her boobs and quickly looked the other way when he thought she had caught him at it. He was soon drawn back to them.

Rachel often wondered why men were so obsessed with tits. Every woman had them to one degree or another. It was not like they were rare. She happened to be blessed with a pair of large, firm round ones that dangled whenever she bent over. They often got in the way. What she did know was that they started tingling whenever Thomas looked at them. What was even more surprising was that the nipples got hard, very hard and demanded attention.

The other thing she noticed was that her very private parts got moist. That just didn't make any sense whatsoever.

After a few weeks, Thomas accidentally touched her hand,

and it was like an electric shock. Both immediately withdrew their hands and wished they hadn't. Rachel wanted Thomas to hold her and hold her tight. He was developing into a very good-looking young man with dark hair, piercing blue eyes, a firm chin, broad shoulders, and very sensitive hands. She wasn't sure why but she kept watching his bum and hunted for the bulge in his tights.

A few days later, after thinking about it, he accidentally touched her hand again and, this time kept it there. Their fingers intertwined, and both wallowed in the pleasure of simple hand-holding. Thomas gently let go and touched her face. Lightning bolts shot down her body and ended in her most private place, which immediately moistened. Her body tingled in anticipation. She had heard the washer-women talk about todgers, but she wasn't too sure what they were. What was she anticipating?

Then it happened Thomas kissed her on the lips. She wondered if that meant she was married and would be having a baby. She didn't care and kissed him back harder and then even harder. Thomas was startled by her passionate response. That wasn't how he imagined it. Nevertheless, he wanted to rip her clothes off.

He had never experienced so much lust. His cock ached but not as much as his balls. They were literately throbbing, desperate for release. He was worried that he might come in his tights. How embarrassing would that be?

They separated and then decided that they needed some more. Tongues conversed silently, sending messages of love. Thomas's fingers were starting to explore her body, but they were interrupted, which might have been a good thing.

Both spent the night alone, thinking about the other. Thomas gently masturbated, thinking about her breasts and the mysteries that existed under her dress. Rachel found herself playing with her very private girlie bits. Somehow, she knew what he wanted to do with her. She wasn't sure if she liked the idea of it. But she loved him holding her hand and touching her face. And she would be quite happy if he fondled her tits.

The next few days, they hunted for each other but pretended that they weren't that bothered if they saw each other or not. The world had suddenly become more wonderful, more exciting, more intense. They both wondered if it was love as their tummies had butterflies and worse. They sang and danced when they were alone, but who would make the next move?

Thomas spotted her in the corridor as he was patrolling. The Citadel had been through so much. Both of their lives had been in danger more than once, and their chances of survival were looking quite slim. Most of the women and children had been evacuated, but she stayed behind as she was a front-line magician and a particularly powerful one.

Thomas grabbed Rachel from behind and covered her eyes. She took his hands without looking at him and placed them on her breasts. He instinctively started caressing them through the material until her nipples were rock-hard. She swooned at his touch and just wanted more. He was in heaven. He had never felt breasts before, and they were simply delightful. His prick soon stood to attention.

She took control and, without turning, pulled his tights down to his knees and then lifted her dress up and rubbed his cock against her most private parts. Thomas felt that he was going to explode, and she was getting the most amazing tingling sensations. She was almost at the point of fainting.

She continued to rub his rigid manhood against her cunt, and then suddenly, he was in her. Both immediately screamed in ecstasy. Both felt a climax that they had never experienced before. The combination of intercourse and their magical abilities created a bonanza of feelings and sensations that were probably unique. It was a genuine fusion of mind and body, and from that day onwards, they were an inseparable couple. Love had conquered them both: they became one.

Stuck on the wall where it had all happened was a note:

> *It was a time of war, and a time of love,*
> *It happened, at last, the visit of the dove,*
> *He fitted inside her like a silky glove,*
> *Had it all been ordained from powers above?*

16

Men at Work

Merlin, 'So how was it?'

Thomas, 'What do you mean?'

Merlin, 'Your first fuck.'

Thomas, 'How did you know?'

Merlin, 'Come on, lad, work it out.'

Thomas, 'You know Rachel?'

Merlin, 'Of course, she is my wife. I could hardly keep my hands off her.'

Thomas, 'So you knew that Rachel and I would get together?'

Merlin, 'I said that she is my wife.'

Thomas, 'It's just that this is the first time you have mentioned any similarities in our lives. What can you tell me about my future?'

Merlin, 'I've learnt that it is best not to say anything. Otherwise, it might affect what you do. And if I tell you that something will happen, then you will spend the rest of your life waiting for it to happen.'

Thomas, 'There must be something you could tell me.'

Merlin, 'I'm willing to say that you, or rather us, will have a very happy life together with her. You have found your soulmate. She is the best of all of us. Listen to her. She is wise beyond her years. Accept her council, and you can't go wrong, but above all, love her with all your heart.' And for the first time, they hugged, and Thomas knew that all was well.

The next day Thomas proposed to Rachel, and she said no. She was happy to be his mistress and take his name, but she didn't want to be shackled to any man. That didn't mean that she didn't love him, but her love of freedom was greater.

And Thomas respected that and strangely loved her more for her independent thought. What a lucky man he was.

There was a surprising side-effect. His magic was much stronger, and then he realised that was how Merlin knew that he had lost his virginity.

Notes were left where lovers would find them:

The boy transitioned into adulthood,
Virginity now lost to his childhood,
New magic not yet understood,
On the hills, you will find wormwood.

The girl did well; she did good,
Blossoming into womanhood,
Mysteries unfolded as they should,
The power of sex was motherhood.

17

Women at Work

Rachel had been brought up in a very strict household by her aunt and uncle. She never knew if they were her true relations or not or what happened to her parents. It was a taboo subject, and there were a lot of them. She had no siblings and few friends. That was a lie. She had never had a friend.

Her uncle and aunt were good people but not very loving. There had never been cuddles, kisses or any sign of affection. There had never been any presents or attention, but they ate well, and sensible warm clothes were always provided. The main problem was sheer monotony. Every day was the same.

She yearned for excitement, love, affection, and adventure. She wasn't too sure what they were, but she yearned for something. That something was directly opposite to what her guardians wanted, but they managed to achieve it. She couldn't see any way out. There was no obvious future that varied from this one.

Then, one miraculous day, the troopers came with an invitation for Rachel to attend the Citadel for scrutinization. Her guardians had no idea what that was, so they refused. The envoy said that it was a chance to live in the Citadel and learn the mystical ways as talent had been detected. Her aunt and uncle had no idea what they were talking about, so she refused. Already they had invaded their safe, secure little word, and it was not welcomed.

The envoy said that the invitation was not for them but for their niece and did she have a view. They said no, but Rachel jumped in and said that she would willingly go. She quickly grabbed her few possessions, said her goodbyes, and was off. And from that day onwards, she hardly gave them a thought.

Rachel later learnt that they had been consumed by the Slimies. She felt for them as that must have disturbed their daily routine. Her life in the Citadel had not been a bed of roses because of the crisis. But she had made friends for the first time and experienced experiences. And she loved the magic. It came naturally to her. She didn't know how, but it was a bit like speaking; you just did it.

Now she was in love. It was just so right, so perfect. She realised that they had to win this war for her love for Thomas to flourish.

Found on her uncle's house was a note:

> *Goodbye to her uncle and aunt,*
> *Now only their bones do haunt,*
> *Magic welcomes like a chant,*
> *And love beckons like a flowering plant.*

18

The Waiting Game

Lord Malander, 'Why haven't they attacked?'

Commander-General Mainstay, 'Because they don't have to. They want us to be afraid. They want us to taste fear.'

Lord Malander, 'Have they completely encircled us?'

Commander-General Mainstay, 'No, we still have full access to the hills, and our scouts are still out there monitoring them.'

Lord Malander, 'I understand your argument about fear, but that is more likely when there is a full encirclement. No, they are waiting for something or somebody.'

Commander-General Mainstay, 'Could it be Galattermous?'

Lord Malander, 'Possibly.'

Commander-General Mainstay, 'Could it be more siege equipment?'

Lord Malander, 'I was wondering that. It looks like their catapults can throw boulders and things that burn. Our walls are thick enough to withstand most boulders, don't you think?'

Commander-General Mainstay, 'Without a doubt.'

Lord Malander, 'And fire is not that challenging, especially as we have prepared for it.'

Commander-General Mainstay, 'The digging creatures could take a wall down a lot quicker than a catapult.'

Lord Malander, 'I think you have got it. They are waiting for more creatures to arrive. The catapults are just a distraction. The troops will attack when the walls are down, and not before.'

Commander-General Mainstay, 'That sounds plausible. In that case, should we attack them? Their troops are in range.'

Lord Malander, 'Why not. Let's take the initiative. Our objective is to kill as many of those bastards as possible.'

Commander-General Mainstay, 'Have you noticed that their troops just stand there? At one stage, I wondered if they were alive.'

Lord Malander, 'It does make you wonder. I would suggest that we capture one.'

Commander-General Mainstay, 'I will get Major Hogsflesh onto it. What do you suggest we do to kick off?'

Lord Malander, 'Start with our catapults. Let's keep the guns as a surprise.'

Commander-General Mainstay, 'Will do.'

Lord Malander, 'Should we also carry out some long-range scouting just in case the enemy is up to something?'

Commander-General Mainstay, 'That makes sense.'

While that was going on, Merlin tried to detect any magical activity but everywhere was quite quiet. That wasn't like Galattermous. He was always noisy. What was going on?

Flying in the wind, the note said:

Why are they waiting?
For our men, it is quite frustrating,
Catapulting the walls will be captivating,
Hope won't stop the penetrating.

Causing stress is quite aggravating,
But our fighters don't need motivating,
To kill the zombie hoard from locating,
The secrets of our mass annihilating.

19

Women and Men at War

Commander-General Mainstay ordered the catapults to fire in sequence and to target the enemy machines. One by one, they sent large boulders hurtling towards the enemy, and the devastation caused was immense. The enemy soldiers were simply bowled over.

It wasn't that easy targeting the catapults, but the operators were getting nearer as they measured where the boulders landed. That didn't help too much as the boulders varied in size and consequently had different trajectories.

The enemy made no response. Their catapults remained inactive, and the soldiers were simply horizontal or vertical, with the horizontal ones being broken. That word was used because it was becoming increasingly apparent that they weren't alive.

The catapulting continued smashing the dead soldiers to pieces. It almost seemed a bit pointless as they were doing nothing: just being destroyed. In the end, Mainstay decided to send out the cavalry to decapitate all those left standing. Over two thousand men left the citadel to attack.

To the cavalry's horror, halfway through the decapitation process, the enemy zombies came alive. The decapitators became the decapitated. A giant worm then smashed through the open gates, and all of the enemy catapults started firing fire-bombs. Confusion broke out as the cavalry fled back home to find a giant worm in front of them and thousands of sword-whirling skeletons behind them. It was a carve-up.

There wasn't much that Commander-General Mainstay could do to save the mounted soldiers, but he had a row of cannons protecting the gates. The cannons literally made mincemeat of the giant worm. Sadly, some of the cavalry were also killed by friendly fire. It didn't seem that friendly to them.

They just managed to shut the gates in time, but the skeletons simply climbed up the walls. The defenders were ready for them.

Merlin shouted, 'Track down the controller.' It was obvious that someone was controlling them, probably Galattermous or one of his henchmen. The magicians worked together in an attempt to disrupt the controller, and it started to work. The attackers simply stopped in mid-kill. Then the controller regained power. Rachel joined the team and held sway over the enemy.

Whilst they were stationary, the defenders decapitated as many zombies as possible. Out of ninety thousand enemy fighters, there were only about twenty thousand left. And some of those were operating the catapults, which were causing negligible damage. However, one boulder had damaged Lord Malander's collection of pressed flowers, something he had kept secret for a long time.

The controller made numerous attempts to regain control, but Rachel was too strong for him or it. The defender's catapults were also improving their aim and were systematically destroying the enemy's infernal machines.

Commander-General Mainstay was reluctant to order more cavalry out based on what happened last time. Still, he knew that a commander in the field had to be unemotional: soldiers were just a resource. The cavalry attacked as he commanded and revenged their brothers. The zombies were effectively eliminated, and they had gained an awful lot of catapults.

The burial details carried out their funeral work, but what do you do with ninety thousand sets of bones?

One set of bones contained the following verse:

> *Were they fighting flesh that was known?*
> *Or fighting living skeletons of bone,*
> *Were they dead zombies or a clone?*
> *Controlled by someone unknown.*
>
> *Were they fighting for a king's throne?*
> *Whilst boulders overhead were thrown,*
> *Rachel won whilst she was in the zone,*
> *Almost beating the controller all alone.*

20

Is it Over?

Celebrations broke out throughout the Citadel. Once again, human forces had won. But Merlin had to remind everyone that the enemy's target was the farming of souls. They had lost no one, and we experienced about three thousand deaths. So who was the real winner, and Galattermous was far from being defeated.

The women and children started returning despite Merlin's warnings, but nobody wanted to listen to him. Humanity can only take so much, and that point had been reached.

Thomas Merlin and Rachel spent most of their time in bed exploring each other's bodies. Sometimes the exploration took place two or three times a day. Rachel was now very familiar with the nature of a todger, and Thomas knew what to do with it.

Lady Malander returned larger than she left, but she still had a few months to go. Her husband was really pleased to see her, partly because he loved her and partly because he had needs. And it wasn't long before those needs were being satisfied. It was often the case that war seemed to make both men and women randier. Perhaps it was a direct result of confronting your mortality.

Lady Malander was also trying to work out where the enemy bones came from. Were they from the already dead, or were they humans that had been deliberately killed to form a zombie army?

What was strange was that every skeleton was identical. It was effectively one skeleton that was replicated. She tried to remember the old days when everything was normal.

Both Lord Malander and Commander-General Mainstay were attending the funerals of the fallen and welcoming new regiments that were arriving from the regions. Old friends were meeting up, but Lord Malander kept remembering Merlin's words about the farming of souls and that they had lost no one. Were these new regiments just more souls to be farmed? So far, that had not met the real enemy: Galattermous.

Major Copson, the newly appointed Commander of Engineering, had a massive job understanding the new technologies. He didn't have Major Staniforth's ingenuity, but he was much better at managing the manufacturing processes. The cannon had saved the day and was his main priority. He had also had a major breakthrough regarding chainmail jackets, although the manufacturing process was slow.

His colleague, Alice Marshall, the new Quartermaster-General, was also having some teething problems. Her predecessor Fay held all of the stock information in her head, or she gave the impression that she did. There were no records. Alice was the opposite, and the new pencils made record keeping a lot easier. She was a stickler for getting it right: everything had a place, and there was a place for everything.

Major Hogsflesh was spending time with his favourite lady playing dip the wick. It was one of his favourite games. His scouts had performed well, and he was determined to have a well-earned rest.

And then the next challenge appeared.

But not before a note arrived in the stock room:

*The ladies of the court did return,
To find love, caring and concern,
It was joyous, but few had time to burn,
Jobs to be done, and old loves to spurn.*

21

It Certainly Isn't

One of the look-outs lit a fire which nearly always meant trouble. Lord Malander, Major Hogsflesh and Merlin went to the battlements to investigate. On the horizon, there was a vast black cloud moving fast towards the citadel.

Lord Malander, 'What do you think it is?'

Major Hogsflesh, 'Trouble. I think we can guarantee it.'

Merlin, 'I will get a viewer onto it.'

Lord Malander, 'I haven't seen much of Thomas recently.'

Merlin, 'He has got a new hobby.'

Major Hogsflesh, 'I'm not sure if you can call it that. He has discovered the pleasures of the female form.'

Lord Malander, 'Has he now? I hope that he is being careful.'

Merlin, 'You don't have to worry as he is going to marry her.'

Major Hogsflesh, 'How do you know?'

Merlin, 'Because I'm married to her.'

Lord Malander, 'Wait a minute. Thomas's girlfriend is your wife?'

Merlin, 'Yes, that's right.'

Lord Malander, 'Don't you mind.'

Merlin, 'How can I? Thomas is me.'

Major Hogsflesh, 'I will never understand the anomalies of

time-travel.'

Lord Malander, 'Fair enough.'

Merlin went off to get a viewer, and Thomas's sister turned up. She quickly opened up a viewing portal for them all to see. It wasn't good.

Lord Malander, 'What is it?'

Robin, 'It is a swarm of flying creatures. I'm not sure what they are. They look a bit like grasshoppers.'

Merlin, 'They would be locusts. Their swarm contains millions of insects that will strip the land of all its foliage.'

Robin, 'Do they eat animals?'

Merlin, 'Definitely not.'

Robin, 'Well, this lot seem to have sharp teeth.'

Merlin, 'Locusts don't have teeth.'

Lord Malander, 'That suggests that they are not your normal locusts.'

Major Hogsflesh, 'How big are they?'

Robin, 'About the size of a rat.'

Merlin, 'That's considerably bigger than a locust.'

Lord Malander, 'Ring the alarm bell.' He called his aide and issued the following orders:
- Everyone to enter the citadel
- Bring all livestock and foodstuffs with you.
- Shut all windows and doors
- Cover all openings
- Lock the stables
- Avoid open spaces.

He told his aide to hurry as the swarm would be here in a few hours.

Most of the actions were carried out, but some people just

ignored them. That was the way of the world.

    The viewer didn't spot the note on her back:

> *From afar, it looked like a dust storm,*
> *But viewing indicated it was not the norm,*
> *Who was trying to misinform?*
> *That it was not another killer swarm.*

22

They Come

Lord Malander watched the swarm get nearer using his telescopnots. They certainly didn't look friendly, and he was proved right. He spotted a man in a field running for his life. A few seconds later, every piece of flesh on his body had been stripped off, and he collapsed as a skeleton. A few minutes later, the entire field had been stripped of all vegetation including substantial oak trees.

The onlookers almost felt sick as anything edible was rapidly consumed, whether it be fauna or flora. Then the swarm crashed into the building, looking for any way to get in. All the inhabitants could do was to defend their actual location, house by house and room by room. Those who hadn't taken reasonable precautions were simply consumed, and many were.

Lord Malander was in a safe room within his personal suite along with his wife and the two Merlins. He hoped that they would be safe, but he had no idea what was going on. They had established a viewing screen, but all you could see was what looked like millions of the creatures flying around the citadel.

Periodically they would throw themselves at apparent weak spots. Usually, the attack would fail, but occasionally you would hear a high-pitched scream followed by deathly silence. On one occasion, there were twenty-odd screams then nothing. It was terrifying as there was little that could be done.

Lord Malander, 'You guys must have some ideas between you?'

Merlin, 'We are not even sure what they are.'

Thomas found it hard to concentrate because he was so worried about Rachel. He logically worked out that she must be safe as they got married in the future, but perhaps the future could be changed.

Lord Malander, 'You must have a spell that could convert them into oranges or lemons.'

Merlin, 'I wish that it was that easy.'

Thomas, 'What about slowing time down so that we could investigate them?'

Before they could do anything, some worms came crashing into the citadel. This time there was no one to man the cannons, and the swarm had entered the inner sanctum.

The interior rooms were far less protected, and the screaming became an almost continuous sound as one property after another was compromised. Death lurked everywhere. This looked like the end.

Then Thomas stopped time except for those in the safe room.

Merlin said to Merlin, 'I didn't know that you could do that.'

Merlin said to Merlin, 'I wasn't sure myself.'

Lord Malander, 'Now what do we do?'

Merlin, 'Let's go and get ourselves a specimen.'

They opened the outer doors to Lord Malander's suite to find thousands of rat-locusts stuck in mid-air.

Thomas plucked one of them out of the ether and killed it with his knife, and they went back indoors, making sure that everything was secure. Then Thomas had to release time. It had truly been an immense task that almost drained his magical battery.

The dead thing was placed on the table. It was hard to tell whether it was a rat that looked like an insect or an insect that looked like a rat. It had mammalian legs and insect-like mandibles. It had a rat head with grasshopper eyes. There was both fur and scales covering its body, and it had bright green blood.

The screaming outside continued. Thomas wanted to rush out to hold Rachel's hand, but he realised that he wouldn't last a second. The swarm would consume him in no time at all, even with his magical skills.

Merlin could tell that the creature was a construct that had been designed to complete this one savage task, but what clues could he ascertain from pure observation? As it was a construct, he wondered if he could unconstruct it.

Merlin tried a simple spell, but it failed. The screaming continued, and he felt under pressure. A second more complex spell also failed, and the pressure intensified. The screaming was getting nearer. It sounded like the rat-locusts had got into the plumbing or the cavity walls. There was every chance that they were vulnerable.

It then dawned on Merlin that the spell would probably work if he were in the line of sight of the ratty beasts. In other words, he had to confront them in the flesh before they consumed his flesh. To stop that from happening, he needed a simple protection spell. That was something that Lady Malander could do.

The alternative was to get Thomas to stop time again, but he was fast asleep.

Merlin and Lady Malander walked to the front door again. The sound of screams was pervasive, and quite honestly, it was terrifying. Lady Malander found that her hand was shaking. She cast the spell, prayed, and opened the door. A huge quantity of the ferocious creatures attacked, but the spell held them off. It was like looking through a window at five hundred mandible-ripping, teeth-chopping snarling orifices that were intent on digesting you. It was pure unadulterated hatred.

Merlin cast his spell with a few embellishments and waited. Nothing appeared to be happening, and then slowly, the scales fell off the creatures. This was followed in quick succession by the eyes, legs, fur and eventually the wings. The bodies collapsed onto the floor, but they still continued to attack, and then they started devouring each other, and then they simply stopped.

The bells were ringing to announce the all-clear, but the inhabitants encountered one horror after another. Whole buildings had been stripped of every piece of flesh. Both skeletons and half-eaten people were found in the strangest of locations in failed attempts to escape. A hospital was devoid of any living person: both patients and medical staff had been consumed.

Ponds were found with fish skeletons floating on top of the water. Stables contained horse skeletons attached to the walls. Some even had saddles on them. Possibly the worst thing of all was the nursery. Over thirty tiny baby skeletons were found. Some still had dummies where their mouths used to be.

Tears rolled down Lady Malander's cheeks. She wished that she hadn't returned. Some of the visions were just too much to bear. Would she never be able to forget what she had just seen?

Lord Malander tried to appear tougher, but he too was suffering. His well of tears was at breaking point. He also realised just how much they all owed to Merlin, both of them, who were really the same person.

They had carried out a series of clean-up exercises, but this was the worst by far. There were tons of dead animal carcasses, and this time you couldn't eat them.

Once again, it was time for bed.
A note was found on the dead:

Was it a locust or a rat?
Perhaps a wombat or a gnat.
Or even a wise, old alley cat,
No, it's a construct like a vampire bat.

But our Merlins sorted the copycat,
With trusty spells from the diplomat,
Nothing was lost to the acrobat,
Except an all-clear from the bureaucrat.

23

They Rest

The whole community was exhausted, both physically and emotionally. Their elaborate plans had probably saved lives but not enough of them. The last attack was probably the worst of all in terms of sheer terror and loss of life amongst the civilians. Whole families had been wiped out, helpless to do anything in their last few seconds.

And to make things worse, their food stocks had been decimated. The surrounding fields had been stripped bare. There was not going to be any harvest this year. They couldn't even eat the giant worms as they had returned to where they came from. That suggested that they were needed for the next attack.

Lord Malander realised that things couldn't go on like they were. A new strategy was needed. He sent messengers out to the regional Governor Commanders requesting them, or rather ordering them, to attend a War Council. They were told to bring food with them if they wanted to eat.

Thomas was still recovering with the help of Rachel. He had literally saved everyone in the Citadel. He couldn't believe how fatiguing the spell had been. Once completed, he was fast asleep and even now, his body ached. But not enough not to enjoy her company.

As a thank you for saving her, he was allowed to choose three different positions without thinking of her. He started with her on her back with her legs wide open. He enjoyed seeing his member enter her sweet little pussy. It was such a tight but delicious fit.

Thomas then had her bending over with his cock embedded deep in her cunt whilst he fondled her dangling breasts. He enjoyed their firmness and the even greater firmness of her nipples. He almost came but decided to wait for the coup de grace where he had her laying on her stomach. His cock then burrowed past her buttocks back into the fanny. In that position, the sides of her pussy grabbed his cock and provided some token resistance, but his manhood wasn't having any of that. He ploughed away and had a truly magnificent orgasm.

As they lay there cuddling, Rachel said that she had a very unpleasant dream while hiding from the rat-birds. A young man suddenly appeared who looked a bit like my father, ripped my clothes off and raped me. The similarities in appearance were uncanny, but he was aggressive and literally pulled my legs apart and had his wicked way. There was no conversation, just a work-like determination to fuck me, and as soon as his seed was in me, he disappeared.

Thomas explained that it was probably a reaction to the rat-bird attack. She agreed but emphasised that the dream was the most realistic that she had ever experienced. It actually felt that she had been violated, but nobody was there. Then she showed him a bruise that was on her thigh. They fell asleep, and nothing more was said about it. Perhaps she should have shown him the ripped clothes, but she was too embarrassed.

He loved Rachel with all his heart, but she was a huge distraction, and he had many jobs to do. He only had these thoughts after he had been satisfied, and strangely Rachel had similar concerns. But those that understood knew how important first love was, and both had earned their time together.

Lady Malander was starting to recover from the shock of the last few days. She was surprised by how emotional and tearful she had become. Her husband suggested that it might be down to her pregnancy. He thought that she might have a nasty case of hormones, but she knew that was Merlin talking. Apparently, women get a lot of them. 'Balderdash,' she thought.

Anyway, the young man in her womb was eager to see the world. She hadn't told her husband yet that it was a boy and a strong, healthy one. That was one of the advantages of being a sorceress: you knew things. He hadn't quite reached the stage where the foetus could communicate yet, but that wouldn't be long now.

She had named her son, but it was still a secret. She wasn't sure if her husband would like it, but she had ways, female ways of persuading him.

24

They Meet

The once pristine conference room was not quite the same. One corner had been ripped open by a giant worm. There were stains everywhere from the rat-locusts. Wooden furniture and doors had been half-eaten in their hunger. The massive round table was scratched, and its veneer had been ruined by a variety of bodily fluids from the enemy incursions.

The attendees had arrived and were shown to their seats. The usual bowl of fruit was not there to greet them.

The meeting consisted of the following:
- Lord Malander, Commander-in-Chief
- Lady Malander, Commander Mystical Arts
- Commander General Mainstay, Malvern
- Governor Commander Winterdom, North
- Governor Commander Mannering, South-West
- Governor Commander Walsh, Wales
- Governor Commander Dragondale, South-East
- Governor Commander Bandolier, Midlands
- Abbott Frogmore, Planning
- Major Hogsflesh, Commander Intelligence
- Major Copson, Commander Engineering
- Alice Marshall, Quartermaster General
- Merlin
- Thomas

The minute's silence was held as usual, but there had now been too many tragedies to give it meaning.

Lord Malander, 'Thank you all for attending in these very difficult times. Those of us at Malvern have almost reached the end of our tether. Is that not the case?'

The Malvern contingent all nodded and made supportive comments.

Lord Malander, 'The attacks have been relentless, and in most cases, quite terrifying. This is not a normal enemy by any stretch of the imagination. I'm concerned that both the military and civilian populations are on their last legs.'

Commander General Mainstay, 'My Lord, I'm convinced that we can hold on. My men will stand.'

Lord Malander, 'Is that you talking or them?'

Commander General Mainstay, 'We are as one.'

Lord Malander, 'Those words are well-meant, but that is not the reality. Let's look at the facts:
- The citadel has been breached by at least twenty worm tunnels
- Probably 30% of the building, if not more, is in ruins
- We have lost 40% of our horses
- There are practically no food reserves
- There will be no harvest this year
- The steel-making factory is in ruins
- The stores are in disarray
- Every attack reduces our strength by at least 15%
- The gatehouse needs rebuilding.

'I could go on.'

Commander General Mainstay, 'What are you proposing?'

Lord Malander, 'I'm proposing that we re-think our

strategy.'

Abbott Frogmore, 'If you are proposing that we leave, there is every chance that we will be decimated.'

Lord Malander, 'We are being decimated now, drop by drop. Galattermous is winning. He is getting the souls he wants at no cost to him. We can sit here and wither.'

Abbott Frogmore, 'So you are proposing that we leave.'

Lord Malander, 'Not exactly. I'm proposing that as a group, we come up with a new strategy.'

Abbott Frogmore, 'But you are not putting anything forward yourself?'

Merlin, 'Can I jump in, please.'

Lord Malander, 'Of course.'

Merlin, 'Lord Malander is right. Galattermous is using the citadel as a killing zone. I hadn't realised that at first. We are effectively sitting here waiting to be killed. He knows exactly where to find us.'

Alice Marshall, 'What does he do with the souls?'

Merlin, 'I haven't been entirely honest about this in the past, as it's quite horrible.'

Lord Malander, 'Please tell us the truth.'

Merlin, 'Well, as you know, the soul is the life-essence of a person. It is what and who we are. It is what animates your body.

'He takes this essence and divides it into thousands of pieces. It is these pieces that power the Slimies and the giant worms and even the rat-locusts.'

Lord Malander, 'Does that mean we are killing ourselves?'

Merlin, 'Yes and no. The original life essence is changed when Galattermous divides the soul up, you could argue that we are killing ourselves, but what's the alternative?'

Alice Marshall, 'I still don't understand why he is doing it?

He captures souls, animates constructs and then loses souls in the attempt to get more. What is the point?'

Merlin, 'You are asking questions that I have spent years trying to answer. Who is he? Where does he come from? What is he trying to achieve? How does he actually get the souls when someone is killed?'

Governor Commander Walsh, 'How did you first meet him?'

Merlin, 'Firstly he came to me in a dream, but it wasn't a dream. It was halfway between a dream-state and reality. He said that he was there to collect my soul. I told him that he couldn't have it. He said that they all say that but that he always won in the end.'

Thomas, 'So I've got this to come.'

Merlin, 'Yes, my boy. But you will be prepared for it.'

Governor Commander Walsh, 'What happened next?'

Merlin, 'He tried to take my soul, but he failed. He looked remarkably surprised and said that we would meet many times again. And we have. For him, it is a game. For us, it is life and death.'

Governor Commander Walsh, 'So how do we end this game?'

Merlin, 'I wish I knew.'

Commander General Mainstay, 'If we left the citadel, where would we go?'

Lord Malander, 'I'm not sure that it matters. Ideally, we want to track him down and engage him in battle.'

Merlin, 'He may not be on this world. He will track you down and attack when he needs more souls.'

Lord Malander, 'Does that mean that he will leave us when he has enough?'

Merlin, 'Possibly, but I wouldn't bet on it.'

Lord Malander, 'So you are saying that if we stay here, we will die and if we leave, he will track us down and we will die. Talk about rocks and hard places.'

Merlin, 'I wish I had some better ideas.'

Lord Malander, 'How have you defeated him elsewhere?'

Merlin, 'By resistance, more resistance and even more resistance. Eventually, the return is not good enough, and he looks for easier pickings elsewhere. That's how we defeated the Slimies.'

Lord Malander, 'But he came back.'

Merlin, 'That's because the pickings still looked very good, and he seems to like human souls.'

Lady Malander, 'It's time to break for lunch.'

It wasn't the normal lunch, but the soup was very good. It would have been better with some meat in it and a chunk of bread.

Under the table, there was a note:

Should we stay or should we travel?
Across the long, windy paths of gravel,
Only time will tell, when will it unravel?
And more of a chance to bedazzle.

25

More Troubles

Halfway through sipping the soup, the alarms went off yet again. It was interesting to see how different people reacted to the warnings. The military proceeded in an orderly manner to their allotted positions. The nervous, which made up half the population, ran for cover, causing distress and panic in their flight. The other half just took it in their stride on the premise that what will happen will happen.

No one was sure what was happening as the fire was lit on the hill. Then there were screams and shouts. The Hills themselves were being invaded by Slimies. They were back. The bad news was that no one had bothered to maintain the stocks of Tanylip. But at least they were an enemy that they understood.

The supporting castles had been infiltrated and captured, and now thousands of Slimies were firing arrows into the Citadel from above. The Malvern regiments were all out of position as they had fought off a series of frontal assaults. However, it didn't take long for Commander General Mainstay to get the formations changed and to return fire.

This time they had secret weapons. The Musketry regiment lined up in three rows: one kneeling, one standing and the final row on a step. The captain ordered a continuous barrage row by row. The Slimies were literally torn to pieces. They really didn't like musket balls in them. In fact, the lead had the effect of turning them crystalline and consequently very fragile.

Whilst this was going on, Slimies on horse-like creatures attacked the front of the citadel. It just showed that Slimies could learn. But a few rounds of cannon fire soon dispersed them. All in all, it was a fairly feeble attack. They had no answer to the disciplined use of gunpowder.

Commander General Mainstay sent troops armed with muskets to clear the hills of the vermin. He was particularly proud of his musketeers, and the easy victory certainly improved morale. The Governor Commanders were very impressed by the power of the gun.

Lord Malander made it a priority to get the steel production plant re-working as it was clear that they needed more weapons as soon as possible.

Stuck on the head of one of the dead Slimies was a note:

The slippery, sleazy Slimies were back,
But muskets fought off the attack,
They failed in their attempted bushwhack,
And mighty cannons became their drawback.

26

The Meeting Continues

The meeting of the War Council continued.

Governor Commander Winterdom, 'John, I must say that I'm very impressed with your musketeers. Fine weapons and a very disciplined performance.'

Commander General Mainstay, 'That's the first time that they have been in action.'

Governor Commander Winterdom, 'Why was that?'

Commander General Mainstay, 'A few reasons. We were still training the men both in the use of a musket and in tactics. Then we wanted to surprise the enemy with our new secret weapon, and lastly, most of the recent attacks have been of a non-military nature.'

Governor Commander Winterdom, 'Well done regardless.'

Commander General Mainstay, 'Thank you. I will pass on your compliments to my men.'

Governor Commander Bandolier, 'And what about those cannons? We have changed warfare forever.'

Commander General Mainstay, 'I agree, we still need archers, but their days are numbered.'

Lady Malander wasn't sure if the change was a good thing or not, but they needed the edge that guns would bring.

Lord Malander, 'So colleagues, where were we?'

Commander General Mainstay, 'My Lord, we were

discussing the possibility of a new strategy rather than just sitting back and taking it like a captured animal.'

Lord Malander, 'You mean just like the Slimie attack.'

Commander General Mainstay, 'Exactly.'

Lord Malander, 'I would be happy to go on the attack if we had someone to attack.'

Lady Malander sat there thinking, 'What is the point of all this?'

It was getting her down, or was it just the time she was living in? She was built for joy and happiness. She wanted long walks in the sun, romance amongst the stars, beachcombing, laughter, fine foods, live music, scintillating conversation, and then it happened.

It was a very quiet voice, 'I will never know my father.' The tears poured down the side of her face because she knew that it was true. She couldn't stay in the room and left in a flood of tears. She was struggling to control the sobbing. She didn't want to control it.

And then there was another comment, 'Don't worry mummy, I will survive.' And then there was silence. She was concerned that there was no mention of her.

Lord Malander wanted to run after his wife, but he was too embarrassed to. The meeting continued going around in circles. There was no sign of any decisions because decisions were rather difficult. There was, in fact, no obvious clear-cut way forward, and that's why we need leaders.

Lord Malander stood up and said, 'I have made a decision. We are leaving Moelbryn.'

There was a quizzical look around the room.

Lord Malander, 'That is the ancient name for Malvern.'

Commander General Mainstay, 'Where are we going?'

Lord Malander, 'We are going to the mountains.'

Commander General Mainstay, 'Why there?'

Lord Malander, 'It's an ancient land populated by an ancient people. Eryri is a natural fortress. We can rebuild, regain our strength, and then fight on. Major Hogsflesh, I need you and your men to scout the area for a temporary home. Please seek the permission of the Druids, but we are going regardless of their response. It is not our intention to stay there; we will return to Moelbryn at the right time.'

Major Hogsflesh, 'Yes, my Lord, but what exactly are we looking for.'

Lord Malander, 'Somewhere in the mountains where we can defend ourselves. We need access to raw materials for our factory and running water. You will know the right place when you see it. I'm sending Thomas with you.'

Merlin, 'It might be better if I go as I know the place already.'

Lord Malander, 'Of course. What else can you tell us?'

Merlin, 'The mists of time do not permit me to divulge the future, but you are making the right decision.'

Lord Malander, 'Major Copson, we need that factory, can you move it?'

Major Copson, 'Yes, my Lord.'

Lord Malander, 'We also need a plan to move all our stocks, equipment etc. We are going to need more carts. Can you do it?'

Major Copson, 'Yes, my Lord, but I will need more labour.'

Lord Malander, 'Alice, you will have a lot of work getting all of the stock ready to move. Can you do that?'

Alice Marshall, 'Yes, my Lord, but I will also need more labour.'

Lord Malander, 'John, can you provide the labour?'

Commander General Mainstay, 'Yes, my Lord.'

Lord Malander, 'I also need your men to requisition anything edible from our surrounding area for the journey, but please treat the locals with respect. We will pay for everything in gold.'

Commander General Mainstay, 'Of course, my Lord.'

Lord Malander, 'Thomas, can you organise the magical team to let the locals know what is happening? They don't have to leave with us, but we would recommend it. They will have to carry anything they want with them. We can't guarantee that there will be any spare space in the carts.

'Tell them that it is going to be a hard and arduous journey.'

Thomas, 'Yes, my Lord.'

Lord Malander, 'I think the time has come to temporarily abandon our regional strategy. We are all moving to Eryri.'

There were no objections.

Lord Malander, 'Lastly, while we are preparing to leave, there are still likely to be further attacks. We must be vigilant.'

As was the normal pattern, a note was found:

Follow the gallant decisive leader,
With wife in tow, now a breeder,
Scouting ahead so no misleader,
To the mountains of the great cedar.

Off to Eryri, in the sun,
With arrows, cannon, and gun,
We won't stop for anyone,
We will finish what we have begun.

27

Preparations

The task of moving a whole community was remarkably complex. Major Copson had his hands full just taking the factory apart and designing special carts for its transport. In the end, it required twenty-two carriages. The stocks of arrows, guns and ammunition took another fifteen carriages. And four horses were needed to pull one cannon.

When you added the other carriages, the convoy would be nearly a mile long, and Major Copson was pretty sure that much of the route would not be suitable for wheeled transport.

Alice first had to decide what stocks were needed and what could be left behind. There were strong arguments for taking almost everything. Part of the problem was that she couldn't determine what she could buy locally. Two of her provisioners joined Major Hogflesh's scouting party to investigate. She was worried that provisioning would be somewhat difficult on top of a mountain.

To make it worse, she was under pressure from every head of department. The medical team wanted all of their stocks of medicine. The magicians wanted all of their herbs and magical paraphernalia. The culinary staff needed every one of their pots, and so it went on. She envisioned a march to the mountains where the route was littered with abandoned material. It made her heart sink, but then she was a professional stock controller.

The Magical Services Team were probably not the best at talking to the local population about leaving. They lacked the common touch in most cases. Generally, people don't like change. Most don't want to leave their homes unless it is absolutely necessary. The young were a lot easier to convince than the elderly, and it was obvious that some couldn't or shouldn't make the journey.

There were difficult questions about what to do with the very old, the infirm and especially the seriously injured soldiers. In a number of cases, the journey would kill them. It was probably best that they retired into the countryside, but there was no vegetation or food for miles around.

The foraging had not been particularly successful as the rat-locusts had done their job well. However, the scouts reported that there were ample stocks available until they got to the borders of Snowdonia. On that basis, Alice issued food to anyone who wanted it as transporting it was just too cumbersome.

Eventually, by hook or crook, every problem was solved, and it was decided that the procession would leave. There were still nearly fifteen thousand troops. The convey was structured into mini-convoys so that each one had a mixture of carriages, infantry, civilians, and cavalry. There was a vanguard, outriders and a rear-guard.

Everyone knew that the road ahead was going to be seriously hard work, but they didn't really appreciate just how hard.

On a large boulder, the following was found:

The road ahead was very hard,
Not a bit like our Malvern backyard,
With rocks and tracks so very scarred,
Not knowing what to keep or discard.

28

More Preparations

The regional forces were also making their preparations. It was decided that the Welsh regiments would head across country to Porthmadog and set up camp there. The Northern troops were to head towards the northern coast of Wales and make camp at Llandudno. The Midland regiments would make camp at Bala.

The South-Eastern forces planned to meet up with the South-Western contingent and head to Malvern to pick up any remaining items of value and then follow the main army. Once in Snowdonia, a proper defensive plan would be put in place.

It was surprising that there had been no sign of the enemy since the decision was made to abandon Malvern. For some time now, Lord Malander had suspicions that something was wrong. He wondered about Merlin, but he had been critical to our defence, and none of us would have survived the rat-locust infestation without him.

He decided that the problem he had with Merlin was that he knew the future. He knew what was going to happen. He was playing the same game as Galattermous. But was that game one that helped his team, or were we just expendable pawns in Merlin's game of life and death? He had no problem with the younger Merlin, only admiration.

Lord Malander was also worried about his wife. Whenever he looked at her, there was a tear in her eye. She was hiding something, and that something was coming between them.

Lady Malander had not received any further communications from her unborn son despite her attempts to kick-off a conversation.

No one knew, but practically everyone did. Rachel was pregnant, but the older Merlin had no children. Did that mean that she was going to lose the child or that the timelines were different? The older Merlin was very silent on the subject.

The Elders, who were becoming more and more irrelevant, were shipping off to hiding places in Monmouthshire. They weren't really fit enough to travel much further than that.

29

Sky High Spies

They said that it was a hard, hard road ahead, but that was an understatement. The path where it existed had to be smoothed, widened, and levelled in many places to take the carriages. Frequent rest stops were needed for both the horses and the civilians.

The hills were a particular challenge as the infantry had to help the horses with the load on the way up. They then had to unhitch the horses and use men as brakes on the way down. It was slow, back-breaking work, but they were making progress. It was fortunate that the scouts had planned the route as there would have been many dead ends without them. Bridges had to be built to cross the rivers. They were left in place as the others were following.

As promised, there were frequent places where food could be purchased, and the water supply was never a problem. Lord Malander was concerned about progress as they were making less than twenty miles a day. So far, there was no pressure on them as there was no sign of the enemy, but that could change at any time.

Neither of the Merlins could detect any unwelcome magical activity.

Thomas, 'What do you think of this trip.'

Merlin, 'It is necessary.'

Thomas, 'What makes you say that? And don't give me that time-travel clap-trap.'

Merlin, 'Do you want to know the future?'

Thomas, 'I wouldn't mind if I did.'

Merlin, 'Are you sure?'

Thomas, 'You confuse me. You say you know the future, but you act like you don't. When we, or rather you, defeated the rat-locusts, how come you didn't know what to do beforehand?'

Merlin, 'That's a good question. I had never seen them before.'

Thomas, 'But you are my future.'

Merlin, 'Am I?'

Thomas, 'I thought you were.'

Merlin, 'I was your future when we met, but we have changed the future.'

Thomas, 'What do you mean by "we"?'

Merlin, 'I mean all of us. This current history is steadily varying from what I remember, but there are broad similarities. A good example is Rachel. In my timeline, Rachel was hurt in one of the attacks, which prevented her from having children. In this timeline, Rachel is pregnant. So my knowledge of the future is somewhat suspect.'

Thomas, 'In your timeline, did we go to the mountains?'

Merlin, 'We certainly did.'

Thomas, 'And did it make a difference.'

Merlin, 'It certainly did,'

Thomas, 'You are not being very helpful.'

Merlin, 'I've answered your questions.'

Thomas, 'But you haven't provided any embellishments.'

Merlin, 'That's a big word for a boy.'

Thomas, 'What's your problem?'

Merlin, 'You are, with your young woman and your youth.'

Thomas, 'You can't be jealous of my age.'

Merlin, 'You remind me of what I've lost.'

Thomas, 'But look at what you have gained.'

Merlin, 'A bad back, aching legs, failing eyes and a somewhat dodgy memory.'

Thomas, 'But what about the magic?'

Merlin, 'Ah yes, the magic. It stops you from sleeping at night. It gives you terrible dreams. It takes you away from your family. It gives you responsibilities you don't want.'

Thomas, 'I see.'

Merlin, 'You know with great power comes great responsibilities. Everything is a potential threat, even that little spider on your jacket.'

Thomas quickly brushed it off.

Thomas, 'What can you tell me about Snowdonia?'

Merlin, 'It's beautiful, majestic and very magical. You will love it and feel quite at home.'

Thomas, 'But Malvern is beautiful.'

Merlin, 'You can't compare them. They are very different. But in Snowdonia, you will become a man. You will know what I mean later.'

Then there was a shout from the front of the convoy, and everyone looked up. It was a giant bird with possibly a wingspan of thirty feet. Snowdonia was meant to be the land of the eagles, but we hadn't got there yet.

It wasn't an eagle. It was an unknown, but it meant that the enemy had spotted them.

A note attached to the bird's feather floated down:

> *We think we know the past,*
> *But the present is here at last,*
> *But is the future quite steadfast?*
> *Or is its truth quite overcast?*

30

Trekking

Lord Malander called a meeting of the convoy leaders and asked, 'Should we change our tactics re the convoy?'

Captain Jericho, 'My Lord, it's the classic question of where do you put your slowest component. If you put the carriages at the front, the whole convoy has to slow down and travel at their speed. If you put the carriages in the middle, then the convey gets split into two. If you put them at the end, they are left behind by the rest of the convoy.'

Lord Malander, 'So what's the answer?'

Captain Jericho, 'You have to find a way of speeding up the carriages, but I don't see how we can do it.'

Lord Malander, 'So what do you suggest?'

Captain Jericho, 'If you are worried about safety, I would send a large portion of the army and the civilians ahead. Leave the carriages to follow but with a good defensive force.'

Lord Malander, 'Let's do that.'

Captain Jericho, 'I should point out that you will have increased the risk of the carriages being captured, but I agree with you.'

And it was done.

The giant bird creatures continued to follow the trekkers. There were about a dozen of them. On closer inspection, they looked like a cross between a rat and an eagle but on a much bigger scale. It was astonishing that they could fly.

Gradually their numbers increased. There were now a few hundred, and they were getting braver, flying closer and closer. Men with loaded muskets were now sitting on the carriages. As far as their colleagues were concerned, they were having an easy time until one of the rat-birds swooped down and took one of the musketeers away.

The south-east Division met their south-western colleagues at Gloucester and proceeded towards Malvern. When the advance guard got near, they discovered that the citadel was now a giant aviary containing thousands of flying rat-like creatures.

Commanders Dragondale and Mannering discussed what to do. Their orders were to collect additional stocks from Malvern and avoid any engagement with the enemy as they had civilians with them. Consequently, they decided to retire from Malvern and follow the River Severn up to Worcester. They sent riders ahead to warn the main army.

All of the human forces were now dangerously exposed. In total, there were about fifty thousand military personal and twice that number of civilians. It would be difficult providing for them all, but they still had extensive gold stocks, assuming that the wagons got through.

It may have been the largest human trek in history up to that point. It naturally experienced the full range of human activities: births, deaths, accidents, joy, sorrow, love, anger etc., but so far, it had been relatively peaceful, and then they were attacked.

At least a thousand rat-birds went in for the kill. Both parts of the main army were attacked. The musketeers sitting on the wagons held their own with men below reloading for them. Their barrage of lead balls certainly interfered with the rat-birds' flying ability. They were falling out of the sky like dead birds. Much to the amusement of the troopers.

The main part of the convoy was less lucky. The path was narrow, and it was difficult for the musketeers to get by to assist the civilians. The rat-birds picked their targets with precision aiming for women and children who were obviously lighter. The musketeers took most of them down, but most of the captives were killed as they fell to the earth. Each death was a tragedy, but there was no time for burials. The convoy had to move on.

The attacks continued on a regular basis, but the musketeers were too much for them, and the attacks eventually petered out. They then stopped to make camp.

In the firelight, they found a note:

Was it a rat, or was it a bird?
Flying overhead, my vision was blurred,
It must be a mammal as it was all furred,
But surely that would be completely absurd.

Malvern was an aviary containing a herd,
And then the commanders conferred,
To a new route, they transferred,
But it wasn't what they preferred.

31

Nearly there

The scouts had done a good job finding some reasonably flat land in a very mountainous area. There was running water nearby and better grazing land than they expected. The Druids had been helpful but nervous of such large numbers of people moving in. They kept emphasising that it was their land.

The actual spot was near Capel Curig and was easily defensible. There were relatively good communications with the other outposts that were being established. The word 'relatively' had to be used sparingly as, in the winter, the roads would be impassable.

Fortunately, the rest of the journey for the army was almost incident-free. But most of the civilians were not too impressed with the rugged, wind-swept environment that they had been delivered to. It was hard farming land, and the winters were going to be very challenging.

Nevertheless, the animals were released, tents were erected, and the engineers started constructing buildings. The wagons were cannibalised, and the scouts had purchased large stocks of timber from the Druids, which was particularly helpful.

Major Copson's engineers were mostly focusing on building shelters for the civilians, but there were many hands to help them. A small group were already erecting the framework for the factory. Lord Malander wanted the manufacturing of guns to be a priority. Fortunately, the raw materials required were nearby, but it was still extremely hard to collect and transport them.

The Magical Services Team were retuning their powers to the new environment. They had full access to the ley lines, and the magic was strong, very strong. Merlin had been right; Thomas was in awe of the landscape. He loved the mountains, and it felt safe.

The convoy of carriages arrived, followed by the southern forces. They all immediately set to work. It was astonishing how quickly a town appeared. Work started on some wooden fortifications, and a small dam was created to trap water for the town's use. The town that was now called Malander, which amused Lord Malander no end.

Alice was a lot happier when her stocks were placed on shelves. And work even started on the building of a small hospital. The town of Malander looked like what it was: a frontier town. Over the next few weeks, the wooden buildings would be replaced by stone in preparation for the winter.

As far as Lord Malander was concerned, the move had gone a lot better than he expected, and then he saw the blue army in the distance.

A young boy found a note:

> *In the mountain, they made a town,*
> *For one destined to wear the crown,*
> *In Capel Curig, with hills so brown,*
> *It was a place for all to bed down.*

32

Blue, Blue, my Love is Blue

The blue army approached steadily, waving banners, and making a form of music that was more discordant than melodic. It didn't look to be aggressive, but the Druids were famous for being unpredictable. Commander General Mainstay put his men on alert but ordered them not to initiate an engagement. He wanted them to be on their best behaviour.

As they approached, one could see that they were singing and dancing. Perhaps singing was the wrong word. It turned out to be an ancient Celtic chant. In fact, it was an ancient Celtic welcoming ceremony that could easily have started a war.

Then three carts were brought forward containing fruit, vegetables, and cooked meats. All of which were very welcome. Then three young maidens with their faces painted blue were pushed forward. They were wearing flowing robes that were suddenly ripped off to expose their naked bodies. Before anyone could say anything, their handlers ripped out their hearts, and the three bodies collapsed to the ground.

One of the fur-covered handlers started digging a hole in the rocky ground to bury the three hearts, which still seemed to be beating. The onlookers were shocked as human sacrifice had never been part of the Malvern culture. It didn't stop there. Some druid women sliced the girls up and drained their blood into large black cauldrons. They then walked around the circumference of the town, splattering blood everywhere. Apparently, the town was now protected from evil spirits.

Thomas felt sick and disgusted at such an awful display of religious stupidity. It was also a terrible waste of three beautiful girls.

The Druid leaders came forward, wanting to parley. Lord Malander asked his wife, Major Hogsflesh, Commander General Mainstay, Abbot Frogmore and the two Merlins to join him. Lord Malander suggested that they went inside one of the new huts, but the Druids always met in the open regardless of the weather, and so they did.

The Druid Leader introduced himself as Vortigern. His five warlords were also introduced, but their names were far too difficult to pronounce.

Vortigern, 'Welcome to our lands, people of the dales.'

Lord Malander, 'Thank you Lord Vortigern.'

Vortigern, 'I speak to men of power, not you.'

Lord Malander was going to object when Merlin said, 'And how is my old friend?'

Vortigern, 'It's good to see you again, Myrddin or is it Maizhin?'

Merlin, 'I've been called many things over the years, but what's in a name?'

Vortigern, 'Everything, a man's name is his history, his past and his future, but why are there two of you?'

Merlin, 'This young man is a younger version of me.'

Vortigern, 'But he doesn't share your destiny. He is on a different path.'

Merlin, 'Yes, that's true; we are rapidly becoming different Merlins.'

Vortigern, 'Those dale-lovers, can we trust them?'

Merlin, 'You can, my Lord. They are fine and honourable men.'

Vortigern, 'I will take your word on that, but they have set-up multiple locations. They look a bit like conquerors, but they won't be able to stay here for long as the blood-rite will stop them.'

Merlin, 'They have no plans to stay here long-term. They have their own lands.'

Vortigern, 'You mean Moelbryn, the home of the dragon that never sleeps and the waters of eternal peace.'

Merlin, 'That's right, my Lord.'

Vortigern, 'Those lands are now cursed by Galattermous.'

Merlin, 'They have fled to Eryri to recoup and then continue their battle against the great destroyer.'

Vortigern, 'So why come to the land of the eagles?'

Merlin, 'Lord Malander made that decision, but it felt right to me. They want to confront Galattermous but have no idea how to track him down.'

Vortigern, 'But you know.'

Merlin, 'Of course, but I'm constrained.'

Vortigern, 'That would be the Lot Law. But I'm not constrained.'

Merlin, 'That is true. You could divulge Galattermous's location.'

Vortigern, 'And if I gave them that, they would go?'

Merlin, 'Why don't you ask them?'

Vortigern, 'So Lord Malander you know of the Merlins.'

Lord Malander, 'I have that honour.'

Vortigern, 'And if I tell you where Galattermous is, how can I be sure that you will leave?'

Lord Malander, 'A lot depends on your answer and the

condition of my people. I might have to leave the civilians behind whilst my troops go off to war.'

Vortigern, 'I understand that. I will give you the destroyer's location if you can meet my three conditions.

'Firstly, will you guarantee your departure on the life of your unborn son?'

Lord Malander, looking at his wife, 'I will, but at this stage, I cannot agree on a date.'

Vortigern, 'I understand that. My second condition is that young Merlin stays with us for five years and learns our ways.'

Lord Malander, 'I cannot agree to anything on behalf of Merlin.'

Thomas, 'I accept.'

Vortigern, 'My third condition is that one hundred of my warriors join your campaign against Galattermous.'

Lord Malander, 'I'm more than happy to agree to that.'

Vortigern, 'The deal is done. It will be sealed tomorrow at mid-day.'

And the Druids left with gifts of mead and Malvern water, the waters of peace.

And the day was done, but a note was found:

> *On a mountainside, three paid the price,*
> *A gruesome death, a sad sacrifice,*
> *To gods unknown in paradise,*
> *Or were they just fertiliser for edelweiss?*
>
> *Was it just a throw of the dice?*
> *Or was it their naked bodies to entice?*
> *That led to a ghastly compromise,*
> *To find that girls are made of spice.*

33

Red, Red my Blood is Red

Lord and Lady Malander sat around the table with the two Merlins and Abbot Frogmore.

Lord Malander, 'Merlin, you obviously know those blue savages quite well.'

Merlin, 'It would be wrong to call them savages.'

Lord Malander, 'But what about those young girls?'

Merlin, 'They had been bred to be sacrifices.'

Lord Malander, 'That doesn't make them any less savage.'

Merlin, 'They knew what was going to happen.'

Lord Malander, 'Why would they need handlers if they were happy with it?'

Merlin, 'I'm not trying to make excuses, but of course, you are right.'

Lord Malander knew that Merlin was just pandering to him. In the scheme of things, everyone and everything was just a pawn in a much bigger game. But that wasn't the sort of game he wanted to play.

Lord Malander, 'Can we trust them?'

Merlin, 'No, certainly not. Did you notice that they kept the girl's intestines for divination?'

Lord Malander, 'I didn't spot that.'

Merlin, 'In the past, they used an animal. They ripped its guts out to foretell the future. Never understood it myself. Didn't want to. All a bit mucky. But as their magic got weaker, they found that they got better results from a human.

'They tested different types of human, and found that virgin girls gave the best results. Then there were disputes about the readings, so they decided to take an average. They need three girls to get a sensible answer.

'So to answer your question, they will read the guts tonight, do some mathematical averaging and decide on the course of action tomorrow. It could be war or a party or anything in between.'

Lord Malander, 'What's this Lot Law?'

Merlin, 'It's the law that prohibits releasing information about the future. If I break it, I could be severely punished or even killed.'

Lord Malander, 'Why do they call Malvern the home of the dragon that never sleeps and the waters of eternal peace?'

Merlin, 'Malvern is the lair of the white dragon that historically has fought the red dragon of Wales.'

Lord Malander, 'And you believe that?'

Merlin, 'Yes, I've seen the dragon.'

Lord Malander, 'And the waters of eternal peace?'

Merlin, 'Malvern has the finest and purest waters in the known world. One day people will come to Malvern just for the waters.'

Lord Malander, 'You joke.'

Lord Malander sent an aide to get Commander General Mainstay. It wasn't long before he arrived.

Lord Malander, 'John, how is it going?'

Commander General Mainstay, 'Worse than expected. It's amazing how some people only see problems. Anyway, how can I help you?'

Lord Malander, 'Merlin tells me that the Druids are honourable people, but their religion is partly based on divination. If the runes look bad, they might even attack us.'

Merlin, 'I'm not saying that they will be aggressive, but there is a possibility. They are unpredictable.'

34

The Blues are Back

Lady Malander had managed to convince herself that the words spoken by her unborn son were just her imagination. But then it happened again.

Unborn Child, 'My father will never know me, and I will never know him. That makes me feel sad.'

Lady Malander, 'Don't feel sad, my little one. It's just the circle of life.'

But they both knew the truth as the tears ran down her cheeks. What made it worse was that her husband had talked about how much he was looking forward to raising their child. He would have made a great father. He still might, but there was truth in her son's declaration. A truth that she couldn't ignore. Lord Malander had less than two and a half months to live.

Commander General Mainstay had his troops in position just in case. The camp was on full alert, and there was a tense atmosphere. The druid's slaughter of the three young girls had not helped them make friends with the rank and file or the civilians.

The blue band of brothers arrived in much the same way as yesterday with a considerable amount of noise and much banner waving. Merlin and Lord Malander were there waiting for them.

As usual, they met outside. There was no hand-shaking as that was not their custom, but kissing was, and it was now permissible as they were now officially friends.

Vortigern, 'The runes are on your side, but I wish you to confirm the following:
1. That your tribe will leave when your mission has been completed
2. That young Merlin will spend five years with us
3. That you will take a hundred of our warriors on your journey.

'And that you agree to the above on the life of your unborn son.'

Lord Malander, 'I agree.'

Vortigern, 'And now we mix blood.' He cut his hand so that it bled. An aide handed over a knife to his lord, who repeated the operation. Blood was mixed, and the deal was done, except he still didn't know where Galattermous was.

Vortigern walked over to Lord Malander and whispered something in his ear. Lord Malander couldn't and wouldn't believe it, but somehow, he did.

Lord Malander shouted, 'Arrest Abbott Frogmore immediately.'

But he was nowhere to be seen.

Lord Malander couldn't believe it. He instinctively trusted this man. He regarded him as a good friend and a confidant. He had even put him in charge of planning.

He also had the job of analysing the prophecy, which he failed at miserably. Thinking about it, he didn't provide a single analysis.

Then he wondered how many men died because of his planning. He knew everything we were doing.

Lord Malander put his head in his hands and wished to be swallowed up.

Merlin came over to comfort him.

Lord Malander, 'You knew, didn't you?'

Merlin, 'I'm ashamed to say yes, but I wasn't totally sure. I thought that he would eventually give himself away or that you would work it out, but as time went on, you got closer to him.'

Lord Malander, 'Vortigern, why did you insist that I took a hundred of your warriors?'

Vortigern, 'When I saw Galattermous in your camp yesterday, I decided to save everyone's lives. If you tried to arrest him then, he would have killed us all in a blink of an eye.'

Lord Malander, 'So you knew that he would disappear.'

Vortigern, 'I guessed and hoped he would.'

Lord Malander, 'But isn't killing us what he wants?'

Vortigern, 'He needs and wants souls, but he has to follow the rules of the game.'

Lord Malander, 'What is this fucking game?'

Vortigern, 'It's the game that every living soul is playing. Most have no idea that they are participants, and frankly, they don't want to know.'

Lord Malander, 'So how do we defeat Galattermous?'

Vortigern, 'You don't defeat Galattermous. You have to create a situation where he can't be bothered to carry on. Merlin knows the rules, most people would consider themselves lucky if they had one Merlin, but you have two.'

And two verses were discovered

> *He was a well-known curator,*
> *And a prophecy translator,*
> *We thought he was a great debater,*
> *But he was the main perpetrator.*

Many died because of the terminator.
A beast who wanted to be a dictator,
The Druids exposed him as a collaborator,
But now we know him as a cursed traitor.

35

The Game

Lord Malander called a meeting of the senior personnel at Capel Curig to discuss their future strategy or, rather, short-term tactics. The attendees were as follows:
- Lord Malander, Commander-in-Chief
- Commander General Mainstay
- Governor Commander Mannering, South-West
- Governor Commander Dragondale, South-East
- Major Hogsflesh, Commander Intelligence
- Major Copson, Commander Engineering
- Alice Marshall, Quartermaster General
- Merlin
- Thomas

Two of the Governor Commanders couldn't make it because of distance, and Lady Malander wasn't feeling well.

Lord Malander, 'Firstly, I need to apologise to everyone here and absolutely everyone in our community, and especially those who died. I recruited Abbott Frogmore, and I accept the consequences.'

Major Hogsflesh, 'He totally fooled me, and that's not easy.'

Commander General Mainstay, 'Let's be honest, he fooled us all. He even took his own medicine and became a hog for a while, and we took the piss out of him.'

Merlin, 'I didn't detect it, but there is a possibility that we were all affected by a glamour spell. Thinking about it, it must have been the case as Galattermous is not naturally a warm character.'

Lord Malander, 'I'm struggling to cope with the number of deaths that were caused by having him on-board.'

Governor Commander Dragondale, 'My Lord, you need to balance that against the number of lives you saved. Without you, we would all be dead by now.'

Governor Commander Mannering, 'I agree with that, but I'm struggling to see why Merlin didn't let us know.'

Merlin, 'As I told Lord Malander, I had my suspicions that something was wrong.'

Governor Commander Mannering, 'Did you suspect that he was Galattermous?'

Merlin, 'I have to be honest, I did suspect that he was Galattermous.'

Governor Commander Mannering, 'And you didn't tell us?'

Merlin, 'I had to be sure. I knew that the Druids would know. He is very dangerous. If Vortigern had exposed him yesterday, we would probably all be dead.'

Governor Commander Mannering, 'Would that include you?'

Merlin, 'Possibly not, but obviously, I don't know.'

Lord Malander, 'To use an unfortunate term, we can carry out a witch-hunt later. Now we need to consider our next step.'

Governor Commander Mannering, 'That's true, but Merlin could tell us so much more as he knows the future.'

Thomas, 'You need to know that it's not true any more. Our history is heading in a very different direction to the one Merlin experienced. Tell him about Rachel.'

Merlin, 'In my timeline, I married Rachel, but she couldn't get pregnant. In this timeline, Rachel is pregnant. There are countless other variances.'

Lord Malander, 'Let's get back to our mission. Vortigern said that you couldn't defeat Galattermous, but you need to convince him that his effort is not worthwhile. How can we do that?'

Thomas, 'We have lots of things at Malvern that belonged to the Abbott. I'm sure that we can use those items to track him down.'

Merlin, 'You are right. We could just hound him off this world.'

Lord Malander, 'That sounds positive. Is there anything about the Abbott that we could use against him?'

Major Hogsflesh, 'I vaguely remember that he hated cats.'

Alice Marshall, 'Isn't there a verse to that effect?'

They looked and found the following:

> *The Master of all is for all a master,*
> *With the Abbott onboard as forecaster,*
> *Progress will be much faster,*
> *As strong and clear as alabaster,*
> *That won't help avoid a disaster.*

> *The Man of God was so fat,*
> *In his cloak and crooked hat,*
> *Don't let him corner you like a rat,*
> *Remember, he hates the regal cat.*

Merlin, 'It doesn't make great reading. It clearly warns us against him. And it clearly documents his dislike of cats.'

Lord Malander, 'But can we use cats against him in any

way?'

Thomas, 'We can generate magical cats.'

Lord Malander, 'I suggest that we do the following:

- Send a team to Malvern to collect the Abbott's things or anything that he had close contact with and bring them to Capel Curig
- Produce spells to track Galattermous down
- Develop cat weapons that we can use against Galattermous
- Agree on a force to track him down
- Use some of the Druid forces
- Use cat spells against him.

'Any comments?'

There weren't any, and everyone was dismissed. On the way out, Lord Malander found the following verses:

> *The lord apologised for the cul de sac,*
> *Stating never fear, they will be back,*
> *Was it the king, the queen, or the jack?*
> *That got the humans on the attack.*

> *They will track him down like a wolf-pack,*
> *Which sign will it be on the zodiac?*
> *Back to Malvern, they will ransack,*
> *Until the evil one faces the flack.*
> *Best to put your money on black.*

36

A Holiday in Malvern

Lord Malander and Commander General Mainstay agreed that Commander Dragondale and Major Hogsflesh should lead a party of forty troopers, including musketeers and half a dozen engineers, to collect Abbott Frogmore's personal possessions from Malvern. One magician was also joining the party.

They would travel as one group, but when they got to Malvern, they would operate as two separate groups to improve their chances of success. Detailed operational planning was down to them. Lord Malander lent Commander Dragondale his telescopnots.

They rode on horseback, backtracking their earlier journey. They were all quite looking forward to going home, although they dreaded what they might find. There was the odd rat-bird, but they showed no interest in them. In fact, the journey was incidentless, almost boring, although the scenery was superb.

They made camp twice as it was seriously tough going for the horses. They made their final camp at Worcester. The few surviving locals had nothing to report. There was no sign of any enemy activity.

The next day they had a quick dry breakfast and then travelled the final ten miles to Malvern. They climbed the North Hill from the Herefordshire side to ascertain the latest position. It all looked very quiet. Elsie, the magician, checked for any magical activity, and there wasn't any.

Commander Dragondale ordered her team to proceed straight down the hill into Malvern. Major Hogsflesh's group were to enter via one of the worm tunnels. Two soldiers and Elsie were left to mind the horses.

Both groups almost entered the wide-open citadel at the same time but from different directions. The place was completely deserted, but painted on the wall in blood was the following message: *you will never find me, signed G.* Had Galattermous defeated us before we started?

Anything and everything linked to the Abbott had been removed, scrubbed clean or destroyed. There was no furniture, books, documents, clothes, cooking implements, or anything uniquely his. It appeared to be forensically clean.

Commander Dragondale and Major Hogsflesh sat down and drank some of the water they collected from the hill.

Major Hogsflesh, 'There must be some trace of the Abbott.'

Commander Dragondale, 'I agree.'

Major Hogsflesh, 'There is probably some crockery or cutlery that he used.'

Commander Dragondale, 'But we would need a dozen wagons to take that back.'

Major Hogsflesh, 'What about the washing facilities?'

Commander Dragondale, 'How would we identify his?'

Major Hogsflesh, 'Elsie might be able to assist.'

Commander Dragondale, 'It's worth a try. Did he have any romantic relationships?'

Major Hogsflesh, 'There were rumours about a stable lad, but I thought he was celibate.'

Commander Dragondale, 'Did he gamble?'

Major Hogsflesh, 'Not that I know of.'

Commander Dragondale, 'We are not getting very far, are we?'

Major Hogsflesh, 'What about the Prophecy team? They might have something.'

Commander Dragondale, 'Where were they based?'

Major Hogsflesh, 'Wasn't it Colwall? I vaguely remember that the Abbott wanted peace and quiet for his team. We certainly know better now.'

They collected their horses, and all forty-odd riders took the Colwall road through the Wyche Cutting. They found the deserted prophecy offices in the middle of the village. Again they found the words: *you will never find me, signed G*, written in blood on the wall.

Commander Dragondale, 'It looks like we are too late.'

They looked around, but the place was clean. It was starting to look like their trip was a waste of time. And as they were thinking of going home, a man with long straggly hair came out of the bushes holding some thick volumes.

Major Hogsflesh, 'Who are you?'

Professor Dayton, 'I was one of the experts working on the interpretation of the prophecies.'

Major Hogsflesh, 'But you didn't get anywhere.'

Professor Dayton, 'We certainly did. I have the evidence in my hands.'

Major Hogsflesh, 'Was any of it written by the Abbott?'

Professor Dayton, 'Yes, we wrote the preliminary interpretations, and he liked to produce the final document in his hand. I must admit that he was a very stylish writer.'

Major Hogsflesh, 'And you have got that book?'

Professor Dayton, 'Yes, just here.' He waved the volume in the air.'

Major Hogsflesh, 'Please hand it over.'

Professor Dayton, 'No way, it's never going to leave my sight. There are important messages in here.'

Major Hogsflesh, 'I must have that volume. The survival of the human race may depend on it.'

Professor Dayton, 'You can't have it, but I could go with you.'

Major Hogsflesh, 'Can you ride a horse?'

Professor Dayton, 'No, but I will learn.'

Major Hogsflesh, 'In that case, let's get moving.'

Professor Dayton, 'Goody, I've always wanted to go to Snowdonia.'

Major Hogsflesh, 'How did you know that?'

Professor Dayton, 'I've read all of the prophecies.'

Major Hogsflesh, 'You could be of value to us.'

Professor Dayton, 'I hope so.'

Inside the front page of the volume was a new prophecy:

Back into the land of the cannonball,
Went our troopers, determined above all,
To collect the Abbott's trace, however small,
That may lead to the bastard's downfall.

No luck in Malvern to enthral,
Off to the tiny village of Colwall,
With success in a volume free-for-all,
They now had victory's wherewithal.

37

Back to the Mountains

The trip back to Eryri was a pleasant stroll, and Professor Dayton was exceptionally good company. He entertained around the camp-fire at night with elegant stories of academia and his suspicions of the Abbott. He had wondered why the prophecies were of no interest to Lord Malander when they held so many irrefutable clues.

He highlighted the following verses:

> *The dark one of the prophecy,*
> *Left his home to aristocracy,*
> *Fleeing from the cat morphology,*
> *To where catnip has no sovereignty.*
>
> *Was it simple animal neurology?*
> *That the cat beat the rat constantly,*
> *Or was it just a strange oddity?*
> *That felines defeat the evil theocracy.*

Commander Dragondale, 'Hardly the most satisfying rhymes.'

Professor Dayton, 'I will give you that, but it is not easy finding acceptable rhymes when you are predicting the future.'

Major Hogsflesh, 'I still don't understand where the verses come from?'

Professor Dayton, 'People have argued that it was God or the gods. Others thought it might be Galattermous having fun giving us clues, or it was just the Fates.

'I think that it is Merlin. Not the Merlin or Merlins that we know, but a future Merlin trying to get past the rules of time travel by sending notes back into the past. But they were important enough for Galattermous to put himself in a position to limit their potential damage to him.'

Commander Dragondale, 'Those rhymes seem to suggest that cats and catnip are a way to beat the beast.'

Professor Dayton, 'I originally assumed that everyone had read the verses and knew that. It's always been there in black and white.'

It wasn't long before they could see the mountains of Snowdonia. They were excited to see what Merlin could do with the tome in terms of tracking Galattermous down. And Commander Dragondale wondered where they were going to get stocks of catnip from.

38

Magical Locationalism

Lord Malander and the two Merlins met with the two returning commanders. There was genuine excitement in the air.

Major Hogsflesh, 'I would like to introduce Professor Dayton to you all.'

Lord Malander, 'Good afternoon, Professor, I think we met on a couple of occasions.'

Professor Dayton, 'Let's say that we have been in the same room before. The Abbott was always keen to keep us out of the way. The move to Colwall was to stop us accidentally interfacing with anyone.'

Lord Malander, 'I was constantly surprised by how little prophecy work was actually done.'

Professor Dayton, 'That certainly wasn't the case. This tome is the equivalent of ten man-years of work. It contains a full analysis of the prophecy, although it is a full-time job keeping it updated.'

Lord Malander, 'And do you believe the contents have value?'

Professor Dayton, 'At first I was hugely sceptical, and although we have magic in our lives, I have always thought that there is a rational answer for everything. But the more interpretations I carried out, the more I understood. So the answer to your question is yes.'

Lord Malander, 'What if I asked you to tell me where Galattermous is? Could you do it?'

Professor Dayton, 'I believe I could.'

Lord Malander, 'Go on then.' Professor Dayton started turning the pages in the book.'

Professor Dayton, 'Here we are:

He pretended to help beforehand,
But deceit was his to command,
Never an Abbott, needs to expand,
Home of the oaks near at hand.

Learned books full of sand,
Forever watch the second hand,
Bishops live in a fairyland,
Still, they need to be banned.

Now it's time for the minute hand,
As time waits to reprimand,
Send the devil to his motherland,
And free the Master from demand.

It says it all.'

Lord Malander, 'What does it say?'

Professor Dayton, 'I will interpret it for you'. And he got a pen and paper and wrote it down:

Rhyme	Meaning
He pretended to help beforehand	Abbott Frogmore was not helping you in any way
But deceit was his to	The Abbott deceived you and

command	probably gave you false information, but you gave him a command position
Never an Abbott, needs to expand	He never was an Abbott but needed to be more, let's say a bishop, but it could be another religious position
Home of the oaks near at hand	Oak trees are nearby. What's the name for a place of oaks?
Learned books full of sand	That refers to this tome. Sand refers to the Sands of Time
Forever watch the second hand	The Abbott needed to be watched. And Watch also refers to time.
Bishops live in a fairyland	This refers to the Abbott's real home
Still, they need to be banned	This obviously relates to sending the Abbott back home
Now it's time for the minute hand	Time travel again, and the need to get moving
As time waits to reprimand	This relates to the time travel rules
Send the devil to his motherland	This is about sending Galattermous home
And free the Master from demand	This relates to you, my Lord. It's about relieving you of pressure

'So from that, it's fairly obvious where he is.'

Lord Malander, 'Are you sure. There seems to be a lot of repetition to me.'

Professor Dayton, 'That's because the verses live on their own. They are normally found singularly by many different people. And I've always assumed that there are lots of missing verses.'

Lord Malander, 'Fair enough. Can you summarise your findings for us please.'

Professor Dayton, 'Of course:
- The Abbott is a lying, deceiving cad
- He must be sent back to his home
- This will involve time travel

The lines relating to his current whereabouts are as follows:
- Home of the oaks near at hand
- Bishops live in a fairyland

'What is the name for an area of oak land?'

He looked around the room like a professor lecturing to students. It was hard to change your ways. Lord Malander and the others all had blank faces.

Professor Dayton, 'I will tell you it's Auckland, so his current location is Bishop's Auckland. I've never heard of a place with that name.'

Lord Malander, 'And you are confident of that analysis?'

Professor Dayton, 'I'm confident of the analysis, but I've no idea if he is there or not.'

Lord Malander, 'Merlin, can you do your magic on this book to track him down?'

Merlin, 'Of course, but I will need a couple of hours to do it.'

Lord Malander asked his aide to find some sleeping quarters for the Professor, which was easier said than done.

The Professor was proud to see that he would now be in the tome:

> *The Master conversed with the Professor,*
> *Is he now the Abbott's successor?*
> *He is a man of words, not a confessor,*
> *But when spurned, he can be the aggressor.*

39

A New Adventure Starts

Merlin, 'I've done my locationalism, and he is in County Durham at a place called Shildon.'

Lord Malander, 'Does that mean that the Professor was wrong?'

Merlin, 'Not at all. It appears that the two places are less than three miles apart.'

Lord Malander, 'Does he know that we know?'

Merlin, 'Possibly. The problem with any magical activity is that it can be detected. He may also know the future; who knows?'

Lord Malander, 'By the time we get there, he might be gone.'

Merlin, 'That is a distinct possibility, but then we track him down again and then again if necessary. We just keep hounding him.'

Lord Malander, 'I'm pretty certain that we need to go in strength as he might have a fair amount of protection.'

Merlin, 'I agree. It could be a long, drawn-out campaign.'

Lord Malander, 'We need another meeting of the War Council to agree on a strategy. We can't take all of the civilians with us.'

Merlin, 'They could stay here, although I wouldn't trust the Druids, or do they go home?'

Lord Malander, 'Where would they be the safest?'

Merlin, 'No one is safe with Galattermous around. Why don't you ask the people?'

Lord Malander, 'If we let the rabble make their own decisions, why would they need the aristocracy?'

Merlin, 'My lord, I have to ...'

Lord Malander, 'Merlin, I was joking.'

Merlin, 'Yes, my Lord. Many a jest ends in tears.'

Lord Malander got his aide to call a meeting of the War Council in two days. Couriers were sent to the remote outposts. He also told him to tell Alice that we need large stocks of catnip and as many dead cats as she can find.

Aide, 'Did you say dead cats, my Lord?'

Lord Malander, 'I did.'

Aide, 'We can always make some if you want?'

Lord Malander, 'I don't want any cat killed on my account.'

Aide, 'I understand, Sir.'

40

Yet another Meeting of the War Council

This was one of the first meetings of the War Council where the news was positive. It made a very pleasant change.

The meeting had the following attendees:
- Lord Malander, Commander-in-Chief
- Commander General Mainstay
- Governor Commander Winterdom, Northern Region
- Governor Commander Mannering, South-West
- Governor Commander Walsh, Wales
- Governor Commander Dragondale, South-East
- Governor Commander Bandolier, Midlands
- Major Hogsflesh, Commander Intelligence
- Major Copson, Commander Engineering
- Alice Marshall, Quartermaster General
- Merlin
- Thomas

Lord Malander, 'Let's get down to business. I'm pleased to say that we believe that we have tracked Galattermous down to a place called Bishop's Auckland, or more specifically Shildon.'

Governor Commander Winterdom, 'That's excellent news. I know that part of County Durham well. The River Wear runs through the area.'

Major Hogsflesh, 'Assuming that we are going there, what's

to say that he will still be there when we arrive?'

Lord Malander, 'We know that we can track him now. On the way there, we will stop and check his location again. We will go where he is going.'

Merlin, 'As discussed with his Lordship earlier, we will keep tracking him down until we can confront him.'

Major Hogsflesh, 'That's excellent news.'

Lord Malander, 'We need to decide what we are going to do with the civilian population. The options are to stay here, go somewhere else, or go home.'

Alice Marshall, 'I can tell you what our people want. They want to go home. They don't like it here. It's too cold and windy, and its crap land for farming. And they certainly don't like the Druids.'

Lord Malander, 'Is that the general view?'

Merlin, 'I'm a bit surprised as there must be some bad memories of that place.'

Alice Marshall, 'That's true, but there are also good memories. Our kind are buried there. We still have folk there. It's our home.'

Major Hogsflesh, 'It sounds like you want to go home.'

Alice Marshall, 'I do, I really do.'

Lord Malander, 'But is it safe?'

Governor Commander Dragondale, 'It was deserted when Victor and I went there.'

Merlin, 'But the enemy could come back.'

Alice Marshall, 'That's true of here. They could attack us tomorrow.'

Major Hogsflesh, 'I must admit that Malvern looked as safe as anywhere else.'

Alice Marshall, 'So is that a decision, are we going home?'

Lord Malander, 'I think it is, unless anyone objects?' No one did.

Lord Malander, 'In that case, we need a force to protect them. Any volunteers?'

Governor Commander Winterdom, 'My recommendation would be that the Welsh and Midland divisions take them home and stay to defend Malvern.'

Governor Commander Bandolier, 'I would prefer to go to Bishop's Auckland with any of my troops who want to come with me.'

Lord Malander, 'Any objections?' There were none.

Lord Malander, 'Governor Commander Walsh, are you happy to take command of the returning forces?'

Governor Commander Walsh, 'Yes, my Lord.'

Lord Malander, 'Then I think that is settled. Major Copson, we are going to need your services again. We will need wagons to assist the civilians on their journey and to return some of the stores.

'The main army will need wagons for the artillery and our stores. I'm sure that you know what to do.'

Major Copson, 'You can leave it to me, Sir.'

Alice Marshall, 'My Lord, did you still want the catnip and the dead cats?' Everyone, except the Merlins, looked intrigued.

Lord Malander, 'I guess that you are all wondering about that. The prophecy suggests that Galattermous hates cats and catnip. He might even be allergic to them or worse.'

Merlin, 'I was talking to our professor, and he was postulating about the name Galattermous. The first few syllables might relate to the word "Galatian", which was an ancient Celtic tribe, and the second being a derivation of the word mouse. Perhaps that might explain his aversion to cats? Just joking.'

Lord Malander, 'Commander General Mainstay, can you plan our route and prepare for departure, please.'

Commander General Mainstay, 'Yes, my Lord.'

A verse was found on Alice's shoe:

Men of Malvern are going home,
Snowdonia was far too far to roam,
So not all roads lead to Rome,
Whilst the rest go to the catacomb.

41

Underway

The main Army cheered and waved as the civilians left Capel Curig. There were also hugs and tears as husbands said goodbye to wives, and lovers made their final farewells. Some knew that they would never see each other again.

One of those was Lady Malander. She was totally convinced that she would never see her Lord and lover again. And her unborn son remained silent. She was disappointed that her husband wouldn't be there for the birth of her son, but then he probably wasn't going to be there anyway. Now she had to focus on her baby.

Major Hogsflesh, with his scouting team, led the procession, followed by Major Copson and the Engineers. They were needed to pave the way for the main force. The vanguard followed them under Governor Commander Winterdom's control. He took that role because he knew the destination quite well.

Lord Malander and his personal guard, along with the two Merlins and the Professor, were next. They were followed by Governor Commander Bandolier's Midlands Division. About 70% of his troops remained with him.

Commander General Mainstay, with the bulk of the army, came next. They were followed by the convoy of wagons pulling the artillery and their stores. Governor Commanders Mannering and Dragondale provided a significant rear-guard.

Musketeers were placed throughout the convoy in case of an aerial attack, but none was experienced. There were few unanticipated problems on the way. It was just one long slog with regular stops to rest the horses, forage for food and check that Galattermous was still at Bishop's Auckland.

The route took them past Chester, Manchester, and Leeds. They stopped when they reached Darlington. As far as they could tell, they hadn't been spotted. It might be that they were being overly optimistic. Merlin was fairly sure that Galattermous knew that they were coming. He was far too experienced a player not to know.

A proper camp was built near Darlington at a place called Blackwell, which was close to the River Tees. Pickets were placed at regular points, but there was a general feeling that an attack was not imminent. Merlin checked again and confirmed that Galattermous was still at Shildon.

Major Hogsflesh led his scouts towards Shildon via Newton Aycliffe. The full scouting core was being used, nearly three hundred men in all. They had no idea where the enemy was based, but the scouts were well spread out, and Shildon wasn't that large a place.

Then one of the scouts spotted a small tower immediately above a cavern. It had a large entrance with sturdy pillars on each side. The interior was pitch black. The scouts decided that it was probably the entrance to hell. Major Hogsflesh suspected that they might be right. It actually reminded him of the opening on the South Downs.

Scouts were sent back to update Lord Malander and the main army. Most of the remaining scouts took up different locations to monitor the target. A few scouts were directed to investigate further afield in case there were other installations.

Major Hogsflesh also ordered the capture of a few locals to obtain information on their visitors, but there wasn't any. Then it dawned on the Major that the whole area was bereft of people. It wasn't unusual for locals to steer clear of armies on the move, but this was strange. He knew in his heart of hearts that Galattermous was responsible.

A couple of hours later, Lord Malander, Commander General Mainstay and the Merlin twins arrived with three hundred troops. They observed for a while, but not a lot was happening. In fact, nothing happened in a five-hour period. As night was closing in, they decided to leave a few scouts behind and return to the encampment. They all agreed that it was turning into a bit of an anti-climax.

Next to the cavern entrance was a note:

The scouts arrived with gun and axe,
Loaded down with their military packs,
They were dealt a handful of jacks,
But so far, it had been an anti-climax.

42

Let the Cannons Roar

Back at the encampment, they discussed their next move. It was decided to return to the location, set the cannons up and investigate the cavern. So it was early doors as it was going to take a few hours to transport the artillery and get it ready.

When they returned, they found that nothing had changed. The cannons were set up, ready to bombard the entrance if required. A group of about twenty, including Lord Malander, Major Hogsflesh, Commander General Mainstay and the two Merlins, ventured forwards, but there was no reaction whatsoever.

Once inside the cavern, they lit their torches and unsheathed their swords. Once they got used to the light, they could see that there were at least five man-made tunnels. They all looked identical. They considered splitting into separate groups, but in the end, they decided to stick together.

Nearly everybody wanted to go down the middle tunnel, but Lord Malander insisted on the first one as it was the most unlikely choice. Merlin wasn't sure what criteria his lordship was using, but it probably didn't matter, but then he reflected that he was usually right.

The tunnel went on for nearly half a mile. They sent one of the troopers back to update those waiting outside. At least they knew that their rear was being guarded. As they proceeded, the tunnel got hotter and narrower, and then they could hear noises.

They carried on without saying a word and, at the same time, trying to keep as quiet as possible. There were definitely muffled human voices ahead of them. They stopped in an effort to understand what was being said, but it simply wasn't clear enough to comprehend. Lord Malander realised that their lights would give them away, but without them, they couldn't see, so they just carried on.

The tension was getting hard to bear. The darkness, the cramped conditions, the putrid air, and the noises ahead were simply adding to the strain. Everyone was sweating, and breathing was getting more difficult. It wouldn't be wise to go on that much further, but the voices weren't that far ahead.

To make it worse, the smoke from the torches was irritating everyone's eyes. With each step, the tunnel was now getting narrower and damper. Ancient waters were running down the side of the wall. Lord Malander was ready to call a halt as he was starting to experience claustrophobia, and he was sure that he wasn't the only one.

Meanwhile, back at the cave entrance, the Slimies were pouring out of one of the tunnels, and the cannons and muskets were mowing them down with an avalanche of ordnance. The human army didn't expect to see Slimies, and the Slimies didn't expect to be up against that type of military firepower.

The outpouring of Slimies stopped. It was hard to tell if they had simply run out of them or whether it was a tactical move.

Governor Commander Winterdom took control and ordered the following:

- Move the cannons nearer to the cave entrance
- Commander Dragondale take fifty men and investigate tunnel two

- Commander Bandolier do the same with tunnel three
- Commander Mannering, you've got tunnel four
- Major Copson, I think you know which tunnel is yours
- Captain Green of my Division put two battalions on top of the cave and investigate that tower
- Captain Shelley, prepare your musketeers to protect the cannons
- Captain Davies take fifty men down tunnel one to join his lordship.'

They all shouted, 'Yes Sir,'

The main bulk of the army was about a mile away, probably having a good brew-up.

Governor Commander Winterdom was surprised to find a note:

> *The old master is so brave,*
> *Not a king but more than a knave,*
> *His master he intends to save,*
> *But sadly, he is meant for the grave.*
>
> *Guns and muskets do behave,*
> *For too many a very close shave,*
> *Those Slimies kill and enslave,*
> *Give us hope for the next wave.*

43

Time and Space

Lord Malander's team could hear the guns behind them and the voices in front of them. And all around them was a mixture of solid rock and coal. They were in a coal mine, probably a disused one. Taking unprotected torches into a coal mine wasn't probably the best idea.

They decided to struggle on a bit further. They were grateful that they did as they walked into the cathedral-like cavern, which had a swirling circle of mist in the middle of it. It was hard for the eyes to focus on it as it was swirling in every direction at the same time.

Merlin told everyone to stand back while he investigated it. He knew that it was an interdimensional portal fixed to a specific time. He began to suspect that each tunnel had a different destination or a different destination/time combination. Merlin was wondering how he was going to explain this to the others.

But where were the voices they heard coming from? There was no one else in the cavern, so the sounds must have come from the portal. Merlin decided that he had no choice but to enter the portal. As he got nearer, he could see their world as it was twenty or thirty years ago. He realised that he was looking at Malvern and a specific event.

He was watching a complete stranger handing over a young baby to Thomas's parents. He could see the happiness and joy in their faces. Thomas walked forward to share the vision.

Merlin, 'What made you enter the portal?'

Thomas, 'As soon as you saw that event, it somehow changed my memory at the same time.'

Merlin, 'That doesn't make sense. If you saw it first, it would change my memory but not the other way round.'

Thomas, 'But you told me not to be fixated on time being linear. But why did the portal show us that? It must have been pre-determined. It can't be chance.'

Merlin, 'If you walked further into the portal, you would be transported to that time period, but I can't guarantee that you could find your way back.'

Thomas, 'So who are my parents?'

Merlin, 'I thought I knew, but perhaps I was wrong.'

They both walked back to the others.

Merlin, 'Lord Malander, hold my hand, and we will walk into the portal. I want to know what the portal is going to show you.' They walked to the edge, and immediately before them was Lady Malander giving birth. They saw her pushing and grunting during the final minutes of delivery. Her handmaidens and an old birthing mother were assisting. It was proving to be a difficult delivery, but Lady Malander was showing true grit. It was a boy. Lord Malander had a son and heir.

Merlin pulled him back as he knew that there was going to be some bad news.

Lord Malander, 'Why did you pull us back.'

Merlin, 'Because exposure to a portal can make you ill, seriously ill.'

Lord Malander accepted that logic but now he was full of joy. He was a father. His heart was racing with excitement.

Merlin, 'It's your turn, young John.' Commander General

Mainstay walked forward, and Merlin held his hand and walked him to the portal's edge.

Before them was a vision of a beautiful young lady dying with an arrow in her heart.

Merlin, 'Who is that?'

Commander General Mainstay, 'It's my younger sister who died in a hunting accident.'

Merlin, 'How did it happen?'

Commander General Mainstay, 'I was hunting for deer, not knowing that she was secretly following me. I saw what I thought was a deer and shot her with my cross-bow. It was and still is the worst day of my life.'

Merlin, 'I'm sorry that you had to see that but did you see her lips?'

Commander General Mainstay, 'No.'

Merlin, 'I can lip-read, and she said that she forgave you. Go on and have a happy life.'

Commander General Mainstay, 'She really said that?'

Merlin, 'Yes.'

Commander General Mainstay, 'That has taken such a burden off me.' And they walked back.

Merlin, 'Victor, do you want a go?'

Major Hogsflesh, 'No thanks, the past is the past.'

Merlin, 'You are a very wise man, Mr Hogsflesh.'

And at that point, one of the troopers ran into the portal and disappeared. Merlin followed him to the edge, but there was no vision. He had vanished somewhere in time and space.

They decided to return. None of them was looking forward to the tunnel experience.

Just then, Captain Davies and a troop of at least fifty turned up.

Lord Malander, 'We weren't expecting you.'

Captain Davies, 'Well, we are at war against the Slimies again, my Lord. Governor Commander Winterdom sent me here in case you were in trouble. He has also sent parties down the other tunnels.'

Merlin, 'We better get back. Who knows what hell they might have unleashed?'

They decided to return as quickly as they could.

Near the exit, there was a note:

> *The past is hidden in a portal,*
> *Now the master's line's immortal,*
> *But what about the shortfall?*
> *The soldier's sister is still mortal.*

44

Bandolier to the Rescue

Governor Commander Bandolier liked nothing more than some action. He took his fifty men and rushed into the middle tunnel. Like the other one, it gradually got narrower, hotter, and damper as they progressed. It seemed endless as they trampled down the twisty path covered in coal dust.

His men were gradually finding it harder to breathe as there was no fresh air coming into the tunnel. It also smelled of dry dung, stale beer, and old farts. But they continued at a much faster rate than Lord Malander's team. They had to duck every now and then due to protrusions from the roof.

Like the previous tunnel, it opened onto a massive, coal-faced cavern with a swirling circle of mist in the middle of it. Unlike the last group, Bandolier led his men straight into the spiral of cloudy fog and disappeared. To their amazement, they found themselves somewhere near Cirencester in a battle with the Slimies.

Bandolier knew that this was the battle where nearly three thousand archers were killed, and only two thousand made it back. Fortunately, he and his men had arrived behind the Slimie lines with their muskets ready for action. Although there was only fifty of them, their muskets ripped the attacking Slimies to pieces.

The Slimies were totally confused and disorientated. It was

partly that human troops were behind their lines, but mostly it was the muskets. They had never seen or heard anything like it. The Slimies were simply being mowed down, but unlike before, they were more resilient.

The Slimies, prompted by their new leader, attacked Bandolier's small force en mass, completely overwhelming them. Governor Commander Bandolier and his men died, showing great fortitude and bravery. Their sacrifice saved at least two thousand human lives and allowed the human forces to continue their struggle.

No one back at Malvern knew what had happened, although some of the archers who survived talked about heroes coming out of the sky and saving them. In military circles, the 'Miracle of Wishanger' is still talked about to this day.

Stuck to Commander Bandolier's body was a note:

Remember, remember our brave bandolier,
He was always the first to volunteer,
The stunning hero of many a year,
He was a true soldier, not a veneer.

He saved so many in his career,
A man of the people we do cheer,
The military rules he did adhere,
Mr Bandolier was a man to revere.

45

The Battle of the Mine

Governor Commander Dragondale wasn't as rash as Bandolier. She took her fifty men and women into the tunnel at a steady pace but then met a horde of Slimies coming the other way. A strategic withdrawal was required as they fled out. They ducked to one side as the muskets and cannons let loose.

Governor Commander Winterdom had things well organised. The cannons were firing grapeshot, and that combined with musket fire was decimating the Slimies. Whilst that was going on, he ordered the rest of the army to march to the sound of the guns.

Archers that were further back shot flaming arrows on to the Slimies, which caused them to explode if they caught on fire. Despite all of this, the sheer number of emerging Slimies forced Winterdom to withdraw his cannons a few hundred yards. The musketeers protected the batteries. Fortunately, more musketeers were arriving by the second, securing the position.

The troops on top of the mine threw down a considerable load of catnip bombs, but they had no effect at all. But the Tanylip worked a treat. The Slimies became a seething mass of blue, multi-limbed slime-buckets itching themselves to death.

But still, more Slimies exited the mine. There seemed to be no end to them, and Winterdom was forced to retreat once again partly due to the increasing pile of dead and dying blue bodies.

The stench was disgusting, with Slimies exploding from catching fire and their bodily fluids rolling down the hill.

Then from behind the human army came legions of green Slimies. The musketeers soon changed their focus, but it was impossible to move the cannons quickly enough. And then they were shocked to find that the greenies were not affected by Tanylip.

The massacre of the human army began. They were outnumbered ten to one and were fighting on all fronts. Gradually the Slimies completely encircled them and started pushing the humans closer and closer together. It was becoming almost impossible to load the muskets in the crush.

Almost by accident, one of the troopers, who couldn't load his musket, threw some catnip at a green Slimie. It was like strong acid that immediately melted the nearest Slimie's face. They had a weapon, but it was probably too late, especially for Governor Commander Winterdom, who had just been ripped in half.

And then the coal mine exploded. It was always a health and safety risk with all those flaming arrows flying around.

Tucked in Winterdom's pocket was the following verse:

> *Who argues with the gods of war,*
> *Mars and Athena we do adore,*
> *Winterdom's name we can't ignore,*
> *He was the battle's matador.*

46

The Battle of the Mind

Captain Davies led his battalion of men back down tunnel number one to rejoin the main army, followed by Lord Malander's group. The old men were gradually being left behind as they weren't as fit. Merlin blamed it on too many pies that he had been forced to eat.

Their tardiness saved them when the mine exploded. They felt the heat and the shock waves. The roof over their heads remained intact, but it had completely collapsed further along. Lord Malander would have rushed to Captain Philips's aid if it was even vaguely possible that they survived.

Instead, they decided to run back to the cavern as they were worried about the air supply. They also knew that they could escape via the portal if it were absolutely necessary. When they reached the cavern, they saw figures emerging from the portal.

It was the giant figure of Galattermous. He stood there ten foot tall with a flowing golden cloak and an ornate staff in his hand. Some would say that he was an imposing figure, but it's hard to admire a multi-limbed green vertical slug with beady eyes.

He had twenty-odd armed Slimies with him, although the first thing he did was to paralyse everyone except the two Merlins and Lord Malander.

Galattermous, 'We meet again.'

Merlin, 'We do indeed.'

Galattermous, 'I wasn't talking to you, old man.'

Thomas, 'You mean me?'

Galattermous, 'Yes.'

Thomas, 'What do you want me with me.'

Galattermous, 'Your soul would be very useful. If nothing else, it would catch a good price.'

Thomas, 'You will never get it.'

Galattermous, 'That is still to be seen.'

Thomas, 'How come you speak our language?'

Galattermous, 'Because I'm human.'

And he gradually turned into a human being, not unlike Rachel's father in appearance.

Galattermous, 'And now I have both of you just as planned. When I absorb your magical abilities, I will become unbeatable.'

Lord Malander stepped forward to apprehend Galattermous when one of the Slimies, moving very quickly, literally picked him up and sliced open his guts. Lord Malander was held dangling in mid-air when his intestines fell onto the floor.

Galattermous, 'I can see that this wretched creature means something to you.'

He nodded, and the Slimie pulled Lord Malander's head off. Lord Malander's eyes carried on, moving for a while, and his lips were trying to say something.

Thomas, 'You fucking bastard.'

Galattermous, 'Thank you, I enjoyed that.'

Thomas rushed forward to attack Galattermous, who simply froze him in mid-air.

Merlin, 'Leave the lad alone.'

Galattermous, 'And how do you intend to stop me?'

Merlin, 'With this.' There was a dazzling light, and Merlin

grabbed the paralysed Thomas and jumped into the portal. Thomas became unparalysed once he was out of Galattermous's direct range.

Floating through the portal came the following verses:

> *The Master of cause is dead,*
> *His heroic story won't go unread,*
> *Gutted and headless, he bled,*
> *A fate that all would dread.*
>
> *Worried now about what's ahead,*
> *Perhaps the prophecy was misread,*
> *The Master was never going to die in bed,*
> *Leaving a wife who is now unwed.*
>
> *Always the hero until his deathbed,*
> *An officer and lord, a real thoroughbred,*
> *A prince amongst men, the aforesaid,*
> *His prize in heaven, a regal godhead.*

47

No Babies

Thomas, 'Where are we?'

Merlin, 'The portal takes you to where you want to go or where you need to go. In this case, it has taken you to a time and place when you can save humanity.'

Thomas, 'What do you mean?'

Merlin, 'I was hoping that you would work it out for yourself and then make the right decision.'

Thomas, 'I can't be that thick, or I would never become you.'

Merlin, 'You are not thick at all, but you haven't learnt how to put two and two together to make five. Let me take you through it slowly.

'Firstly, do you love Rachel?'

Thomas, 'You know I do.'

Merlin, 'And Rachel loves you?'

Thomas, 'Yes, I'm sure of it.'

Merlin, 'Have I ever had a child?'

Thomas, 'You said that you couldn't have children.'

Merlin, 'And why is that?'

Thomas, 'I've no idea.'

Merlin, 'You are lying.'

Thomas, 'It is said that male magicians can only fire blanks.'

Merlin, 'And what are you?'

Thomas, 'I might be an exception.'

Merlin, 'You are clutching at straws.'

Thomas, 'But Rachel loves me.'

Merlin, 'I know, but we are being logical.'

Thomas, 'I can't believe that my loving, honest Rachel has slept with another man.'

Merlin, 'Now think. Has Rachel mentioned anything that was sexually unusual?'

Thomas, 'That's private. That's between Rachel and me.'

Merlin, 'I know that she likes her nipples covered in jam and sucked.'

Thomas, 'How did you know that?'

Merlin, 'I am you, for god's sake. I can't believe that I used to be that dim.'

Thomas, 'Wait a minute, she did mention that she had a strange dream once where she was stripped and raped.'

Merlin, 'When was that?'

Thomas, 'About six months ago.'

Merlin, 'And how long has she been pregnant?'

Thomas, 'About six months. Oh my god. So it's not my baby.'

Merlin, 'I'm really sorry, Thomas.'

Thomas, 'Does she know?'

Merlin, 'She probably has her suspicions, especially with her magical abilities.'

Thomas, 'So who is the father?'

Merlin, 'I'm pretty sure that I know. Rachel is a powerhouse of magical abilities. Her children would almost certainly inherit them. A powerful magician would want her powers.'

Thomas, 'You are not saying that Galattermous raped her?'

Merlin, 'I'm suggesting an impossible paradox. Galattermous raped Rachel, who then gave birth to

Galattermous.'

Thomas, 'That's utterly preposterous.'

Merlin, 'I know. It's the old dilemma. Could you go back in time and kill your father?'

Thomas, 'Of course not, because I wouldn't be alive to kill him in the first place.'

Merlin, 'You have travelled in time. In fact, there are two Thomas's and two Merlins at this exact moment in this very place. The fact that we are here doesn't stop them from being here. I could kill the other you. Would that stop you being here?'

Thomas, 'These paradoxes are impossible.'

Merlin, 'So what do we need to do?'

Thomas, 'We need to stop Galattermous from raping Rachel.'

Merlin, 'We probably need a more permanent solution.'

Thomas, 'You are not suggesting that we kill Rachel?'

Merlin, 'I wasn't planning to be that drastic.'

Thomas, 'The only other way is to stop her from having children.'

Merlin, 'Exactly.'

Thomas, 'Can't he rape someone else?'

Merlin, 'He needs Rachel.'

Thomas, 'But it's not fair on Rachel.'

Merlin, 'If she loves you, she must know that she can't have your children.'

Thomas, 'So you are saying that if we stop Rachel from having children, then Galattermous ceases to exist.'

Merlin, 'Yes, he can't be born, and consequently, he can't rape her.'

Thomas, 'So do we tell Rachel or just do it?'

Merlin, 'This sounds really awful. We tell Rachel

everything. If she agrees to be sterilised, then everything is fine. If she objects, then we have to force her, or worse, kill her.'

Thomas, 'I can't do that.'

Merlin, 'No one wants to, but it's either Rachel or the whole human race. There can be no alternative. And we need to confront her today.'

A note was found in the ether:

> *The paradox was caused by rape,*
> *There was no way she could escape,*
> *Left in a very different shape,*
> *As Tom and Rachel are left agape.*

48

The not so Moral Maze

Thomas and Merlin knocked on Rachel's door, and she invited them in.

Rachel, 'You are not my Tom.'
Thomas, 'How can you tell?'
Rachel, 'A woman knows, a magician knows more.'
Thomas, 'I am your Tom to be in about six months' time.'
Rachel, 'But you have aged, by more than six months.'
Thomas, 'That's probably true.'
Rachel, 'And you are not my Merlin.'
Merlin, 'I've been caught.'
Rachel, 'I know why you are here.'
Thomas, 'That's very unlikely.'
Rachel, 'You have come from a time where we have lost. Lord Malander is dead. Commanders Bandolier and Winterdom are dead. Our final army has been defeated. And I have waited all my life for this moment.'
Merlin, 'And what moment is that?'
Rachel, 'The moment I hold mankind's destiny in my hand and I can join Galattermous in ruling the world.'
Thomas, 'You don't mean that.'
Rachel, 'I certainly do.' She opened the door and in walked Galattermous.
Merlin, 'How did you know that we would be here?'

Galattermous, 'I could say that you were so predictable or that I was remarkably clever. Both of which are true, but I've seen the future.'

Merlin, 'What happens now?'

Galattermous, 'You both die and Rachel and I live happily ever after.'

Both Galattermous and Rachel positioned themselves for the ultimate magical showdown. The mystic war of wars to decide everything was about to begin. World domination was the prize for one side.

The evil duo fired off their first round, but it had no effect on the two magical holographic projections. They had put all of the energies into making their appearances absolutely perfect. They thought they had been caught at first when Rachel said that it wasn't her Tom.

The note slipped under Rachel's bed:

To the slaughter went the lamb,
The winner took the grand slam,
And the losers lost the exam,
Because in the end, it was a hologram.

49

The Week Before

The real Merlin and Thomas were actually in Malvern a week before their holograms met with the two evil conspirators. They discussed at length how they were going to kill Rachel. Thomas was amazed by how his love had turned to hatred. Regardless of previous emotions, he knew what had to be done.

In the end, they decided to just barge into Rachel's suite and knife her to death. Their only chance was surprise. The use of magic would alert her. Both were nervous as they weren't natural killers. But they would kill if they had to, but it was repugnant to them and their magic.

They silently walked up to her room, and Thomas kicked the door in to find a startled Rachel. They had caught her by surprise. Both rushed towards her, but she managed to kick Merlin in the balls, which completely winded him. Thomas had his knife out. Rachel kept screaming at him to stop and that she loved him. She was edging towards the bedroom when she pulled a knife out of her stocking.

She threw it at Thomas, who ducked, and the knife made its way into Merlin's chest. Thomas threw his knife in response, and it struck gold. The blade pierced her heart as Galattermous opened the bedroom door. Rachel collapsed on the floor dead, and Galattermous simply dissolved and then everything dissolved.

The final note was everywhere and nowhere:

The hero of the day was Tom,
Whether with gun, knife, or bomb,
A butcher who showed great aplomb,
But is it time for Merlin to embalm?

50

Is it the End or the Beginning?

Suddenly Thomas was back in the butcher's shop in Malvern with a full memory of everything that had happened to him. And he still had his magical powers fully intact.

So was this the end of one reality and the start of another, or was it just a continuation of the pre-Slimie existence? He removed his butcher's apron and decided to stroll around the town.

Everything and everywhere had reverted back to his childhood memories. Malvern was now the Malvern of old. An important market town famous for housing the Elders. There was no citadel, no military installations, fewer buildings and certainly a lot less people. It was much quieter, calmer and more rustic.

Most importantly of all, there was no fear. No fear of oncoming doom, no fear of annihilation to come. No need to militarise the civilian population. Apart from the odd guard, there was no military. There was peace throughout the land.

In fact, there was so much peace that it was boring. Thomas wasn't sure if he could cope with the drudgery and the lack of excitement. His mind had been expanded: he had seen the world and he had been at the fulcrum of world-changing events. He mattered. He had lived, loved, and experienced the joys of brotherhood and comradeship. He was now a man and never a butcher again.

He learnt that Lord Malander and his wife were still managing their estate. He assumed that all of his long-dead friends were now alive: Lindsey, Tindell, Fay, Victor, Annie etc. But he would probably never see them again. If he did track them down, they wouldn't know who he was. Now he was back to being a nobody, which on reflection had its benefits.

It dawned on him that he could exercise his magical powers to scan for his friends, and he did. They were all alive, including Rachel. What are we going to do about her?

But his magical powers couldn't detect Merlin. Did he survive? Somehow, he knew he did, but who knows?

He wandered back to the butchers as he had nowhere else to go. When he got home, one of Lord Malander's valets was waiting for him with two horses. The valet said that his master wanted to see him.

Thomas wondered if the prophecy had ended when he picked up a note:

Is this the beginning or the end?
For the boy who lost his girlfriend,
Things are back we can pretend,
There is no need to condescend.

And the world can start to mend,
So, all men can be my friend,
But future dangers we must apprehend,
Before these days come to an end.

The End